15p

James Burke

THE
FIREFLY
HUNT

Collins
ST JAMES'S PLACE, LONDON
1969

The lost child cries and, crying,
still he clutches at the Fireflies.

RYUSUI

One

Besieged.

No doubt of it.

Ordinarily, a castle can be under siege for years, for generations, without the proprietor suspecting that the walls are mined, the scaling ladders at the parapet and a traitor holding the key to the gate. For all the king of the castle may know the defenders may have been completely infiltrated by the enemy; and how is he to distinguish the armoured defender from the mailed enemy?

I suffered under no such uncertainties.

I heard the engines and thought they belonged to a formation of propeller driven warplanes but upon reflection I realised that it was not a holiday and therefore unlikely that the populace was being titillated by previews of mechanical destruction. And be-sides, the noise did not have that normal aeronautical rising and falling thrum and was approaching much too slowly. I went out on the rampart. The sky was clear. I peered into the street from between the battlements. They were coming from the east; four greeny-black tanks, Juggernaut Mark IVs; enormous cannon, perhaps one-o-fives, projecting, half erect, anticipatory.

From my height, almost a hundred feet above the street, they looked squatter, blacker and more insectivorous than at closer range; more repellent. The bumbling of their engines grew louder, to a roar, to an insane drumming. That's the frightening thing, I said to myself, like the big bass drum in a parade. The sound envelops you. It traps you. It no longer seems to come from a precisely identifiable source. You are surrounded.

I began to tremble and my heart to pound and I felt frightened

7

even though I could look at the machines analytically and note how lightly they slithered over the pavement due to the calculated distribution of weight—forty or sixty tons—over their exaggeratedly broad treads. And I could tell myself that they had nothing to do with me. Probably only the militia out on Sunday morning manœuvres. A few bank clerks and plumbers' mates indulging in their weekly booster shot of omnipotence.

No. Nothing to do with me and my Castle.

The individual tank commanders stood waist deep in the hatches of the gun turrets. Did they still kick the driver? Right shoulder for right turn; left for left turn? No . . . That was probably a couple of wars ago. There was a sudden change in the attitude of the tank commanders, as though an order had been given and received. Nothing more.

They began to turn to the right—not only the commanders but the turrets. The guns were traversing and rising swiftly until, in an instant, I was looking down the barrels of four enormous cannon whose apertures dwarfed their masters behind them, each of whom was staring at me with a severe military expression.

Yes, I thought, this extraordinary precision is the result of some mysterious gyroscopic device which maintains the gun on target though the tank may be rushing at forty miles an hour over trenches, bodies, shell holes, etc. I have read about it somewhere. No. Not *Popular Mechanics*. *Illustrated London News*, perhaps. Longitudinal schematic drawings of new P. & O. ocean liner showing boiler rooms, bulkheads, ballrooms, bunkers, stabilisers. Yes. The *News* is very strong on cross sections and exploded views of shipboard fighters showing bomb racks, arrestor hooks, navigational devices, gun sight. Or: archaeological strata, millenium by millenium. Thighbone of proto-human; flint scraper. Then our kind of people. Civilisation. Mystic designs on potsherds; skulls crushed by blunt instruments; femurs cracked for the marrow; spear and arrowheads of great refinement; domestic articles of hasty crudity; warclubs of polished alabaster; chariot wheels of gold; finally, in the upper strata, art works emerge—of the most

8

piquant elegance, depicting slave quarters and the slaughter of prisoners of war.

Yes, without a doubt, I had seen the cross section of this tank in a library copy of the *Illustrated London News*.

That I should think in these terms with cannon staring me in the face indicates how paralysed, how frightened silly, I was. But perhaps there was more to it than that. My mechanical interest was genuine. As a boy I took my bicycle to pieces almost every week. I understood the functions of sprocket, chain, ball bearing, coaster brake, although precise adjustment seemed to elude me and the chain developed tendencies to involve itself with the wheel spokes. That was probably a matter of manual dexterity or, rather, lack of it, and had nothing to do with my intellectual appreciation of the logic of mechanical processes.

There is something wrong with that statement.

Perhaps not.

No. I mean, simply, that any logical, mechanical process can easily capture my interest. I give as much attention to a Rube Goldberg cigar lighter—(dog seizes bone attached to string which trips lever which releases ball which weighs down cup which engages gear which turns tap which fills bucket which slowly sinks on pulley tightening lamp's chain turning out light by which dwarf is reading and who lights match to see what is happening which attracts moths tied by thread to chair on turntable which turns man so his cigar is in match-flame light by dwarf)—as I give to the Caryatids holding up Erectheus's porch which, of course, are the pillars of pillars. But at the same time I am aware, in an engineering sense, that only the cross section of the neck provides effective support and that this region may unwisely act as a focus of stress. However, æsthetically, male figures couldn't have done the same job. No.

The wide-arsed female centre of gravity is exactly right to give the perfect sense of poise, serenity, stability. Just think of the buildings they erect to-day on a few stilt-like legs. Enormous masses held up by a slide rule. Yes, perhaps this expresses the enormous, precarious threat under which we live but just wait until some runaway revolutionary girdles a few of those columns with a plastic explosive charge. Just wait.

Admittedly, these are not the most useful thoughts to flash through one's mind in the face of four enormous cannon (one-seven-fives, probably) aimed absolutely between one's eyes. But those fake stone battlements, a foot thick, would stop nothing even if I had the presence of mind to fall down behind them. Besides, I'm the type who would refuse the blindfold on facing a firing squad. I would still be interested in the reactions of the riflemen.

So I looked down the barrel of the third tank's cannon to the lieutenant in the turret hatch; a sandy-haired little fellow with a wispy moustache and light freckles; eyebrows somewhat bleached from the sun; beret dashingly pulled down on the side and clamped to his head by the earphones and mike set. His left hand was on the rim of the hatch, his right on the microphone in front of his mouth, as though ready to switch it on. His little blue eyes had that murderously impersonal look a man gets when aiming a gun, just to get the feel of it, without a real live target in sight.

Surely they couldn't have ammunition in the breach, trailing through peaceful Sunday city streets. And yet I was dreadfully shocked. Yes, that would be the purpose, I now realise—to shock me, to frighten me, to indicate a little the size and the power of the forces aligned against me.

I'll admit it was foolish; childish, even. But it seemed in its spontaneous impulsiveness to be the only appropriate reaction I could make to this enormous threat. I pointed my index finger at the little lieutenant, back down his gun barrel. I pointed it like a child playing cops and robbers, thumb cocked up and ready to fire.

I did not speak the words because I knew they would be lost in the roar of the engines.

'*BANG—YOU'RE—DEAD!*' I mouthed distinctly, so that he

might read my meaning if he had any talent that way. And I clicked down my thumb as though firing at him.

As I mouthed '*BANG*' the tip of the cannon approached the cross-bar of a utilities pole. The lieutenant's eyes widened to take in this unforeseen factor. As I mouthed '*YOU'RE*', the tip of the gun barrel splintered the ceramic insulator, and the cross-bar and fitting tore away as the high tension line stretched and broke with a great, leaping blue spark. For what seemed a long minute the high tension line whipped through the air with a giant, elastic recoil and wound itself around the gun barrel, its broken end finally darting into contact with the barrel like the strike of a cobra and emitting enormous lightning-like arcs of flame.

'*DEAD*' I mouthed as the lieutenant was flung back against the edge of his hatch, smoke emerging wispily from under his left hand which had been grasping the rim. He lay against the edge of the hatch like a flung doll. Yes. Exactly like a doll, a limp doll, a soft-bodied doll. Yes. Whoever invented that expression knew exactly what he was doing. Yes. A hundred feet below me, at the end of my lethal finger, the lieutanant was a dead rag doll. And the tank had gone out of control. It sidled left with that jerky, slithery motion tracked vehicles have, and crunched over a new Chrysler hardtop parked on the other side of the street in front of Senator Reserpine's house, leaving it a compressed heap of jagged trash. Still maintaining its mindless eight miles an hour it mounted the sidewalk, crossed the Senator's lawn, and without hesitation pushed through the north-west corner of his house, the erect gun barrel with its hotly sparking high tension line still attached sweeping part of the second floor along with it.

With one-third of the Senator's house reduced to a rather insubstantial pile of bricks and boards the tank continued across a rose garden until it struck a concrete retaining wall too high for it to climb. It kept grovelling away at the base of this wall, churning up the turf and rose bed until it stalled, at which point a black, greasy smoke began to emerge from the lieutenant's hatch. Before it engulfed the Senator's home I saw him come to the broken edge of his second floor, lathered, a straight razor in his hand and suspenders hanging down. His prosperous and well-inflated gut was holding up his trousers.

He looked at the destruction and turned back into the remnants of his house. A few minutes later, when the burning tank had set fire to his eaves, he came out of the opening where the front door had been, and collapsed at the foot of his front steps. A heart attack.

So, some good came of it, after all.

At this point I have a confession to make. One of the most difficult statements I have ever uttered. There is no need for me to reveal this information. No one saw me. It is not particularly to my credit. It may even make me appear heartless in the circumstances. Perhaps it only illustrates my tendency to let myself become involved in the logical continuation of events when there is no real necessity to do so. Perhaps it is the self-indulgence of an over-active imagination. In any event, when the tank had come to a standstill against the retaining wall I noticed that I was still aiming my finger at it. It seems incredible to me now but I raised my index finger to my lips and *blew the smoke from the muzzle*! the way they used to do in old cowboy pictures. Or was it in gangster films when the thug has callously committed a particularly wanton murder and turns his attention to the tools of his nefarious trade. And not only that. I then thrust my hand down the side of my thigh as though holstering my gun. That made it cowboy, I suppose.

And additionally: *I began to laugh.*

I laughed almost silently in that doubled-up, stomach-knotted, spastic-breathed despair with which Charlie Chaplin afflicts me when he breaks the tragedy barrier. I convulsed myself to such an extent that I began to feel an excruciating necessity to empty my bladder, but with the tank burning below me and the flames igniting the Senator's roof and the lead and rear tanks having swung broadside to the roadway, blocking all traffic and a ser-

geant from the second tank heroically endeavouring to attach an
enormous chain to the burning vehicle at risk of instant incinera-
tion and the swelling sound of sirens in the distance and with the
Senator collapsed in his undershirt on the lawn and his wife in
hair curlers ministering to him under the shadow of the smoke
pall now drifting distantly to the south-east, I did not dare go
inside so I relieved myself through one of the ports in the floor of
the parapet—the sort of thing through which in ancient days they
used to pour boiling lead upon the enemy attempting to scale or
undermine the walls. This was an act neither as public nor as
shameless as it sounds. At the top, the parapet was built out several feet from the wall to allow for these ports or machicolations,
and the battlements provided a chest-high screen of privacy except where they afforded gaps or notches through which only
someone on my own level could see, and there was no high building to the south for nearly half a mile. Still, this had later consequences unrelated to the military débâcle below me.

Perhaps it was the most fitting thing I could do. Certainly it
was enormously more significant than any reaction of the crowd
of spectators. What were they doing? Standing about, open-
mouthed, while the charred bodies of the tank crew were removed. Thrilling to the thought that they were on the scene even
as the press photographers blasted the disaster area with their
flash guns while these, in turn, strode from one vantage point to
another conveying the impression that it was all in a day's work;
that if their next assignment were a Baptist wedding where the
breakage promised, in contrast, to be non-existent, their attitude
would be the same.

On the next day, when the newspapers came out, how many of
those spectators, at work, at home, in a bar, on a street corner,
would say, 'I was there five minutes before the photographers
arrived.' Or: 'The firemen were afraid the ammunition would
blow up, that's how the fire got such a good start on the Senator's
house. Now if I . . .' Or: 'There's not a bit of difference between
a sick Senator and a sick ditch digger. All the classic signs . . .'

Or: 'No trouble keeping that crowd back, with the ammunition and gas tanks ready to blow at any instant . . .'

They would become actors in the drama, interpreting for their friends and acquaintances the tragedy upon which they had stumbled. And of course the police, with their powers of control and inquiry, had taken an active part. The firemen, once they had been assured by the tank captain that no munitions were being carried, were spectacularly active with fog nozzles, pressure nozzles, etc., wetting down neighbouring roofs and knitting the scene together with a skein of hose lines. The tank crews had been truly heroic, leaping upon the flaming tank which could have exploded at any moment since the gasoline tanks must have been warming up swiftly, and dousing the flaming hatch, the dead lieutenant and every visible surface with foam from their fire extinguishers. A dozen youths, refusing to participate in the adults' folly, clustered about the crushed Chrysler. With brutally sudden vulturine pecks they wrenched off a side mirror from the carcass at one moment, a licence plate at another, or a hub cap, and gulped it into the secrecy of their windbreakers.

It seemed to me that I was the only real spectator present; that everyone else, prime actors and audience alike, was actively involved in the drama as part of a chorus of mental defectives: 'Is he dead?' 'Give him air.' 'What are they doing that for?'

'Stand back. Stand back.'

'I saw it all.'

'There'll be hell to pay.'

Strophe. Antistrophe.

Every man an actor. And the contemporary playwright retreats two and a half centuries to bring up the vanguard.

But no one is able to upstage the blackened corpses.

As the sole true spectator of the tragedy only I could manage the classic purgation; the catharsis. That the absurdity of the tragedy had convulsed me with laughter rather than tears, had initiated micturition rather than a more symbolic spiritual cleans-

14

ing, did not seem to invalidate my reaction as the only sincere one at the scene.

Of course, there is the matter of the pointed finger to consider. Perhaps, it could be argued, I was the true protagonist of the drama. Is it possible that my pointed finger distracted the lieutenant momentarily from his task of intimidation, blanketing that split second in which he could have altered the elevation of his gun in time to avoid entanglement with the high tension line? And had my mouthed *Bang You're Dead* the psychic force of a surprise tactical flank attack that completely overthrew, in its absurdity, every military tenet permeating the lieutenant's highly organised personality? Had I chosen to counter-attack with the most feared of all the conquered nation's remaining weapons—childishness?

Yes.

What is the first action of the modern conqueror upon entering the subdued town? Seek out and ravish the women? No. Dig for gold? No. The shells have already dug up and scattered any treasure. Organise the firing squads? Not immediately. No. The most urgent task, once the army public relations photographer has arrived is to round up the children—or a child—undamaged and winsome, and snap her as she reaches for the chocolate bar—or perhaps offering a simple and straggly bouquet of roadside flowers to the dust-covered, tired but human-looking hero.

Yes. The hero most fears the charge of cowardice hence the vanquished display their maimed children, their babies spitted on bayonets. The victor flourishes his magnanimity, his humanity and warmth by petting a child—and, occasionally, a dog for the benefit of the childless. Yes, a most potent weapon; strong enough to create a hesitation—fatal in war.

But no.

The gesture was anything but childish. It was purely and simply a spectator's gesture.

Yes, I had been momentarily frightened by the noise, by the astonishment at finding myself the focus of the cannon, but I had not fled, I had not taken shelter. That would have made me an actor co-operating in the ridiculous drama, assuming a role. Instead, I had maintained my status as spectator and my right to make a judgment, to point a finger in demonstration if not in accusation. I had reserved my right to say, No, I refuse to participate in your farce. I refuse to mouth the mouthed words of your mindless prompter. I refuse to dance to your fiddle. Nor shall I supply you with the next cue. I refuse to be conscripted into the anonymous safety of your chain gang shuffle for when one stumbles all fall. No, I refuse to play your epicene games with mechanical, priapic playthings. In fact, I am a spoilsport. I point my finger at you in derision. I have caught you in the naughty, naughty act. You fumble, you wilt in guilt and flee in confusion. There is more potency in my extended finger than in a whole squadron of your tanks and their inert gun barrels. You live so close to the grave that it takes only a word, *bang*, to tumble you in, *dead*.

No, this is not all afterthought. This and more lay behind those three critical words and their simple gesture. Does not the veiled dropping of an eyelid contain, often, more of hatred than the public ravings of a froth-mouthed degenerate?

If I regret anything about the incident it was that the lieutenant had to go off to his Valhalla with the eternal vision, burned into his mind, of his death by what would seem to him to be my absurd, make-believe gesture. Still, who can die a hero's death to-day? The Shakespearean wound that allowed time for realisation and a significant comment (The rest is . . . much ado about nothing) is to-day opened, transfused, sutured, opiated and sterilised until, with boots off and in a wet sheet, the hero is cancelled in triplicate in the midst of a clinical stupor.

Of course, there was an immediate investigation—a Court of Inquiry by the Armed Forces—*in camera*. They didn't call me as a witness. Public relations issued a statement to the effect that, through a technical failure that could occur only once in stellar billions of times, the traversing mechanism had gone out of control but that the error had been corrected and the tanks were now safe as churches. So they hushed that up.

Senator Reserpine received a handsome settlement (out of court) for his house and medical expenses. It must have been a baronial sum. No figure was given out. They hushed that up.

Mayor Waugh mentioned in Council that the tanks had roughed up a considerable expanse of municipal asphalt during man- œuvres to block off the street during the incident but his remarks were given only three lines on the comic page along with several fillers (The Caspian Sea contains thirteen trillion, trillion tons of salt. The Deadly Nightshade is related to the Tomato). And they repaved the street the next day. So that was quickly hushed up.

The lieutenant and the two sergeants who had given their lives for their country were awarded the E.C.M. (Extraordinary Conduct Medal) which carries with it a pension of one dollar a day for life which the Government saved since the award was posthumous. Four widows showed up to claim the medals but that was hushed up, too.

The speed, efficiency and dignity with which the whole inci- dent was handled, and the elevation of the victims beyond criticism as sacred patriotic martyrs indicated that someone was frightened. I estimated that I would have peace for some months.

It is not easy to quell an undefended fortress.

Two

An orgy of happiness!
  An orgy of happiness!
  It was a phrase that had stuck in my mind, perhaps years ago.
It seemed appropriate.
  I murmured the phrase silently to myself all day. . . .
  I drifted.
  I drifted smiling. Again, to myself.
  I put on my tweed suit. Old, very thick, very coarse, scratchy
material in the best styleless English style under which one wears
a heavy sweater. I regretted, but not deeply, that the trousers
were ordinary trousers and not plus fours. I would have liked
that. Ribbed knee socks and the plus fours bagging down to the
calf.
  I drifted and ambled. I ambled all over town. I bought a tweed
flat cap. I wore it in spite of the fact that it abolished my forehead and stressed the Great Leap Forward made by my nose at
the best of times. And in the shade of the peak my eye had a tendency to look a touch more beady than is consistent with good
humour. But I didn't care. I didn't care that the bulk of the tweed
jacket backed by the bulky sweater, backed by my not incon-
siderable belly drew an appraising look or two.
  I am of an old-fashioned shape. A heavy gold chain stretched
across the vest is my natural style—two generations out of date.
Yes, a plug hat and a cut-away. I'm tall enough for the plug hat:
six-foot-two. In another age I might have made my mark but
to-day the leaders have been over successful in insisting they are
18

but common men, so we are led by a seedy pack of cost accountants, impassive, bespectacled.

But I was drifting, ambling, wandering amiably. I looked well. I was deferred to. A paunch improves the posture—at least, a high paunch does. It is scientifically impossible to carry a paunch and hang one's head. Gravity is against the idea. A head held high gives a certain confidence to the eye and the over friendly find it impossible to breathe in one's face over one's outer defences.

Yes, confidence, amiability and prosperity cast an aura about me that was immediately apparent.

It looked almost as though they had guessed that I had inherited the Castle but I was saying nothing. I hadn't even acknowledged the lawyer's letter. In fact, I had almost thrown it away unopened but it had been registered and signed for by my landlady, Mrs. Peake.

'Aren't you going to open it?' she demanded as I thrust it, crumpled, into my coat pocket.

'Bad news,' I said. 'I don't want to know.'

'But it's registered. It must be important.'

'Not for me. People register letters and send telegrams when it's important to them. As Father Bunyard says, "Bad news drives out good".'

'Your wife may have died,' she said, hopefully.

'No. She wouldn't allow it.'

'It's from Cutter, Mandrake and Swingle,' she put in, tentatively. 'They're a very big and important legal firm . . .'

'Then it's very bad news. They can't be suing me because I haven't a dime. I've been bankrupt for years and my prospects, I'm happy to say, are zero. And small wonder. Everyone over forty should be replaced by a machine. Less obsolescence that way. . . .'

'Oh, I don't know,' Mrs. Peake protested stoutly. 'You're at the prime. Mature. You know what things are about. Not like some young fellows nowadays who are interested only in what

they can get . . . right now. I'll tell you, I wouldn't settle for anyone under forty. . . .'

'I agree entirely,' I said. 'I'm with you, absolutely, on that. Up
to that point there is simply too much energy to be dissipated.
How much energy can Love absorb? Three per cent, perhaps?
And most of that is vanity; and half of the rest is the drive to be a
winner. And, averaging out youth and age, I wouldn't be surprised if more time were devoted to constipation than to love.
Say, twelve per cent. It's an enormous industry—from Chuck-A-
Luck baby nappies to senile clysters and all the diets, chologogues,
suppositories, natural herbs and pile ointments in between. If I
were a psychologist I suppose I'd have to make that figure twenty-
five per cent to include certain classes of art that come under
the heading: Look Mommy What A Nice Mess I've Made For
You.'

'Oh, I agree. Some of this modern stuff is horrible. Rubens . . .'

But I wasn't going to let her trap me in the meat department.
'Business, of course, takes only about one and a half per cent of
man's energy and is so undemanding that the most elaborate
conventions and rituals must be invented to fill the enormous
gaps between the few times when real business is done. Hence,
the enormous number of apparent errors. Everything must be
done twice and in the most inefficient manner . . .'

'Yes, yes! Just the other day I ordered a can of hair spray from
Pennywise's and do you know . . .'

'Yes, I know. Any executive in any year dictates more wordage
than Shakespeare wrote in his whole lifetime. It all has to be filed
at both ends, initialled, passed on, replied to, which, in turn,
evokes another reply which, in turn . . . Well, you see how many
people are involved quite uselessly. File clerks, people manufacturing file cabinets or microfilm machines, typewriters, dicta-
phones, copiers, the whole postal system and the telephone
system—all resting on the bedrock of tranquillisers and barium
meals with attendant clinical staff and their ancillary services—

all designed to fill in time, to absorb excess energy. Yes, as you say, Mrs. Peake, the thing to do is get along to middle age as fast as possible: get things slowed down, otherwise there is this frantic, desperate business of trying to use oneself up with fornication, marriage, child rearing, sports, murder, rape, watching television and a thousand other delinquencies.'

'But that's not what I meant . . .'

I knew what she meant. Having lived for seven weeks at Mrs. Peake's enormous rooming house I was prepared for her when I heard her knock. Her technique was, as soon as I opened the door, to plunge in with clean towels over her arm or a pillowcase she had forgotten and, once into the room, assault me with a mixture of mothering (an eagle eye for sieved socks) and arch seduction.

Not that she was unattractive. Quite the contrary. At thirty-eight (she admitted to thirty-three) it was obvious that she was a full-blown blossom; not a velvet rose; more like a chrysanthemum or a tough and gaudy zinnia whose faded petals wither behind ever flourishing and renewed blades of colour. But her archness and the elaborate make up of her eyes, totally rimmed by mascara, made me feel that I was in an old silent movie and this set up a jerkiness of response in me that made me both want to laugh and to flee at sixty-four frames a second.

So this time, at her knock, I stood at the side of the doorway and her impetuous entrance left her standing farther inside the room than I was. I had only to sidle a little to the left as I prattled on to be on the way out. 'Good God! Look at the time! Lock up for me, will you, Mrs. Peake?'

And I departed.

I would not be quite truthful if I said I did not have a good idea of the contents of the lawyer's letter. Ten days earlier I had mailed out a few clocks and this, I was certain, was a response.

Ah, the clocks.

Yes.

A very simple matter. My favourite mode of expression, of criticism, of comment.

For there are no effective channels of opinion or retort open to the individual nowadays. Marching is tedious—a footsore and weary business even when it is not cold, wet or sweaty. And I cannot see myself, at my age and with my generous proportions, lying-in, sitting-in, spreadeagled on the pavement lik e a stranded Moby Dick—if I may mix a metaphor. Much too ludicrous. That sort of thing is all right for youth. We are used to seeing them flop about on football fields, lounging about coffee shops, slouched in the depths of an easy chair, reading books with their necks bent at ninety degrees. We feel quite tolerant about it for, after all, they are not so far removed from the crawling stage. I recognise that they are, in fact, only partly along the road from egg to fish to amphibian to infant to child to youth to erect manhood and so they use the attitudes and instruments appropriate to their condition and time. But all this going limp under the hand of authority, though an understandable response in girls, seems a mighty suspect matter for boys. But perhaps, at my age, I'm over sensitive about that sort of thing.

No, no. I am being unfair. These kids have been born into a world too grotesque to adapt to, whereas we, one generation removed, were bent, moulded to it under a pressure just this side of intolerable—for most of us. They seem to realise, as I still do not, really, that there is no more standing up; that survival means hitting the deck: more; that this is not enough; that they will soon have to go underground; that the situation is, in a word, grave.

The kids nowadays are highly intelligent and are undoubtedly aware of the casualty figures of all the wars and of how, in spite of Mademoiselle from Armentières and Mademoiselle from Smolensk and Mademoiselle from Nagasaki, and the rising population curve, the production of human beings has dwindled to a trickle. And, of course, they know that the casualties are not only the dead and crippled young men but include the gut-crippled and unfertilised young women and the unborn. They don't believe the old men who are ordering them off to be shot, deballed, incinerated, trepanned and moulded like meat balls into posthumous patriots. They know that square miles won or lost and comparative casualty lists are meaningless and that there are no victors in war. These are clichés so widely accepted and so devoutly to be wished that they are suspect and one must look elsewhere for war loot.

For instance: casualty lists. The greatest number of war casualties are ignored—the stupefying number of separations that are enforced by war—the segregation of whole populations by sex. The growing success of the plan to divide the world into, literally, two homosexual groups with contact allowed on the basis of women's auxiliary groups, degraded to the role of unofficial whores, is apparent. Then there is another, allied area of progress: women are no longer considered war loot. The development of a civilised attitude? On the contrary. Women are no longer considered of value. Not even worth seizing as slaves. Blow them up like bricks and mortar.

Do these two facts mean anything? Do the faces of the Leaders tell the youngster anything? The smooth-rugged, wrong-mouthed, covert, eunuchy faces giving out the orders to mutilate populations.

Mighty queer.

I'm sorry. I didn't mean to go on so long about these ordinary little thoughts of mine that everyone is so familiar with but they help to explain about the clocks. Being constitutionally unable, or unwilling to join any group, even in agreement, and to act in concert and under orders, and yet wanting to express my individual opinion with some impact in order to help stem the flow of sewage spewing over us every minute of the day, I was for a long time desperately frustrated until Mayor Waugh forced through a motion to cut down day nursery costs by thirty-nine thousand and next week raised councilmen's salaries by about sixty-four thousand dollars.

'Someone should set a bomb under that son-of-a-bitch,' I said and the newspaper trembled with my rage.

'You always say that,' Myrtle said with her usual detachment.

'I'll do it, by God! One day.'

'If wishes were horses, beggars would be kings,' she said calmly.

'. . . beggars would ride,' I murmured automatically.

'Well, there's no sense in working yourself up,' she said with absolute reasonableness and truth. 'You won't do anything, so you might as well forget it. You know, Timothy, you're not very aggressive.'

'I know, I know,' I said thoughtfully. 'That's why the bomb is such a good idea. I could simply mail it and when old Waugh opened it up—Boom! Might blow up the whole City Hall.'

'And where would you get a bomb?'

This was said in a much too tolerant manner.

'I'd make it. Anyone can make a bomb. A stick of dynamite, a flashlight battery, a clock for a timer . . .'

'Oh yes. Dynamite. You start fooling with that and you'll anniliate yourself.'

My mouth was shaped to correct her but she had been much too patronising, much too knowing.

'If anyone gets anniliated,' I said, 'it's going to be Waugh.'

'Annihilated,' she said.

That decided me.

I went up to our bedroom, wound the alarm clock as tightly as possible and packed it in a cardboard box. I decided against newspaper as stuffing because it deadened the tick. Instead, I jammed it in with some sections of stiff cardboard so that the tick could be heard clearly through the outer wrappings. Then I addressed it to His Honour Mayor W. C. Waugh at City Hall and also wrote my name and address in the sender's corner.

I came back down to the living-room and held the box to Myrtle's ear.

'There it is,' I said.

'That's the bedroom clock. You'll never get up in the morning,' she said.

'The Mayor doesn't know that. Imagine that slob Waugh, talking all the time he's opening the parcel—and then realising it's ticking. He'll shit himself.'

Ordinarily I'd have said he'll wet himself since Myrtle preferred the more genteel of expressions but I had to pay her off for that anniliate–annihilate business. She ran her conversations, and even her life, like a Siberian troika pursued by wolves. Out went the babies, the red herrings, every three minutes, wolves or no. Even if one did not stop to gobble up these tidbits it was a major feat to maintain the straight line of an ordinary conversation with Myrtle.

'He'll call the police,' Myrtle replied, still cool. Extra cool.

'Then he'll look awfully foolish.'

'They'll . . . pound . . . you . . . to . . . a . . . pulp!'

This time she put considerable feeling into it. And it wasn't all because of the naughty word. She could see trouble coming. Besides the police investigation there would be publicity. My job would probably be lost. They might want to test my sanity by their own mysterious standards. The communists would want to defend me, to close ranks about me—until they found that I had a sense of humour and felt no obsessive responsibilities to any Given Word.

'Yes,' I agreed. 'They'll probably cripple me for life. You'd have to go back to work.'

This, of course, was nonsense but it was easier to have a little exchange like this with Myrtle than to discuss my new idea, for she was totally resistant to new ideas, if not to new styles. My little feint got her mind on to other things. I, too, am an expert troika driver.

Myrtle was somewhat old-fashioned. Her vision of herself went something like this, I am sure: Herself lying on a chaise-longue in a gold *lamé* gown, mules with spike heels of incredible height, a champagne glass on a little table beside her with the caviar, a gold-tipped cigarette in a foot-long holder and a maid bringing a calling card to her on a silver salver.

In actual fact, she was pert, eager, intelligent, energetic, competent and capable of enormous charm and concentration and at her best busily running, say, an office of thirty stenographers or co-ordinating a large market survey bossing without effort dozens of crews, or managing a busy beauty salon—all of which she had done, and happily. But she had certain intellectual and emotional dead spots and at these points she went inactive. With inactivity, I believe, the languorous vision obsessed her. And with inactivity she became hopelessly constipated, hence difficult.

If she had said to me, 'Tim, darling, let's not have excitement this week. I don't feel up to it. Do you mind?' I'd have shelved the whole idea. But as it was, she did want some excitement so she thought she would stir me up a bit. A perfectly normal marital procedure. I, therefore, responded in a like normal manner by throwing the suggestion of work at her—which actually she would enjoy but which would violate her leisure which she felt she was entitled to, even if it killed her with boredom.

Leaving her struggling with these feelings, I went out and mailed the clock to Mayor Waugh.

That was seven years ago and since then I've mailed about a hundred clocks to a wide assortment of similar public nuisances. So when the letter came from the lawyers I was sure it would run something like this: Sir: We have been given to understand that on or about the 17th of April you used the public mails to convey an apparatus of some potential injury to my client J. J. Durrell. May we remind you that there are statutes to control this sort of criminal and irresponsible behaviour and that only the charitable temper of our client towards your mental condition prevents us from prosecuting you to the fullest extent of the Criminal Code. May we remind you that using the mails for purposes of watching, besetting and intimidation constitute a gravamen of the most serious sort as well as being a Federal offence carrying with it the most serious consequences and that a repe-

26

tition of such actions will be prosecuted to the fullest. Yours truly, Arthur Swingle. Mandrake, Cutter and Swingle.

This sort of twaddle is scarcely worth scanning and I had long been used to the sort of windy and timorous abuse that lawyers without real grounds send out for their clients. It wasn't until I had reached the street car stop that I ripped open the envelope and I moved into the car along with the crowd only to be jammed at the entrance door with the tail of my coat squeezed between the closed doors. I was holding the letter above my head, so close was the crush.

I read; Timothy Badger, Esq., 13 Mulberry Place. May . . .

I was shocked. Esquire! They must think I have money.

The car stopped. I read no more. I retreated with a slight qualm for I had not paid my fare. But since I could not force myself physically close enough to the fare box to pay, and since I had no immediate intention of going on to work, I felt that I was not actually being dishonest and, besides, if I continued on to work the company would get its fare though I would make the trip in two stages. I could not continue to send out clocks to the crooks, politicians and other riff raff in our public life if I felt myself to be in any way unscrupulous.

I stood at the kerb and read: Dear Mr. Badger: It is with regret that we must inform you of the death of your esteemed uncle, Sir Moses Muddiman, on Dec. 16 last. We have had some difficulty in ascertaining your present address which accounts for our delay in informing you that you are the sole surviving beneficiary of your uncle's will. If you would be kind enough to consult with us at your convenience we would be happy to inform you of the particulars concerning your inheritance, and proceed to the probate of said will. Yours very truly, Charles B. Swingle.

So his name wasn't Arthur. I'd have sworn his name would prove to be Arthur. Just one of those feelings of certitude of the sort that make us put ten dollars on the nose of Rainbow's End— at forty to one; or that convinces you that of all the females in

27

the world your particular Phoebe is the only possible one for you —odds of one and a half billion to one. Perhaps they will prove, one day, that this sort of feeling is due simply to the detachment of a sulphur atom from a bit of protein somewhere in the brain, which may account for my standing on the kerb, slightly distracted by the fact that this unexpected letter was not signed by a non-existent Arthur Swingle.

I turned for home, musing: This must mean that Aunt Freda is dead. Did she finally fall out of her tree? If not watched she would climb into an old apple tree and have to be rescued by the Fire Department like a stranded cat.

Uncle Wilbur would have been long dead. Epilepsy in the grand manner. Toppling like a log in the middle of the street, half-way up stairways, at the edge of subway platforms, does not make for longevity. Aunt Grace gone too? When last I heard she had been getting forgetful and, knowing this, she remembered half a dozen times a day to take her laxative. So she was probably put away long ago on grounds of untidiness. Uncle Herman gone too? Impossible to believe. No. No. The good die young and Uncle Herman was a wicked old dodger and should have been good for centuries, if my memory for family history was sound.

In this manner I managed to put off acknowledgment of the facts. I busied myself slipping into my room, changing into my tweeds, and slipping out again without arousing the attentions of Mrs. Peake. I rushed off to Fletcher's to buy the tweed cap. It was exactly the sort of weather for a heavy suit, bright, cool, with tulips blazing, hyacinths, squill, forsythia.

I tried to become interested in everything I saw, but it was no use. I had to face the facts. I pulled out the crumpled letter and read it again: 'sole surviving beneficiary'. Stated explicitly. No question about it. Moses' Castle would now be mine. And all his millions. In a way, it was a shock; a peculiar sensation. Like being struck on the head by a child's balloon. Nothing particularly pleasant about it, but certainly nothing dangerous. A blow of a magnitude totally incongruous to the mass involved. I felt a little silly.

And what would the boys say, down at McGohee's Three Minute Car Wash?

Three

I told myself that walking would provide the proper atmosphere in which to examine my dilemma. With the brain properly oxygenated by exercise I would be able to come to a precise, correct and moral solution to the problem of my inheritance.

Not that I am of the Peripatetic School. No. I was probably, at that time, many more thousands of years out of date. Anarchy appealed to me in a semantic sort of way but I was repelled by its high degree of discipline, dedication, logic, order. Like everyone else these days I was probably an Ishmaelite wandering in our over-populated desert, feeding on manna, the original God-given plastic, and whining for a cup of clear water.

My problem was that I was committed; committed to criticism by means of my clocks delivered out of the blue with the implied message: This could as well have been a bomb. Time is running out. Have you thought of your actions, as Baruch Bunyard would say, 'under the aspect of eternity' which may come along for you in the next package.

I felt quite justified and constructive about sending along my clocks to those politicians (all of them) who felt that government was simply management, less ten per cent handling charge, of public money. And to heads of corporations who said, 'My duty is to my shareholders and I'd skin my grandmother alive to keep my power.' And to doctors refusing night calls to bleeding patients. And to members of the new scientific Inquisition who pretend that their search for fragments of temporary truth is not hand in hand with the mortician. And to finicky spacemen who refuse to drink reprocessed urine unless it be their own.

But now I was powerful, if I wanted to be, and obviously so with this monstrosity of a Castle on my hands. Automatically I became one of *them* unless I took some drastic action. I could pass through the needle's eye simply by giving the Castle away, stone by stone, and all the wealth involved. Loaves and fishes to the poor. Or, I could establish a philanthropic fund in perpetuity— the Moses Muddiman Foundation—and feed out all the surplus to some worthy cause that would promote the health and happiness of mankind: A Movement For The Compulsory Surgical Deflowering Of Young Females, perhaps, or The Fund For The Abolition Of All Uniforms or an Anti-Hairdressing League. I most certainly would not turn it over to the Government for I don't believe in the perpetuation of that sort of folly. Governments should be discouraged rather than encouraged.

I soon found that I had strolled into the vicinity of the Old Market. I could not resist the temptation (surely it is not a sin) to go in and feast my eyes on the produce. Ah! The mounds of colour! Orange! Oranges from everywhere—Florida, California, Mexico, Israel. Near-ruptured navels. Flabby tangerines. The green of limes from St. Nevis, Jamaica. The Grenadines. The lemon of lemons from Spain. The dulled yellow of good grapefruit, thin skinned, juicy, dense, heavier in the hand than a great breast. Exotic pomegranates. Bursting portable oases. Grapes from Peru. Pineapples—fragmentation bombs—cruel, comic topknots. Unfortunately, the strawberries, flown in from California, looked juiceless in their green plastic baskets at ninety-eight cents a handful.

I bought three Delicious apples, hoping they had stored well, and a tangerine. I stuffed them in my pockets. Nor could I resist the olives. Great salty barrels from Spain and Greece. I had them fill a tiny cardboard bucket with the best Greek olives—not the bitterly salt ones but the expensive ones with the texture, almost, of soft cheese. I ate them as I strolled from stall to stall, spitting out the pips with a lordly carelessness which astonished me but did not deter me even though, ordinarily, I am most careful about littering.

Ah! The vegetables! Where fruits are gems, vegetables are uncut stones and building blocks. Asparagus, ancient axeless fasces come to life. Broccoli, imported from the moon. No. Surely it's the seasonal sprouting carpet of Mars. Green beans, wax beans, every one guaranteed different. Brussels sprouts with the strength but not the ambition to be cabbages. Cauliflower, an innocent blossom brutalised, keratosed by generations of fall-out radiation. Carrots, great dog peckers. Imperators by the shape of them. Crop-topped celery looking as though it had run out of imagination after a strong start. Smiling sweet corn, mimicking a happy dentist. Eggplant, anarchy in royal purple. Grenade sized acorn squash. Mild vegetable marrow, neck humbly bent. Onions, metaphysically designed so that the last layer peeled back leaves not even a pin to dance an angel on.

I strode smiling through the market. I shall have the time, the money, the space to adventure into some really interesting cooking, I thought. And that surprised me for I had never been interested in food except in terms of sustenance and appetite.

Looking back upon that thought I realise that I had let the sensual impact of all that colour, smell, remembered taste and texture seduce my intellectual position concerning my inheritance—and in the most pleasant way—without my really realising it. Yes, that must have been the entering wedge.

How did Pope Bunyard XXX (1242-1387) put it?

> Moreover, none
> Grow hostile towards riches; and even those
> Who have so grown renounce their enmity.
> For riches have a formidable way
> of creeping into spots inviolable
> And hard to reach; and into places where
> A poor man could not, even if he came thither,
> Obtain what he desires.

And if the vegetable produce could seduce me, think of the preserves put up by farm wives. Peaches, pears, crab-apples, cherries, strawberries enamelled in syrup, glistening in their jars. And the cheeses. From everywhere. No, not everywhere. Mostly from Europe. Why not Africa? Asia? Is there a water buffalo cheese? A Watusi, a Masai Schabziger?

Thank God for refrigerated rail cars, trucks and ships. And thank God there are civilised people all over the world who are aware that here, in the centre of the continent, am I and others ready with our digestive secretions to do homage to their love offsprings, for I believe it must be impossible to pluck fruit in hate.

I bought a small piece of Very Old Canadian Cheddar, some Roquefort and, for the sissy in me, a Boursault. Altogether, not much more than a pound. Just savouring the names was sustenance. Oka, Brie, Muenster, Caerphilly, Cheshire, Double Gloucester, Camembert, St. Paulin, Tilsit, Edam, Feta, Bel Paese, Jarlsberg, Emmenthal.

The old bastard probably has a wine cellar, I thought, but what about cheese. That will be the first thing I'll do. Build a cheese cellar, if that's what they call it. Properly controlled temperature and humidity. A bit of vinegar in the air. Or is that an old wives' tale?

Meat. Vegetables are to meat as serfs are to kings. Magnificent sirloins. Well marbled roasts, prime ribs. Gobbets of stewing beef. Monstrous livers. Stilled noble hearts. Grand uncut tenderloins. A hind quarter on the block. A whole carcass suspended from hooks. Almost beautiful. The butcher, surveying his shambles with a monumental air, seemed a king on a victorious field, robes stained, hand resting on his sword whose point penetrated the block of execution.

I did not buy. Neither the lamb nor the pork. Not even a few double loin chops, nor some back bacon, nor a capon. Not even a few slices of ham. I shuffled through the sawdust, noted the butcher's cuffs. I hadn't seen straw cuffs since the demise of the neighbourhood butcher twenty or thirty years ago. Do they still

c

spread the floor with sawdust behind the supermarket where they package the meat on little absorbent cardboard trays?

I won't speak of the fish. The halibut steaks, the salmon, the Winnipeg Gold Eyes, the Arctic Char, the whitefish, the lake trout, the sole, the shrimp, the roe, the oysters, the live, musing carp, the green lobsters like living, sprouting rocks. No, I refuse to mention the metallic glitter of the scales, the astonishment of the dead eyes, the rankness, the pervading life-in-death pungency of the sea.

I bought a small French stick to go with my cheese and olives and left the Market by the south entrance, not even bothering with the other side with its flower stalls, its poultry and egg displays, its delicatessens with a hundred wursts, a thousand pickles, its dozens of trays of salads, its hams, its smoked oysters, its pickled herrings.

It is easy to say, at this distance, that I was putting a smoke screen of sensation between myself and a hard examination of the implications contained in the lawyer's letter. At that moment it was not so simple. For three years I had sojourned in the wilderness. I had cut myself off from society, which is to say I paid no taxes. I scurried from one rooming house to another as the tentacles of my old life reached out for me. I worked most days as a casual labourer at one or another of the instantaneous car washes that dotted the city. As a casual labourer I could show up for work or not, as I desired. I was paid at the end of each day. No one could garnishee my wages, make deductions or sue me. I did not even have to change my name since I was not on any payroll. But since I was self-supporting I could not be found in the hostels for down-and-outers, nor in welfare offices, nor at government clinics.

I owned no wallet. I kept about fifty dollars in my trouser pockets—my total capital. I had given up my driver's licence and with it my insurance liability card. I belonged to no clubs or associations and possessed no credit cards. I owned no health or hospital insurance card, no identity card, no union card, nor birth certificate. I carried no document to attest to my blood type; no warnings that I was cataleptic, diabetic, anginal or allergic. And no insurance salesmen called.

In short, I was not being continually processed.

Thus, I could pass for a free man, in some quarters, or at least for one who was on the loose, temporarily, until I suffered a stroke, or fell down in front of a bus or emerged from a washroom with my clothing unbuttoned just as the Ladies Auxiliary marched by.

Now, with a crazy and monstrous, if valuable, castle on my hands and probably several millions of dollars I could no longer feel free. If the plumbing were to clog, or the roof to leak, I should have to call workmen. And see to it that the grass got cut regularly and the windows washed and the garbage put out. One does not ordinarily think of garbage in relation to a castle but undoubtedly garbage is produced there as well as in every other area where humans encamp.

In a great place like The Castle I was sure that bats would be a constant menace as well as birds nesting in chimneys; and since there would be extensive cellars in such an establishment rats would probably abound and, possibly, mysterious smells.

As a single man all these tedious, complicated and detailed chores would devolve upon me and I did not feel equal to it. The household duties of the world have always been in the hands of women and they have managed them with extraordinary capability, being of a much more logical and practical turn of mind than men. Where a handful of dust must be disposed of, a man will draw upon untapped sources of energy, develop metallurgy, physics, lubricants, plastics, papers, textiles; will study a thousand disciplines and invent the vacuum cleaner. A woman, on the other hand, will decisively and without moral disturbance, sweep the dust under the nearest rug and get back to living. The best that men can do in keeping an environment tidy is to organise an army and impose a rigorously disciplined order under pain of horrific penalties, beginning with death.

I would, therefore, be tempted to include a woman in my household simply to cope with these matters. And with money, I would be a marriage temptation to many a woman, if not all.

But I could not frighten myself with these musings. I was feeling more and more buoyant. That damned expression 'an orgy of happiness' kept bubbling to the surface of my mind and I brushed away my imagined problems with the magic fly whisk of millions. It was all so simple. Cutter, Mandrake & Swingle could manage my financial affairs and turn over whatever residue accumulated. They could also hire a housekeeper for me—preferably a woman who had held this position in an hotel, or even a prison wardress; someone who would take no nonsense from the staff and who would make sure that no maid would ever ask me to lift my feet while she swept the rug as I sat by my log fire.

I was passing Clyne's window when a display of watches caught my eye. I went in. I had been using a chromium plated pocket watch, the sort that used to be called a dollar watch but which now sells for three-ninety-five in the catalogue. I put my carton of olives on the glass showcase and pointed to a Patek Phillipe.

'That one,' I said.

The clerk looked hesitant. He practically shied at my olives.

'The Patek Phillipe,' I said. 'I won't eat it.'

With careful, ritualistic gestures he removed the watch from the display case and positioned it in front of me, beside the olives.

'Help yourself,' I said, shoving the carton towards him. 'Delicious. Best quality.'

'I never eat during business hours,' he informed me loftily and his left nostril went rabbity at the thought of this foreign fruit standing on his counter. I popped another olive into my mouth.

'I hope you realise,' I said, 'that these olives come from three-thousand year old trees on the slopes of Mount Hymettus? I daresay they have a better pedigree than either you or me or this watch. How much?'

'Eleven hundred dollars.'

Small triumph. But he was still sending out alarm signals with his eyes, all over the shop.

I licked my fingers and dried them under the armpits of my jacket. I picked up the watch and strapped it on. Round, thin, highly under designed, no numerals, not even a sweep second hand. A snooty touch, that. Would have made it too active, undignified.

'No, I won't take it,' I said. 'It occurs to me that this represents the extreme of inelegance. Utterly *nouveau riche*. Watches are for clerks under pain of dismissal: for businessmen—time is money; for factory workers who must punch a time clock or lose wages. What gentleman needs a watch? To catch a train or a plane? There'll be others along shortly. No, I shan't take it,' I said, and thrust my hand into my pocket and broke off a piece of cheddar and popped it into my mouth. Then I broke a chunk from my French stick, leaving some crumbs on the immaculate showcase.

I stripped the watch from my wrist and laid it down.

'The only use I can think of for this watch,' I said, 'is to use it as a timing mechanism for a bomb being sent to, say, a king. In the old days they used to pour molten silver into the ear of a condemned monarch. This would be in the modern tradition, wouldn't it? Sneaky, ignoble, but mechanically elaborate.'

He looked as though he were ready to press the alarm button and drop down behind his counter. I left, depressed. I had forgotten the chilled steel atmosphere and the dead brightness of the fluorescent lighting. I had forgotten the silent clerks and their tightly limited responses, looking as though they were prepared for the day in the mortician's back room.

I was saddened, too, to think of how the rich, and not only the women, are so brutally intimidated, manipulated, scorned, crushed and disfigured by hairdressers, interior decorators, columnists and authorities on every sort of fashion. One week-end, Mrs. Lightbody-Speckle dominates the Sunday supplement with a two-page spread in colour of her alfresco lunch with a Libyan camel saddle for each semi-distinguished guest, herself in Mexican

37

huaraches and peon pants and posed prettily over a Japanese hibachi. Next week she is swept into oblivion by Mrs. Spracklin-Shank in the latest of denim coveralls with solid gold reinforcing rivets showing her remodelled bathroom, with such a civilised bidet and papered in medieval palimpsests, to the Duchess of Parmigiano.

No, I will never fall for that sort of thing, I promised myself as I stopped by the window of a camera store. At most, perhaps, I would buy a modest camera. Not a Hasselblad, nor a Nikon, nor a Leica. A simple reflex: a Minolta or a Pentax with a wide angle and a long focus lens. Then spend a few years photographing all the verge boards and similar gingerbread on the Victorian houses in the area. It would be a project which would hurt no one; would contribute to no form of destruction; would make no pretence of being constructive, creative, progressive, so nothing needed to be cleared away, no one evicted, no one dispossessed in any guise, no ideas attacked or defended. I would simply drive around the country, into small towns, into the older sections of the city, and quickly photograph all these gay details; then, at leisure, study them to discover correspondences, duplications, trends.

Perhaps they were all copied from a pattern book. I suppose, I thought, that I could get an architect's opinion on the matter but that would not satisfy me. I wanted to find out about the air of gaiety exhibited by these essentially simple and sober houses. I wanted to determine, once and for all, whether there ever had been such a thing as innocent gaiety in that time; whether such a thing as a picnic ever had existed with its chicken sandwiches, potato salads, hard boiled eggs, sweet gherkins, dill pickles, exquisitely ripe peaches, chilled wines, cold roast beef, apple, rhubarb, blueberry pies, chocolate cake, celery, stuffed pork sandwiches, home-made bread, crisp lettuce, garden-ripe tomatoes, delicate green onions, chilled asparagus, beer, home-made ice cream packed in salt and ice. And if I should find, as I hoped to, that carpenters of a hundred years ago scorned to

38

slavishly duplicate time and again these patterns of gaiety then I would be confirmed in my opinion that there were once men of self-respect who could feel pride in their work and shame in shoddiness.

It would be a quite harmless and private investigation solely to satisfy my casual curiosity. Doctors of Philosophy have achieved fame for lesser endeavours—and perhaps by reason of them being lesser. At the moment, I could think of nothing more innocent to devote my life to.

I could again indulge in my orgy of happiness. I smiled my inward, Cheshire cat smile more broadly than ever. I knew how completely lacking in grandeur were my innocuous plans and I realised their utter naïvety. But then, all happiness is naïve. Even the saints, dying horribly but happily, would no doubt have writhed in dismay if they could have foreseen their spiritual function encompassing only the return of lost garnet brooches to senescent maiden aunts.

I had eaten my olives, half of my cheese and most of my bread stick and I was thirsty. I would not, voluntarily, have chosen the New York Chop Suey Café in which to be served a cup of coffee but I had seen approaching what looked suspiciously like Charlie Scaliger so I made a quick left turn, plunged into the café, flung myself into a booth and buried my face in the menu.

My happiness had vanished.

Four

'Son of a gun!'

Charlie Scaliger made it sound like an exclamation of surprise, delight and astonishment. He even put a twinkle in those psychopathic washed-out blue eyes of his. He thrust out his hand.

My mistake had been to hang my hat on the rack built into the end of the booth so that although I had buried myself in the deepest corner of the restaurant Charlie Scaliger had only to catch sight of it to make a beeline directly to me. I ignored his hand, looked through him, and said, 'Tea, please,' to the waitress.

He slid into the opposite seat.

'As I live and breathe, Tim Badger,' he said with great warmth.

'I'm afraid you are making a mistake,' I said with the coldest formality and I brought out Cutter, Mandrake & Swingle's letter and, on the back of the envelope, proceeded to list in very tiny letters under the heading of SCALIGER:

(1) brown-noser.

(2) sneak.

'It's Ol' Charlie Scaliger, Tim. Come on, you remember . . .'

'Sir, neither name means anything to me. Now, if you will leave me to my privacy . . .'

I jotted down:

(3) crook.

'Collingwood College,' he suggested, eyeing me with expectation as though I were a TV contestant trying for fame, fortune and a free trip to Brunswick, Ga.

'A fourth rate institution, I believe.'

I noted:

40

(4) bubblehead.

'Ah, they were good times, Tim.'

I wrote:

(5) trance artist.

I couldn't help myself.

'For whom?' I said, without looking up.

Collingwood College was one of Uncle Moses' benevolences. Mother had dragged me, almost by the ear, over to The Castle. Uncle Moses kept fleeing before her, circling round and round his great baronial hall with its hammer beams and hanging banners. Mother kept nipping at his heels, crowding beside him, heading him off should he bolt for a doorway, a corridor. They were speaking in *sotto voce* style (to spare my feelings) but with the volume turned up so that I would not miss one drop of the bloody sacrifice they were making for me. I tried not to listen by thrusting my head out of the enormous casement window and trying to bomb a dry looking geranium twelve feet below me with gobs of saliva. I find it extremely difficult to act dignified in dignified surroundings.

'But Moses,' my mother kept saying, 'it's Veronica. This is your little sister Veronica. . . .'

'That has never proved an advantage to me. . . .'

'Ah, is that what families are for? Advantage?' Sadder but wiser tone.

'That's what you're after, isn't it?'

'Moses, I never thought, when we were little children together, that you would treat your little Veronica this way . . .'

She broke off in a tremolo that implied tears with another word. I could hear Uncle's voice soften into contrition, gentle concern. Although I did not turn around I could visualise him putting a fraternal arm around my mother's bowed shoulders. She was expert at throwing herself into tragic poses.

'Ah, my little Veronica. How old are you now? I'm becoming forgetful. I should pay more attention to these family matters.'

There was a suspicious hesitation on my mother's part.

'. . . I'm thirty-seven . . .'

'You're forty,' Uncle Moses snapped with the ferocity of Genghis Khan sweeping through a village of thirteen yurts. 'And I'm sixty-five and I'm damned if I ever rolled around on the floor with you at the age of twenty-five or thirty. I was not only making a living for my whole family but I was well on my way to making a fortune.'

He raised his voice and yelled at me, 'At your age I was slugging sample cases through the wilds of this god-forsaken province by horse and buggy beyond the range of the railroads. I was the most successful drummer in . . .'

'I'm sorry, Uncle,' I murmured, 'but I'm not musical . . .'

I heard him gasp.

'That boy's a ninny,' he muttered to my mother. 'He's had it too soft. He needs a little toughening up. I'd put him through the mill, if I had him for a year. Just like his father. He's a ninny and I've always said so and I'm damned if I'll subsidise him for the rest of my life. . . .'

'It's not a question of subsidy, but of right,' my mother said in the voice Elizabeth I must have used to the Bishop of Ely when he refused to give up his town house. 'I have scrimped and scraped for eighteen years . . .' (I suffered a hilarious, silent conniption for Mother was an expert at the Big Lie) '. . . and if you think I'm going to turn him into a ditch digger, you are sadly mistaken. Remember there are still The Courts and neither I nor Blanche has ever had a proper accounting of Daddy's store. I'm sure there's still a few dollars . . .'

Uncle Moses plunged off to the left. Mother dashed to the door and spread-eagled herself against it but Uncle Moses was only going to tug a bell pull which flicked dust into the air as he yanked it. Almost immediately, old Shrubsole answered, opened the door behind Mother, steadied her as she slid backward against the opening door and said, 'You rang, sir.'

'Tea.'

'The service, sir?'

'No.'

Shrubsole brought in on a battered tray, three cups, a slightly chipped china teapot and six of the plainest, driest, cheapest nineteen cents a package tea biscuits, placed it on the end of a thirty foot mahogany table and retired. There was no milk, lemon, sugar.

'No use getting worked up about this sort of thing,' Uncle Moses said in a conciliatory tone.

Mother seated herself at the end of the enormous table and, sitting well towards the front of her seat, put on her Duchess's air and poured tea. If Mother was anything she was most definitely a lady. Anyone with an opinion to the contrary was likely to find himself snatched baldheaded and gouged about the eyeball—at least, verbally.

'Now—ah—err—Jim,' Uncle Moses said in his most avuncular manner.

'Tim,' I said.

'Ah, yes, Tim.'

I could see he hated me. I thought he was being polite to me because of Mother.

'Well, Tim, what are your plans?'

'My plans, Uncle Moses?'

'Yes. What are you going in for? Doctor, lawyer, dentist, teacher, scientist?'

He was desperately impatient with me but was making an enormous effort to keep his temper under control. If he had ever hired me, he would have fired me at that moment.

'What I want to go in for is Phyllis Bromley, Uncle Moses. That's all I've wanted all summer, to go in for Phyllis Bromley. I've spent every dime I made this year on her. That's why I have nothing towards my college tuition. And if you gave me or Mother two hundred dollars for college I'd go right out and spend it on Phyllis Bromley. Yes, in one night. I'd crawl ten miles over broken glass just to sniff her bicycle seat.'

That's what I wanted to say to Uncle Moses. He'd have been

43

thrown into a Force Nine epileptic fit. But I suppose I knew, even then, that honesty can exist only in a vacuum so I said, 'A lawyer, Uncle Moses.' Just to please him.

He raised his left eyebrow a quarter of an inch and came within two or three hundred miles of a smile which was his equivalent of doing a back flip with a full gainer, throwing himself on the floor and gnawing the rug, screaming with hysterical laughter and shedding tears half-way between astonishment and disbelief. Anyone could tell, even in those days, that I lacked the moral ambiguity necessary to the successful professional man. 'Dentistry,' he said. 'Perhaps you should try dentistry. One extra cavity per mouth and you're a rich man.'

He said it thoughtfully.

'It is time we raised the tone of this family,' Mother put in regally. 'Tim shall be a Doctor.'

'Tone. There's nothing the matter with . . .' Uncle Moses began.

Mother simply raised her chin another two inches. Uncle Moses faltered. 'He won't be anything unless you do something immediately,' she said.

Uncle seemed to be thinking. He brightened.

'Perfect,' he said. 'That's the solution. Go see Dean Nash. Collingwood College. I have influence there. Just the thing for you, my boy.'

'Collingwood College? Collingwood College?'

'Not good enough for you, Veronica? I could manage Agricultural College. A swine inspector in the family might be just the thing . . .'

It was a threat.

'Well, if you'll give me the cheque, we'll go. Don't think I'm ungrateful, Moses, but I do want the best for my boy.'

'Don't worry about the money. I'll look after everything. You'll see. You'll see.'

I saw.

When I arrived at Collingwood they gave me a job. Assistant to the night engineer. Enough to pay my tuition and about three-fifty a week left over to eat on. Graveyard shift, midnight to eight. Shovelling coal, cleaning boilers, breakfast, lectures, then nearly nine hours all to myself for study, sleeping and such activities as worrying about being hungry all the time. And they wanted me to join the football team. I was big and they needed linemen. It meant about four hours' sleep a night but I joined the team because they laid a training table loaded with steak.

Dear old Uncle Moses.

My temper shortened in direct proportion to my lack of sleep. Coach Carpus did not care for my lack of team spirit.

'You are the leaders of the future. In the next generation, you will be running this country. What you learn on this playing field will stand you in good stead in future competition in your chosen careers. So get out there and win.'

And here I was, already a loser. Singing for my supper. But as that blessed martyr Saint Bunyard said as he forgave the lion gnawing on his left buttock, 'It is easier to enter the gates of Heaven than for a Poor Sport to get a ticket for the Emperor's box.'

After the third game, the one against Talbot Tech, I was voted Poorest Sport of the Year. Before the game, my team mates, not the least offensive of whom was Charlie Scaliger, mentioned that I'd be playing against Buck Paddock on the line.

'Little Ol' Buck's a pushover,' they would say, 'a cream puff.' Then they would snigger like yokels at a freak show.

Ol' Buck Paddock was a pushover, all right, if you had a bulldozer. He was at least two hundred and fifty pounds so he outweighed me by fifty or sixty. That wasn't so bad. What bothered me was his habit, as he tried to break through my position, of slinging an uppercut at me under cover of the scrimmage.

I was shocked, the first time. This was supposed to be sportsmanship, amateurism, it matters not if you win or lose but how you play . . . etc. 'Hey! What's the idea?' I demanded.

45

He gave me a gap-toothed smirk. It also seemed to me that my linemates were enjoying my surprise.

The second time he caught me a stinging blow just under the eye. 'Do that again,' I said, 'and I'll kick your syphilitic teeth in.'

He appreciated the adjective. He kept his smirk but it hardened.

The third time he split my lip. 'Whose what kind of teeth is who going to kick in now?' he sneered.

Scaliger, our quarterback, was calling the signals. I was wondering what the hell we were doing there, grown men, practically, crouched in a field like animals. I stood up and took one step forward. The whistle blew. I was off side. And not only was I off side, I was standing on good Ol' Buck Paddock's hand. My full weight was on my cleats and my knee seemed to have bloodied his nose and he was screaming like a girl.

I released his hand. He held out his bloody, muddy right hand supporting it at the wrist by his left and half-gasped and half-blubbered in shock, 'Uh-uh-uh . . .' while he stared at me in horror.

Someone in Tech's backfield (it's always someone in the backfield) whined, 'He's not getting away with that.'

My Collingwood College team mates faded back, feeling instinctively that I was morally indefensible, while the Tech team piled on.

A Tech halfback and an end seemed to get the idea of a flying tackle simultaneously. I hit the turf and they hit each other before landing on me, then the rest of the team piled on. I hugged my hands to my chest so that I shouldn't suffer Buck Paddock's fate and by hunching my shoulders high, my shoulder pads touched my helmet and so protected my neck. My kidney pads protected that region so that only my ribs and legs were vulnerable to the kicks, punches and gouges that were attempted. I was insulated from most of these by the first layer of the Tech team on top of me and my only real injury was to my knee which was badly wrenched

46

and chipped at the top of the fibula though I did not find out about that clinical detail until several years later.

The referees unscrambled the pile-on, gave me a game penalty and gave Tech a yardage penalty for piling on. On the strength of their vastly superior moral position, and even without Buck Paddock, Tech smeared Collingwood 32 to 0.

Two of the Tech team had to be assisted off the field because of serious injuries suffered from their team mates' ill-directed kicks. I half-limped, half-hopped off the field alone, without a helping shoulder to lean upon. There were cries of rage from the Tech side of the stands, shamed silence from Collingwood's side.

After the game it was Charlie Scaliger who led our team into the Tech dressing-room and made an abject apology to the visiting team for my lack of sportsmanship. Marshall of *The Globe* wrote a highly incensed article with a three-column head, *New Low in Sportsmanship*, and at the end of the year voted me Poorest Sport Of The Year.

My term papers came back, slashed to the bone. Of course, I was suspended from the team and, worse, from the training table. Then, a cutback in staff, they told me, allowed them to dispense with my services in the boiler room and, beginning with the winter term, my tuition was payable in cash.

I took the hint and limped away.

Those were Charlie Scaliger's good old days. Is it any wonder that I blurted, 'For whom?' when he murmured soulfully, 'Ah, they were good times, Tim. We were only kids then, Tim. Carefree. I'd give a million dollars to go back . . .'

'I'd give a million to send you back,' I growled.

The waitress placed my tea in front of me and as she did so Charlie Scaliger picked up the envelope I had been scribbling on. With the utmost coolness he turned it over, noted Cutter, Mandrake & Swingle's imprint and said, 'I see they finally found you.'

He turned it over, read my five notations under his name: brown-noser, sneak, crook, bubblehead and trance artist. He calmly shoved the envelope back at me.

'What are you doing in a place like this, Tim? With all Muddiman's money? This place isn't good enough for you. Leave.'

I slupped my tea in a deliberately noisy and, indeed, disgusting fashion in the hope of driving him off. At college he had always been very strong on decorum, neat dress, grooming and similar deceits. This, with his fair complexion and blond hair made him appear as quite a clean cut kid and few of the staff could have suspected that he was probably the worst cheat in the college, his clean cuffs stuffed to capacity with cribs at exam time.

He was determined not to be driven out though. He leaned back in that excessively relaxed manner that always indicates an enormous unease.

He made a small gesture that took in the whole tea room. 'It's not that there is anything wrong with this, much,' he said, 'but you know, I belong to Les Amis des Goulus.'

'Too bad,' I said.

'The local gourmet club. You know. We've been written up half a dozen times . . .'

'Truffles?'

He nodded eagerly. 'Yes.'

'Hollandaise?'

He nodded again, delighted.

'You have, of course, a pan used for nothing but omelettes?'

'Yes, of course.'

'No smoking before dinner?'

'Yes, yes!'

'One stirs only with a wooden spoon?'

'Absolutely!'

'But there are occasions when even the wooden spoon would prove too bruising and then . . .?'

'It would be sufficient to tilt the pan in all directions. Not enough to swirl the sauce. Just enough to move it.'

He was triumphant. He was drooling to be put through a catechism on sauces: Bordelaise, Mornay, Fennel, Hollandaise, Mousseline, Sabayon, Ravigote. I looked at him directly for the first time. I was shocked. The old Charlie Scaliger was there, all right, but under a not-too-obvious layer of degenerate tissue. Superficially, he looked to be in great shape. He had been a bit of a pouter pigeon back at Collingwood and this cluster of mannerisms he still retained: the way he held his head up and cocked a bit to the side; the jaunty walk; the hint of superiority; more than a *soupçon* of vanity; the nattiness. But the eyes were growing smaller behind puffiness. He didn't give the appearance of jowliness yet his cheeks were so thick that his little ears seemed to spring out of indentations. A broad gold wedding band was in the process of becoming absorbed in surplus tissue like a tree encysting a wound. His nose had lost crispness and his hairline had receded in two lagoons, almost isolating a central patch above his forehead. He looked as though he still thought he was a lady-killer, but I had always known him as a Boy Scout with tendencies towards pocket-pool.

Molloy, whose girl friend was a very young widow, used to torment him in the locker room. Or rather, Scaliger used to torment himself. 'How did you make out with your broad last night, Molloy?' he would ask in his patently false, careless manner. His idea of casualness was not to look Molloy in the eye, and worldliness to him meant calling girls, babes, broads, skirts.

'Christ! She nearly killed me,' Molloy replied on one of these interrogations. 'Feel that.'

Scaliger whirled, looking startled, then with suspicion felt the indicated spot on top of Molloy's head. Molloy's helmet strap had broken in a practice session and it was in that scrimmage that he had acquired the bump.

'She did that? You had a fight?'

'No, no. She's mad about me.'

'But your head . . .'

Scaliger was hooked.

'She must have . . .'

Molloy massaged his bump gently, sensuously. He closed his eyes and let a dreamy expression come over his face.

D

'Well, she did attack me.'

'With what?' Scaliger demanded.

Molloy's eyes flew open then narrowed.

'With herself,' he said.

'What do you mean? My God!' Scaliger's imagination was making his hair stand on end.

Molloy kept him on tenterhooks.

'I don't know whether I've told you,' he said, 'but Sally lives in this rooming house . . .'

'Yes, yes!'

'It has a vestibule about four feet square. Just the front door and the inner door. Enough to kill draughts. And this filthy matting on the floor . . .'

'For Crissake, Molloy, get to the attack. Please!'

'Well, I rang the bell and she opened the door, grabbed me by the wrist and dragged me in, all in a split second. It was strange . . .'

'Strange. Yeah. O.K., O.K.!'

'She had on this gown. It went right to the ground . . .'

'Oh, God! A fashion show. Come on, come on!'

'Even in the dark, in the vestibule, I could practically see right through it. It was some sort of thin stuff. Very thin. Sheer, that's the word . . .'

'Christ!'

'It was hanging wide open, now that I think of it.'

'You're shitting me! In the vestibule? No!'

'She threw her arms around me. I thought she was going to kiss me but we never did kiss last night.'

This shattered Scaliger.

'No. She threw her arms around me too tight for me to kiss her then she gave a little hop and wound her legs around my waist.'

'What! What! You did it that way?'

'Are you crazy, Scaliger? She weighs a hundred and thirty-five pounds. Jesus, she's got an ass on her . . .' And he held his hands as though hefting a great, globular bottom. 'We just sank to that filthy mat in the vestibule.'

'You did it in the vestibule? Right there in the front vestibule of the rooming house?'

A glimmer of incredulity lit the murk of his imagination for a moment. 'Molloy, you're the biggest bull artist I know.'

He made as if to walk away but found it impossible when Molloy silently fondled the bump on his head.

'That vestibule couldn't be more than four and a half feet, corner to corner. I almost think I'd prefer the back seat of a car. Anyway, someone wanted to come in the front door. Banged me right on the head with it. I slammed it shut. They kept trying to open it and every time they banged me on the head . . .'

'Naw, naw.' Scaliger sounded as though he were protesting against an unbearable truth. He was gnawing his knuckles. 'No one. No One. *No One.* In the circumstances . . . Even if it were true. You're a goddam liar, Molloy. Goddam it! No one in the circumstances . . .'

'What the hell was I supposed to do?'

'*No One. No One*, goddam it. Don't you have the least goddam shame? In public, practically? Get the hell out, that's what you were supposed to do . . .'

'But I couldn't.'

That checked Scaliger's panic for a moment.

'But you couldn't? What the hell does that mean? There was the other door. You could have gone out the back way . . .'

'What's the door got to do with it? I tell you I couldn't.'

'You couldn't?' Scaliger was confused. His logic had failed him.

'I was on the bottom,' Molloy said simply.

Scaliger backed away as though Molloy had pulled a knife on him then he fled and we heard him gasping under the hiss of the cold shower.

So this was Charlie Scaliger, trying to look into the waitress's bosom as she served my tea, leaning back with that elaborate casualness that indicated his uneasiness with me, absorbing my insults with calm because, obviously, there was something he wanted from me.

'Be my guest at the next meeting of the Club. Oswald, the chef from Hillier's is in charge. What do you say?' He smiled, for a man, charmingly. It had been his forte in the Drama Society at Collingwood.

'No,' I said. 'Thank you. I've got beyond all that.'

Now, why did I say that? I wondered. The holier-than-thou attitude is, of course, notoriously irritating but I must have had something more in mind than the desire to depreciate Charlie Scaliger and his new found hobby. Fortunately he did not leave me to stew in my own juice (perhaps sauce is the more appropriate term) for long. As with any recent convert, he leaped to the defence too soon.

'Beyond all that?' he asked, nettled, but trying to conceal it. 'You must be off in the far-out realms of Chinese cookery.'

'Not at all,' I said.

'You're not a health nut? Safflower seeds. Organically raised produce?'

He was quite anxious.

'No, no. It's more basic.'

'Well, there are only two schools of cookery. French and Chinese. The rest are off-shoots.'

He was quite firm about this.

I was making a quick geographic tour in my mind, trying to alight upon an eccentric, almost unheard of novelty with which to confound him. I told myself that I must cover the earth, from pole to pole, within an instant. And that gave me the clue.

'You are perhaps familiar with rotten mattak?'

'No,' he said, 'and to tell the truth, I'm not all that partial to high game. It's pretty well passé. In the old days when everyone and everything stank to high heaven it was more acceptable, but there aren't too many who can stomach that sort of thing nowadays.'

'It's a different process,' I informed him gently. 'Probably I should not have said "rotten" but rather "fermented". Yes. Fermented mattak. The narwhal skin tastes quite like walnuts while the blubber has a touch of Roquefort flavour about it. Rather sharp . . .'

'*Narwhal Skin?*'

'Considered a great delicacy among Greenland Eskimos. Of course, it's an aged thing. Fresh narwhal skin, I suppose, is nothing. It takes perhaps three or four years for the process of fermentation to achieve the delicacy required.'

'*Rotten Mattak?*'

'Yes. They cache great slabs of the narwhal skin under rocks for some years and with the prevailing low temperatures even in summer the blubber has no tendency to go rancid although it does definitely turn a decided shade of green . . .'

'*Greenland?*'

'The difficulty is getting it out without exposing it to warm temperatures and this means air transport. It's a bit difficult to mail a casual note to eighty degrees north latitude on the Greenland side of Baffin Bay. To go through Danish channels, I'm afraid, is a bit slow and chancy so I must depend for this sort of thing on a chap named Eric Rasmussen who will make unofficial arrangements with U.S. Air Force personnel at Thule to bring it out in good condition. A pretty penny. A pretty penny . . .'

'*Baffin Bay?*'

'They're not supposed to fly out civilian goods in military planes but, fortunately, I have the resources.'

I had Charlie Scaliger on the ropes: no mean accomplishment. For, although he often carried the ball, he was rarely tackled. In those days of Statue of Liberty plays, Trojan Horses, and end runs, he yielded the ball only when there was no possibility of glory for him, when the play was doomed; then he flipped the ball to the nearest team mate and let him get smeared. So I ground it in.

'I suppose this business of cooking food until all its natural qualities are dead, then gingering it up with allegedly subtle concoctions is all right for the decadent, the toothless and those dedicated to liver trouble. And speaking of liver, did you know that the liver of a properly ripened seal tastes distinctly like sweetened cranberries? That the variation in taste from neck to paw of a polar bear is a veritable symphony? But all this is crude when compared to giviak . . .'

'*Giviak?*'

'A delicacy. Or rather, two delicacies. Frozen and thawed. I see that you are not familiar with it? Preparation is an interesting process. You will note I do not use the term cooking. As with many another recipe, this one would begin, "First catch your seal".'

Scaliger's eyes were glazing. His mouth silently formed the word 'seal'.

'The flensing is the most delicate and demanding of tasks. The skin must be removed from the carcass without the least cut or puncture and this can be done only through the mouth. The forelimbs must be cut with great accuracy at certain precise joints, the body separated from the skin and blubber and drawn out through the mouth. This blubber-lined sealskin bag is then filled with dovekies—a sort of little murre which nests in the arctic cliffs. But this is of the utmost importance: the dovekies must be killed by forcing the thumb under the breastbone and bursting the heart. The wings are braided over the back and the birds packed solidly into the sealskin bag.'

'First gutted?' he managed to put in.

'Oh no! That's throwing away the best part. No. The complete bird is packed in, feathers and all. When the sealskin is full it is cached under rocks where there is no chance of it warming up and turning the blubber rancid in an unseasonally mild summer. Slowly, the oil in the blubber seeps into the birds which ferment the while. A few winters later comes the two part feast—frozen and thawed giviak. The frozen meat dissolves like sherbet. Encountering a formed egg is the greatest of delicious good luck. A taste treat, as a copy writer would undoubtedly say. The liver is like soft ripe cheese; thawed it is somewhat spicy. The blood clot formed by the burst heart is a taste adventure. Gall bladder, intestines, stomach, all have their distinctive flavours, from spice to hops, and should be savoured separately. Feathers and bones one concerns oneself with no more than the shell of a lobster and in the thawed condition the feathers may be stripped off with one stroke of the cupped hands while holding the bird's feet in the mouth. Of course, one must be adventurous. Willing to break out of that hidebound circle of French cookery. Give a French chef enough butter and he'll cook a brick for you. I had hoped for delivery of a giviak in about a month but it is too much to ask you to break the habits of a lifetime and share it . . .'

I had described this Eskimo food with slow-paced relish, mostly because I only half remembered it from an old travel book and had to invent the rest. This must have seemed like sincerity to Charlie Scaliger for he leaped to my half-proffered invitation.

'Delighted. I'd be most anxious. An adventure. Exotic. Never heard of this sort of thing . . .'

'Of course not. A real rarity. I don't suppose there are more than half a dozen men in the Arctic capable of producing a good giviak. And why should they ship off such a gem to us? No. It's not like other cookery. No fakery about it. No possibility of a fad developing—not because of the inaccessibility of the north and the rigorous conditions under which giviak must be aged. Money can duplicate or pay for all that. The trouble is that one must get into training for this sort of treat. Because of the very high fat content. A good gorging of giviak and you'd inevitably come down with fat poisoning.

'Never heard of fat poisoning, of course? Proved it on Canadian troops in the last war when they tried pemmican on them as an iron ration. They all got terribly sick and weak. No one could understand why they couldn't paddle sixteen hours a day and portage three hundred pounds on a pound of pemmican, a quart of tea and a pint of whisky like the old *coureurs du bois*. Steffanson proved they hadn't built up their fat tolerance. The pemmican was half fat. So, I'm warning you, get into training for the giviak.

Build up your diet until it contains fifty per cent fat or there's no point in even trying the giviak.'

Scaliger was somewhat downcast at this news but he manfully vowed to adjust his diet to my epicurean demands. He handed me his business card, first jotting his home phone number on it. He thrust his hand at me with the greatest of apparent good will but fortunately I was fishing in my pocket for change for the waitress and could pretend not to see it.

I thought he went off down the street with a little less bounce in his usual strut. And yet, I was uneasy.

Five

Now, why did I shroud Charlie Scaliger in such a tissue of false-hood, fantasy and fatuity I asked myself as I rushed away from him. Had I already been perverted by even the thought of my inheritance? Impossible. I had indulged in a few random antici-pations, no more. Not to do so would have been unnatural. And yet, in essence, we had talked of nothing but money; extravagant consumption.

It was certainly not envy on my part for even his sports-minded team mates had held him in a not always amused contempt for his tendency to hog the ball. A suspicious element in our meeting was his lack of energy in upholding his stale epicurean views in the face of my esoteric ones. A second and even more suspect fac-tor was his persistence in accosting me. Yes, he wanted something from me. Perhaps only an opportunity to make his obeisance to the money he probably thought I already possessed.

But my reaction? Why was I rushing along the street trembling with rage? Why did I plunge into the nearest hardware store, seize an alarm clock, wind it furiously while I waited for my change then thrust the clock savagely into my pocket without waiting either for its carton or to have it wrapped? Was it that I had learned he headed a bailiff's organisation? That all those newspaper photos of the dispossessed with their scant belongings in the street suddenly had a real (if perhaps unreal) man behind them? Had I simply found a target? No. I felt too vulnerable my-self. It is impossible to mistake the feeling. Even with one's back turned one recognises the entry of an enemy into a crowded room.

It's people, I told myself, and idleness. For three years you have

successfully avoided contact and kept yourself from mischief with
the sound, healthy physical job of washing cars. Now, on the
flimsy excuse of inheriting a fake castle you play hookey, hobnob
idly with the lowest elements of society and end up in the destructive toils of rage.

Long ago, through an analysis of the Monday morning papers,
I had discovered that man has very little tolerance for others of
his species. As soon as he is released from his shackles for the week-
end, he seeks out companionship and this association takes the
colourful form of automobile collisions, drunken brawls, murders,
suicide pacts, stranglings, knifings, abortions, armed robberies,
adulteries and similar aspects of communal endeavour and of
love.

Was it Baron Bunyard—no, I believe it was Mr. Beyle the
gambler—who said, All her virtue returned because love left her.
A clear indication of the murderous insanity involved in the close
communication between men, nations, societies, civilisations and,
perhaps, worlds. I knew all this, as I have said, and yet I knowingly joined Charlie Scaliger in the game of Friend Pelt Friend
With Garbage. It was most disturbing.

So I dashed out of the business district with all the speed I
could muster, short of a run. I slowed down only when I had
entered a quiet neighbourhood of modest homes and tranquil,
almost deserted streets. Men at work, children in schools, wives
engaged in domestic duties or perhaps striving for second-hand
heartbreak in front of television sets. The modest surroundings
calmed me. I began to see more clearly my ludicrous position as
the heir of Uncle Moses' Castle.

Why should I spend the rest of my life, I thought, dining at the
end of an enormously long table and under the public gaze of
servants? Why should I devote hours of my life to waiting on
waiters? Why should I have to make a special request for a stalk
of celery or arrange for it a day ahead? How could I possibly
enjoy an omelette prepared ten minutes before, hundreds of feet
away and perhaps several stories below? Could I carry a fresh

apple in my dinner jacket pocket? Would I ever again enjoy the simplicity and contentment of that picnic to Poplar Point years ago? I mellowed, almost melted, under the recollection.

It had been a day late in spring or perhaps early summer. Warm. Sky milky-blue, somewhat hazy, calm. There was a feeling of diffuseness, a lack of pressure, a loose freedom. Myrtle was feeling easy, compliant. 'To hell with work,' I said. 'Anyone who works on a day like this ought to be arrested.'

I expected her to whirl on me to see whether or not I was serious, for usually I progressed from this sort of statement to a desire to throw everything up, start afresh in a totally unexplored endeavour.

'Smell the garden,' she said mildly. She was leaning out of the window and did not turn around. 'The air is so soft. From the south, I suppose.'

I joined her at the window. The air was indeed soft, rich. It was that time of year when the birches and poplars spew pollen in volcanic profusion into every cranny, on to every miscegenous pistil, into every lung, on to every squirrel mounting his, for once, languid mate, on to every inertly nesting bird, on to our hair, our clothes. There is probably a chemical action involved, narcoticising us with the languid unease of spring fever while the germinal odours of the season vaguely stimulate us without driving us to disciplined action.

'A fishing sort of day,' I said. 'Too bad it's too early in the season.'

My arm was around her waist as we leaned out of the window, my hand on the womanly crest of her hip.

'A picnic?' she suggested.

'A cool picnic. All right. Early for ants, but why not?'

We remained at the window for some time before drifting away from it to pack the lunch.

The food was simple. A delicate ham sausage. God knows where it came from. It had none of the German brutality in its make-up, none of the tear-bringing sentimentality of the Italian sausage, none of the fire of the Polish. The rolls were perfect; perfectly fresh yet with a crust of shattering crispness. There was the rubbery-soft texture of devilled eggs. An inexpensive extra-dry domestic white wine exactly suitable to the occasion, not too chilled. I had brought along our best crystal for it though Myrtle was worried about it being broken on this informal outing. The fruit was both crisp and juicy. Pears, I believe. Imported. Great brown shapeless ones. And cheese, probably Bel Paese. Or perhaps that was the menu of another holiday.

We sat with our backs against the car, trapping a little more warmth from the hazy sun. The lake, tame for once, murmured rather than hissed against the shore in tiny surges and the sand-pipers dithered back and forth, skirting pneumonia. On a distant sandbar gulls had congregated silently except for the shriek of an occasional protestant. This always stirs and delights me—the jeering of the crow, the suicidal melancholy of the loon, the para-noid wildness of the gull's cry. Tweetie birds are nothing to me. Give me the wild calls, any day. This probably says something about me. The psychologists have never given this matter suffi-cient attention.

We walked hand in hand along only a part of the beach's two miles, just to where a tangent to the car must cross the curve of the water. All was flat, calm, gentle—the lake, the shore, the land behind with its occasional gleaming barn roof, the air, the sun, the mistily greening trees.

I leaned lightly against her as we approached a clump of juniper that had crept beyond the foot of a dune. I wanted not so much to lead her into the little brush-screened hollow behind the crest of the dune as to influence her subtly, just suggest the possibility to the lower levels of her mind, of which she had many, that we disappear from sight.

But she leaned rather definitely into my almost accidental pressure; not really in an obvious way but in view of what was in my mind it was quite definite. And at the critical point where we had to veer either to one side or another of the projecting clump of juniper she lengthened one pace just an inch so that my shoulder, should it touch hers, would be behind it and without significant leverage except to urge her on and so we continued along the beach.

Although the pleasant memory ended here there is no known method of abolishing remembrance.

We arrived back at the car untired. We could have trudged along the beach until we became aware of the sand dragging at our feet and then the return would have been a plodding chore, but we turned back before that point so the walk itself was entirely pleasant. We drove back in silence but it was a silence that could have turned sullen with a word; any word. And to make matters worse the front left corner of the car developed a 'crick-crick' which manifested itself even on the smoothest portion of the road. This mysterious 'crick-crick' filled me with a nameless anxiety. I had never heard anything like it before. Shock absorber? Metal fatigue? Dry steering box? Engine mount?

I tried the brakes. Satisfactory.

I slowed to thirty. Sometimes a change in the pattern of vibration . . .

Crick-crick.

I speeded up to forty.

Crick-crick.

Fifty.

Crick-crick.

No pattern to the intervals.

Sixty.

Crick-crick.

Seventy.

Crick-crick.

Eighty.

Crick-crick.

Cured!

No. The roar of the engine and the rush of the air by the open windows almost obscured the sound.

Crick-crick.

Ninety. Might as well blow out the carbon.

Crick-crick.

I had been driving mainly by ear, barely noticing the road. I had forgotten about Myrtle. But over and above the physical tensions which invest a speeding car I sensed another and more dangerous tension. When I put my mind to it I realised I was noting, out of the corner of my eye, that Myrtle was grinding her heels into the floorboards with formidable pressure. Another flick of my eye showed white knuckles on the arm rest. I did not need to look at her face.

Ha!

So this is the Age of Communication.

As Jean-Paul Louis Bunyard says in his Commentaries: It is to laugh.

Any couple, married thirty-five minutes, can give the experts the whole story on Communications, if they dare.

My slight, tentative, subliminal pressure towards Myrtle's shoulder had said, All right, we've had our simple picnic, our quiet, domestic wine. We've had our sniff at the great outdoors in its calmer mood, now, what about a bit of excitement for a change?

And the one inch increase in the length of her stride and the refusal of her shoulder to yield to any pressure as unequivocally said that she didn't think much of the idea; that cold-blooded indulgence was not in her line; that broad daylight made it impossible; that outdoors without the security of a roof it became an insanity, not to mention the sandy nature of the ground and the stunted habit of the shrubbery with the possibility of a mad lepidopterist (perhaps Nabokov himself) obsessively stalking rare fritillaries on the other side of the junipers at this very moment; that the moon was not in phase with a subtle relation to pay day.

And I knew, too, didn't I, that she regarded this wallowing as something fit only for the Eastern Mediterranean race, Africans and the mysterious East and perhaps, locally, the lower classes; that when one must rarely, if inevitably, yield to the demands of the flesh it must be with reluctant endearment, in midnight darkness, in the colour and secretiveness of sin, physically anonymous and impersonal, intelligence allegedly obliterated by the pulse of the blood, with morning amnesia.

But no. Myrtle's amorous peculiarities I leave for another more appropriate occasion. I simply point out how over-loaded with communication we have always been; how the slightest gesture—the flicker of a lash, movement of a muscle variation in a tone too minute to show upon a scintillometer, is freighted with hundreds, thousands, perhaps millions of messages more than any coaxial cable is capable of transmitting. So Myrtle's gesture of lengthening her step an inch contained not only all I have mentioned but also a reproach for a sharp word a year ago last November, revenge for pinching her in the subway and pretending for a moment that it was a fellow strap-hanger, but also a Lysistratian threat for the future, not to mention grating reminders of the hazards of years of married life.

Communication! What we need is respite from communication for communication is only the enormous, tedious, persistent endeavour to change other people's minds whether it is called propaganda, education, advertising, entertainment or public relations.

Aha! What about sex?

Well, what about it? Look at any two long-term communicants such as celebrants of golden weddings. It is a common observation that they look like twins. In two generations of communication they have cut each other down into their own image which in itself was always being modified by the other.

But I was trying to say, not something about the destructive nature of communication, but about fleeing from Charlie Scaliger and entering the quiet residential neighbourhood and relating its calm and peace to the picnic at Poplar Point.

So, either the recollection of this picnic calmed me and made

63

me see the district through which I walked in a pleasant light or the neighbourhood with its untroubled air suppressed my anger by example. In any event, with calm, the solution of my problem appeared to me without stress or struggle or resolution. I would simply put the Castle on the market. Wash my hands of it. Continue my simple life—with a few conveniences and embellishments added—but not so many as to enslave me or to undermine my humanity. This solution restored my frame of mind—not to my former orgy of happiness but to a definite sense of pleasure—so that I smiled again as I strolled along.

I smiled even more as I approached a school crossing. The crossing guard, a stupid-looking woman with iron grey hair and close-set eyes under her peaked cap, flipped up her STOP sign suddenly and brought a car to a squealing stop. The children streamed across to my side of the street, most of them turning towards me and flooding past me, chattering, as though I were a rock in the middle of a current. One tiny figure turned the other way in the direction I was walking and I soon caught up to her I felt myself smiling like a village idiot at a flea circus.

She was probably five years old and small for her age, dressed in a tiny plaid skirt with cross braces over a miniature white blouse. White cotton stockings could not disguise those heart-breakingly skinny, gull-like knees. In her right hand she held out stiffly a sheet of crayon drawings as though she were immediately and purposefully making a special delivery of them. And she wore two little pigtails, no more than four inches long, tipped with tiny red bows and standing out abruptly from the side of her head.

I gave one pigtail the tiniest of tugs.

'Don't do that, mister,' she said without irritation. The matter-of-fact glance she gave me showed great, brown, wide spaced eyes and a missing tooth. A formidable beauty, in her way.

'I'm sorry, sweetie . . .'

'My name is Penelope,' she said evenly. Just giving me the facts.

64

'I'm sorry, Penelope. I hope you will forgive me. My name is Timothy.'

'Willie Bartholomew gives me a candy when he pulls my pig-tail.'

'Does he always have candy?'

'No.'

'What then?'

'I hit him.'

'Oh. Doesn't he hit you back?'

'Boys aren't supposed to hit little girls.'

She was definite about this. She was an absolute knock-out. She had me whooping and hollering with delight, rolling in the gutter in hysterics, climbing trees, throwing my hat in the air. But I dead-panned it, as she was doing.

'I wouldn't want you to hit me,' I said. 'I don't have any candy. Would this do?' And I offered her a tangerine.

'You're too big,' she observed, taking the tangerine.

I watched her as she tried to fit it into the tiny pocket of her skirt. She was all of a piece: perfect, certain, healthy. She showed none of the rags and tatters of the disintegrating adult. No sick-ness in the eye, no backbone bent under guilt, no nervous flutter-ings of fear, no binding chains of excuses. I had completely re-covered my orgy-of-happiness feeling.

One attempt showed her that the tangerine would not fit her pocket.

'Will you carry my orange home for me, Timothy, please?'

'Yes, of course.'

'My mummy likes oranges. Will you give her one, too?'

'Yes, I will.'

She took my hand or, rather, two fingers and we walked on for half a block, then she tugged me to the left. We proceeded up a driveway—to the back door I presumed—but she led me on across a lawn towards a fence at the end of the property.

A hand on my collar thrust me forward and to the side so that I had to throw my hands up against the side of a garage to keep

E

from falling. 'Got you, my lad,' I heard, and then, 'Grab the kid, Walt.'

It was happening with the split-second speed of a nightmare. Penelope slipped through a gap in the fence where a picket was missing. She was screaming, 'Mummy, Mummy, they're hurting Timothy!'

The policeman was vaulting after her but a woman, obviously her mother, came plunging out of her kitchen and snatched her up before the policeman reached her.

'Why are you chasing my child? What do you mean by it?' Penelope's mother demanded.

The policeman didn't meet her eye.

'We got this call,' he said, 'about this pervert hanging around the school and dragging a little girl up a lane . . .'

The other officer had just finished frisking me. I pushed myself away from the garage wall and was flung sprawling on the ground by some judo trick, some quite unnecessary leverage against the knee.

'What sort of brutes are you?' Penelope's mother demanded. 'Is there any excuse for that sort of action—in front of a child?'

My captor had his gun out now. In his other hand he held the clock he had fished out of my pocket.

'Get up,' he ordered.

'They're hurting Timothy,' Penelope wailed.

'I hope you realise that it is you who are terrifying my child,' Penelope's mother stated. 'And I think you have your facts wrong. Penelope comes home this way every day. Coming through the fence saves walking all around the block. Until you came, I could see she was leading Mr. Badger quietly by the hand up to the fence. Do you think if he had any peculiar intentions he would have brought her home like this?'

So she knew me! And she was not hostile. In the circumstances, I found this extraordinary.

The policeman, Walt, was apparently more intelligent than his partner. 'We can't take chances, Mrs. . . .'

'Bellman.'

'We have to check out every complaint like this immediately . . . before anything . . .'

'Well, I don't like your method of checking out.'

'Get up and identify yourself,' my captor snarled.

'I have no intention of getting up and subjecting myself to another criminal attack, even in the presence of a reliable witness. Mrs. Bellman has already identified me. However, just to keep you abreast of your present circumstances . . .'

I handed him the lawyers' letter informing me of my inheritance. It was a threat. He read it very slowly and deliberately and as he read I could see him turn to pale jelly behind his brutal façade. Walt, meanwhile, vaulted back over the fence, delighted to break away from the embarrassing Mrs. Bellman. He read the letter over his partner's shoulder. When they had finished they threw each other minute, desperate glances. They had made the one irretrievable mistake for a policeman. They had abused the rich and the powerful.

Me.

They made a show of noting my name in their black books and then silently handed the letter back to me. I took out a pencil and held it poised over the back of the envelope.

'And now, if you will identify yourselves, officially . . .'

With sickly stiffness they showed me their badges. I, in turn, made my notes: Walter Black and Desmond Stollery.

'Desmond?' I said in an insinuating, unbelieving tone. I got up from the ground, and turning my back on Mrs. Bellman, murmured, 'When I get you before the Commission it won't be the manhandling that will be your problem, Desmond. It will be the frisking. What were you looking for on . . . ah . . . the inside of my thigh—a machine gun? You took an exceptionally long time about it.'

Walter Black threw Desmond an astonished look. Desmond's face, in spite of his beefy outdoor complexion, turned grey. He was too shocked to be murderous. Horror paralysed him. I had

67

dealt him an ice-pick sort of blow. The wound was almost invisible but unquestionably irreparable.

He turned away, perhaps to die, face to the wall.

I called him back.

'My clock, Desmond, if you please.'

My clock was hanging from one hand, his gun from the other. He hadn't noticed. Silently, he handed me my clock, turned and disappeared into the street with his partner.

Mrs. Bellman released Penelope who again slipped through the fence. 'Can I have my orange now, Timothy?'

I handed over her tangerine.

'Are you going to give Mummy her orange, Timothy?'

'Yes. Yes, indeed.'

But in being thrown to the ground I had crushed my last tangerine. I did not attempt to remove it from my pocket but Mrs. Bellman's pleasantly amused expression intimated that this was no secret. An apple, fortunately, was intact. With the obvious gestures of a magician (but really to show that the handkerchief was clean) I polished up the apple and presented it to her with a flourish.

Mrs. Bellman accepted the apple with becoming modesty but Penelope protested, 'That's not an orange, Timothy.'

'Unfortunately, the orange is broken, Penelope,' I said, bringing the tangerine out and breaking its uncrushed portions into sections which I shared with her and her mother.

'Thank you,' she said but before accepting the fruit she looked at her hands, one of which held her own tangerine and the other her crayon drawing. 'You can have my picture,' she said, handing the sheet to me.

It seemed a gesture of gratitude but perhaps it was only a practical method of freeing her hand for the fruit. But it seemed honest and did not prevent me from cherishing this naïve art until to-day. The sheet contained a dozen figures or objects: cats, bears, mother, father, balloons, whistles, beds, tables, chairs, cows, etc. The colour relationships were astonishing. Something like Picasso's when he was doing those two-faced women. A bit on the brutal side. Bodies, limbs, heads had been brilliantly reduced to highly conventionalised shapes. Triangles for women's bodies, horizontal oblongs for animals, vertical oblongs for men. Chairs, tables, beds were inordinately out of scale—as they must appear to children. The child was obviously a genius, although genius at this age tends to be outgrown.

After many pleasantries concerning Penelope's artistic potential I asked: 'Mrs. Bellman, how could you be so certain, so quickly, that I meant no harm to Penelope? I'm sure that, in ordinary circumstances, I'd now be in jail on some incredible charge. Any other woman would now be in her house, trembling behind locked doors with a frightened child too panicky to speak to anyone over three feet tall in the future; perhaps frozen in apprehension for life. How did you manage it? Not just identifying me. You could have seen my picture in the papers. I know I'm notorious. And don't tell me it was intuition. Women are cleverer than that.'

This pleased her, but I wasn't flattering. I sincerely believe in the cleverness of women. I am positive that they have the ability to size up a very complex situation instantly; to weigh to a micromilligram the emotional, practical, economic, social, psychological, political, sexual and intellectual elements; to arrive at a finely-honed, computerised judgment of extreme accuracy, and still have enough sensitivity left deliberately to throw a microscopic quantity of hormones into the balance and choose the course of action they wanted all along.

Mrs. Bellman was reacting well to me, but why not? In a matter of minutes I had brought her a whiff of danger, an outlet for hostility and an occasion for social intercourse with someone whose picture had been in the paper.

She gave me a smiling look of complicity and putting her finger to her cheek in a pretty, thoughtful gesture she bent her brows in concentration. 'As you heard me tell the police, I always expect

Penelope home at this time so I was watching for her. Yes, I was cleaning the lettuce at the kitchen sink which is right under the window, there . . .' And she pointed out the window as though giving evidence. 'A tossed salad always seems so right with spaghetti and meat balls . . .'

'With Parmesan,' I nodded agreement, 'but forget the Chianti. Generally vinegar. Once you have enough of the bottles for candlesticks, forget it. Try an inexpensive Portuguese rosé.'

'I'll remember that,' she said. 'I'll have Fred get some. It's funny you should mention Chianti bottles. I threw them out last month. They really are messy looking, aren't they, with all those candle drippings? When we were first married and didn't have much, they were all right, I suppose, but we've outgrown them.'

'Yes. We started off with Chianti bottles, too. Marriage on a modest basis in those days was impossible without them. I thought by now that perhaps they were out.'

'Well, mine are out. Out in the garbage.'

'And Penelope?' I suggested, knowing that women's conversations have no real beginnings and no ends. They probably began with Eve bringing Adam's attention to the first apple blossom or wakening him to show him the first leaf on the first apple bough. And their conversation has gone on, around the well, over the back fence, on the party line, at the quilting bee. Where men have a thousand religions, theories, philosophies, cultures; a million sciences, formulae, laws, arts, crafts, trades, specialities, dogmas, all tumbling down the attic steps like children's blocks, hard-edged, jumbled, women's dialogue, completely organic, creeps like a vine around the world, softening the outlines of this brutality, gracing that sorrow, bursting with the grape of new love but not letting fall the raisin of the old. Men's dialogues, three dimensional, occupy space and compete for it, hence war. Women's dialogues, four dimensional, extending infinitely in time, bend like light waves around stars and eventually, perhaps, return to their origins. But they accommodate to the roughness of the wall and compromising, vine-like, seek the sun and peace. I have always admired this aspect of women but have not always had the patience, or perhaps the strength, to hear them out.

'And Penelope . . .'

'I'm quite used to Penelope bringing home cats, dragging dogs by the collar who want only to go to their own home. I smiled when I saw her with you. A pretty big catch.'

'A regular whale.'

'And when I saw her tug your hand and you followed her, I knew it was all right. You wouldn't have come right up to her home, would you?'

'No.'

'And then I recognised you.'

'From the papers.'

I was slightly embarrassed. My press notices have not always been admiring.

'No. We used to live in the suburbs. Gotterdammerung Crescent, as a matter of fact. We've met.'

She smiled smugly. We had lived on the next street, Baalbek Boulevard. 'Good lord! And yet I don't remember, exactly . . .'

'I didn't want you to. My hair was up in curlers and I had no lipstick on. I kept my face turned away as much as possible. You helped me when my bag of groceries broke.'

'Yes, yes, I think I remember.'

I didn't.

'I told your wife I thought you were very kind. She didn't agree with me. She said you were sweet but definitely not kind. I didn't quite understand her.'

'Puppy dogs, poodles—they're sweet. Children, even when you could feed them through a meat grinder, present company excepted, are sweet. Doddery old men are sweet, especially when trying to be gallant. But Timothy Badger, sweet? No. I refuse to be sweet, no matter what Myrtle said. What could be unkinder than that?'

'And you left her.'

71

'I?'

'Well, I saw her for a year after that. That's what she said. I didn't see you in the neighbourhood again.'

'As a matter of fact, she left me. In spirit, if you understand me.'

'She didn't tell me that.'

'Given enough time, she'd have told you everything; anything. She ended up in possession, didn't she? But that's only a legal technicality. That was my trouble—ignorance of the law. We had thousands of unwritten contracts between us although I found out about them only one at a time, when I was in default as she saw it. If I raised my voice, she'd burn the toast. If I embarrassed her at a party by insulting a lampshade wearer, she'd invite her mother to dinner. If I watched the Bugs Bunny show on TV she'd manage a two day headache in the interests of culture.'

'But surely there was more to it than that. Every marriage has its ups and downs . . . uh . . . there must have been something . . . something big . . .'

'The straw that broke the camel's back? Playing around? No, no. Myrtle very nearly cured me of your whole charming sex. But there was something . . .'

No. I couldn't tell Mrs. Bellman how, one Saturday afternoon, Myrtle left for the hairdresser's after instructing me to repair one of the little shelves she had built across the dining-room window. There were two of these shelves and on these and the sill and sash between the windows she had collected a display of several dozen glass and china knick-knacks: china dogs, glass herons, porcelain shepherdesses, curled cats, slinky panthers, trolls, gnomes, et cetera.

With the first tap of the hammer I toppled a glass flamingo and it shattered on the sill. I had a moment of real panic as I visualised the consequences: a fortnight with her face to the wall and a frigid back turned to me. Trailing about the house without make-up in simulation of illness. Macaroni and cheese for dinner every second night.

THE FIREFLY HUNT

I hated myself for even thinking in terms of consequences and, since it is dangerous to hate oneself, I also realised I hated and despised Myrtle's kickshaws and I picked up a china shepherdess, placed it upon the sill and tapped it firmly with the hammer. Then I smashed a little glass basket with red, white and blue glass flowers, then three glazed pottery dogs, perhaps airedales, in descending sizes, then a toy cup and saucer, then a boy with a flute, a kitten playing with a ball of china string, saving for the last a Dresdenish couple holding a wreath of roses. When I had cleared the shelves I drove the little nail into the loosened corner. This struck me as strange even at the time but I seemed to have little choice about it. For a moment I felt I understood those maniacs who walk into the street and begin slaughtering perfect strangers.

But I couldn't tell all this to Mrs. Bellman, not on such short acquaintance. It certainly would not reflect to my credit in her eyes and I had no desire to disturb her. She seemed much too gentle and, besides, the smashing of the bric-à-brac was closely related to another matter I felt even less desire to divulge, simply out of delicacy although, if there was a final straw, a watershed from which my life for the past several years had flowed, it was this:

I had just come out of the Cremona Theatre. I had seen, I think, *The Cranes Are Flying*. Granted certain insincerities in Russian peace propaganda, certain non-commercial calculations behind their exports, a certain cynicism in the limited and highly circumscribed picture we get; granted this, I was still deeply affected by the useless death in the mud of the young soldier, of the anguish of his girl, of the waste of it all. Or, perhaps, I had seen *Paths Of Glory* where the French, in cold blood, execute some of their own men at random as a deterrent to their mutinous army. In any event, I came out on to the street suffering seriously from the waste of life and probably feeling, though I had never put it into words, the waste of my own life.

I felt stunned. My mind seemed to be shaking itself. Trying to shake off the blast of bombs.

No.
The crack of rifles.
No.
Hitler.
No.
Stalin.
No.
Chamberlain.
No.
Churchill.
No.
Foch.
No.
Pétain.
No.
Clemenceau.
No.
Mud.
No.
Death.
No.
Tim Badger, Insurance Adjuster.
No.
Love.
No.
Yes, even love seemed too painful, too badly mutilated.

Paralysed, I found myself staring mindlessly into the window of Norm's Novelty Store next door to the Cremona and thinking:
No.
Crooked dice, false noses.
No.
Itching powder.
No.
Miniature toilets for ashtrays.
No.

Monster masks.

No.

Supine figurines. Enormous breasts . . . salt and pepper.

No.

No, no.

No, no, no, no, no, no, no . . .

A Thousand Laffs!

No, no, no, no, no!

Yes, I was seeing it.

No.

Fool your friends!

No.

Gag Of The Year!

No.

Acme International Toy Corp.

No.

But there it was.

No.

A plastic turd.

No.

Stapled to a card.

No.

'The meaning of life? One day that will be revealed to us. Probably on a Thursday.'

No. Wrong. It is Tuesday. And it is impossible that Norm has knowingly bought and stocked this item. It is impossible that a salesman has called and persuaded him, carrying a sample in his case. It is impossible that a salesman could bring himself to cart this sample about the country. No. What did he say when the Sales Manager gave him this sample to add to his line. Did he say 'Hot shit!' to show his enthusiasm? It is impossible to conceive.

No. It is impossible to imagine some jokesmith creating the idea. Sitting down to the draughting board, creating the sketch, the design, the specifications: such and such a length; such and such a diameter; such and such a colour, tone; such and such a finish. No.

And possibly he did research.

No.

It is impossible to conceive a Production Manager calling a chemical company for consultation about the most appropriate plastic for use in manufacturing an imitation turd. What does the Sales Manager of Acme International Chemicals do when such a request comes in? Call the Lab? 'Better hire half a dozen more Ph.D.s in Chemistry. We have this problem of a plastic turd. Better make that Biochemistry. It has to have a certain wet shine . . .'

No.

But the tool and die makers must cut dies of extreme precision and heavy industry must produce the presses to extrude the artificial turds. And they must be inspected for flaws. And forests must be hewn down to provide boxboard which must be printed. And artists must design illustrations for the boxes and the turds must be packed and shipped and freight car loadings must rise and trucks must be manufactured to transport the cartons of turds and men must be hired to handle them and there must be great demand for money to finance all this activity and the interest rate goes up and the flow of capital runs towards the higher interest causing international stresses and new bond issues are floated on the idea of imitation plastic turds.

No.

It is all quite impossible. A whole society cannot be constructed upon plastic turds.

No.

And yet, there under my nose, in the window of Norm's Novelty Shop, was the plastic turd.

No.

Out of delicacy, I could not tell this to Mrs. Bellman so I said, 'One day, Myrtle caught me red handed.'

Mrs. Bellman's mouth made a round, silent 'Oh!' of shocked interest.

'It had been going on for some time.'

'But you said . . .'

'I had been intercepting the mail.'

'An old friend?'

'An old enemy.'

'Oh, dear! I didn't think people had enemies any more, these days.'

'Was breaking up my home.'

She shook her head in sympathy, as though she didn't believe Myrtle capable of anything so . . .

'The sucker list. Third class mail. The *free offer!*'

'I don't understand.'

'Valuable coupon inside! One Package *Free*! Seven *Free* vacation days for two plus five hundred dollars to spend as you wish! Miracle Fluff Dessert (with chemical stabilisers in fine print) Win A . . . Send Coupon With . . .'

'Oh!' She blushed. Another addict.

'She caught me red handed, trying to destroy a free Lucky Number Draw Contest worth $60,000 from *Reader's Digest*. If there were a co-respondent guilty in the break-up of our marriage, technically, it would be *Reader's Digest*.'

' "What are you hiding?" she demanded. "Nothing," I lied. "Then show me." "What?" "The nothing you're not hiding." She was eyeing me with her terrier look. I was a dead rat. "It's this trash," I said, handing her the circular. She snatched it. "Five hundred and fifty prizes for lucky Canadians," she read. "Elegant High Priced Cars—Buick Riviera, Ford Thunderbird . . ." Her eyes were glittering with avarice, her voice dropped to a murmur until, finally, her lips moved in silence as she raced through the colourful folder, shaping words like "*free* Colour TV Sets", "*free* Trips For Two—Paris, Vienna, London . . ."

'I reached for the circular. She snatched it away from my

hand. "Don't you dare . . ." "Look, I hate to see you waste your life filling in these coupons, sending in entries, hoping. You haven't a chance in hell . . ." "What are the chances of your taking me to Vienna?" "About the same as your chance of winning the Lucky Draw—zero," I admitted. "Well, then?" "Don't you know you never get anything free in this life?" "They've even sent a stamp to send in the entry!" It was attached to the *Free Mystery Gift* coupon. I snatched it from her and tore it to fragments. "No!" I shouted. "Can't you see they're leading you around by the nose? You have to buy a subscription before you're eligible for a prize!"

'I was really enraged and often when I'm enraged I shout and as I shouted I thought I tasted again the glue on the Lucky Green Stamps I had been sticking into the coupon book. "Well, what's wrong with that?" she shrieked. "A $2.97 value for only $1.97. And another stamp. And someone has to win those prizes . . ." Her skin had shrunk over her nose, around her mouth—a sure sign of rage or fear—as though she had had her face lifted. I knew there was no arguing with her now that she had decided she could win the contest by sheer determination.'

As a perennial purchaser of sweepstake tickets and a *Free* contest entrant, Mrs. Bellman seemed embarrassed, so I desisted.

'Well, now you see,' I concluded lamely, 'what Myrtle meant by my not being kind. I should have indulged her, perhaps, but that sort of thing encourages belief in miracles, doesn't it? And finally, demands miracles from me. Impossible . . .'

Mrs. Bellman was making mouths of silent protest. It was time to go. 'I don't know how to thank you, Mrs. Bellman, for remaining clear headed and rational under pressure.'

'Just don't send me a clock, Mr. Badger.'

'Ah! I'll send you a medal. If anyone deserves a medal, it's you.'

She laughed.

'Seriously. I send out medals, too. Didn't you know? B.U.C.M.

Badger's Useful Conduct Medal. Yields the acronym Buck 'Em . . .'

'You're impossible, Mr. Badger!'

She went into a spasm of shyly embarrassed giggling.

'It's quite true. Why not? Governments coin them by the ton during wars. For slaughter. For being there, under conscription. For getting dysentery, et cetera. They're quite cheap, you know. And they're almost never given for useful accomplishment. Just for scrambling to the head of the line, usually . . .'

'Oh, but the Victoria Cross . . .' she objected.

'Mostly posthumous. The rest judiciously sprinkled to raise morale. Controlled scarcity hence artificially maintained value. I would think that everyone who advances under fire deserves the V.C.'

'Perhaps you're right there. But what about the others? The extraordinary feats?'

'Skewering thirty-four opponents with your bayonet? That's a lot of death. Something more solemn is called for. I wouldn't encourage a chap like that.'

'How on earth did you ever think of a thing like this?'

'I was impressed by Professor McQuorkerdale, the big researcher in atomic physics. He just quit. Quit cold. Said the only contribution he was making was to destruction. So he stopped. It set me thinking about how everyone agrees that war is no good but they keep on fighting; about how marriages go on in horror but no one stops them; about boozers slowly killing themselves but do not stop; and cigarette smokers and dope addicts and jail birds and shop-lifters and stamp collectors and television watchers. They all know it's no good and they know they'd benefit by stopping but they won't. Yes, I was thinking what a stroke of genius the Professor showed by just stopping. A perfect and elegant solution. And, of course, once certain things stop, others can start.

'As I was musing on the fact of the Professor being the only extant credit to Science I happened to pass Kirk's jewellery store.

They had a display of athletic trophies in the window. In a corner quite overshadowed by enormous silver plated cups was a bronze medal showing an athlete holding up a wreath. You know the sort of thing . . .

'Ideal, I told myself, and I went in and ordered one engraved for the Professor. The clerk must have taken me for a school principal or Member of the School Board for he showed no astonishment when I initiated the Badger Medal. Instead, he suggested a quite reasonable price for bronze medals by the gross and I could have "Badger's Useful Conduct Medal" cast integrally and would then have only to have the recipient's name engraved later. It was a bargain. I accepted—and ordered the ribbon to be two broad stripes of black and blue. Symbolic, perhaps. Apt.

'Of course, there was no chance of hiding twelve pounds of bronze medals in their boxes from Myrtle. She went into one of her sullen rages and I retreated to a profound silence. She thought I had wasted the down-payment on a mink coat. Some things are unexplainable—to some people.

'It could be said that that was the beginning of the end for Myrtle and me but it was really only one of the occasions on which the cumulative speed of the disintegration was obviously apparent. In fact everything, absolutely everything, in the end, contributes to the dissolution of a marriage, to the declaration of a war, to a murder. In our case, the good times, by contrast with their scarcity, demonstrated the general bleakness.'

'Oh dear!' Mrs. Bellman murmured. 'A gross of medals! Oh, dear!'

I could see I had made a mistake. Even so amiable a woman as Mrs. Bellman has needs. And nothing is less consumable than bronze medals. She seemed pained. Perhaps thinking of the waste. Bronze medals when she needed a new washing machine —or draperies—or even a mahogany whatnot for knick-knacks for the corner of the living-room. Before she could resent my improvidence I said, 'You are an amazing woman, Mrs.

Bellman. When you can keep your head when all about you, et cetera . . .'

'What you mean is "If I don't reward you, God will". Think nothing of it, Mr. Badger. I'm not the type to wear a medal.'

'On the contrary. Rewards are in order. A pony for Penelope, perhaps.'

She showed alarm.

'A tricycle then, and roses—and something more substantial. A television set, a hi-fi . . .'

She looked quite cross then, as women do when they feel the impossibility of their avarice.

'Really! Mr. Badger . . .'

'I'm serious. Look, I'm rich.'

And I showed her the letter.

'Oh! The Castle! Oh.'

She scanned me with anxiety, embarrassment, reappraisal. I saw that I had made another mistake. She could no longer dismiss me as an old neighbour, a harmless eccentric. I began to retreat.

'I don't know what Fred would say . . .'

'You'll be hearing from me. Cast your bread upon the waters . . .' I said.

'And you'll have soggy sandwiches for lunch,' she murmured in a distant manner.

The rejoinder itself was terrible enough but what bothered me more was the sense of distance that had come between us, as though she had retreated to a previously prepared position while I myself was abandoning the field. 'Good-bye, Penelope. Good-bye, Mrs. Bellman. Good-bye, good-bye . . .'

I drifted backward waving my hand to them and even, in one of those foolish and precipitate gestures that I never seem able to control or foresee, waving my handkerchief at them as though leaving on an excursion.

I knew I had stayed too long. I was trembling with apprehension by the time I reached the street.

F

The crossing-guard was still on duty. Obviously, she had been the informer who had called the police. She glared at me, foiled of her prey. I stopped and examined her for a moment.

'I know your flat-chested kind,' I said. 'I know what's on your mind. You're sorry nothing happened to the kid. You'll have nothing to talk about for the next ten years. Oh, I know you're just a poor widow woman whose husband is crippled and hasn't been out of bed since '27 and your sons are no help and your daughter's a whore and you've always worked your fingers to the bone to keep body and soul together and make ends meet and the price of everything is sky high and you'll end up in the poorhouse but what has that to do with those filthy teeth of yours? Don't you know they're moss green? Don't you ever put them in a glass of Sani Flush at night? Don't say a word. Anything you say will be taken down in evidence against you. You'll be hearing from my lawyer in the next few weeks. A suit for wrongful arrest and, never fear, if you don't go to jail I'll take every last shingle from over your head and throw you in the street and keep you there, rain or shine.'

I left her shaking with rage and terror.

I suppose I could be accused of hardness of heart towards the old trollop. A great deal is said about compassion nowadays. Usually by the merciless. They love to identify with butchers about to be hanged. My God! they say. They're going to hang you? What do they think we are, barbarians? Have they no feelings? Nothing inhuman is alien to me. Better a thousand innocent jailed than one guilty hanged. Have they no idea how exasperating women can be? Admittedly, thirty-nine stab wounds is a bit much but can we actually make a harsh judgment in the light of the psychiatric evidence: the sadistic withdrawal of the breast at the age of three; the brutal coercion of toilet training at the age of five; extinguishing the night light at the age of fourteen; the continual pressure to be a man. Never fear. We'll spend millions to prevent your hanging. The orphans? Oh.

There's some sort of social service agency or county orphanage to look after that sort of thing. Perhaps.

I make no claim to being a sweetie-pie. Count me out when it comes to mopping up the vomit. My idea is to go for the throat. Choke it off at the source. Put the social sanitation services out of business. So I point a finger, apply standards, make judgments. A very unpopular endeavour, nowadays.

And it's not a matter of hate. In the case of the crummy old crossing-guard not only her actions but her face showed she had long given up the human burden of generosity for the cancerous delights of bitterness. And, just as it is a scientific fact that weeds secrete a chemical which inhibits the growth of neighbouring plants, she obviously had diminished everyone within her circle. Myself only the last. A Typhoid Mary of the spirit. I had simply tacked up the quarantine sign.

I had left her thirty yards behind before I finally heard her gasp. She let out a shriek like a train whistle before the crash.

'You filthy old pervert, you! At your age! There oughta be a law. They oughta cut them off. They'll get you one day. A poor little girl like that. If I was a man I'd show you. Go ahead and sue me. Much good it will do you. I'm on welfare and to hell with you . . .'

It was shocking. If there had been a crowd . . .

I fled.

I came to earth in an all-day movie house. I felt momentarily safe among the unemployed, the footsore, and a sprinkling of discouraged salesmen, hold-up men and old-age pensioners. The oblong silver membrane screened me from the outer world which beat in fantastic fluid shapes against it.

A grey-at-the-temples diplomatic type murmured in upper class accents, 'They are within an ace of perfecting The Saline Ray which, as you know, precipitates into crystalline form all the salt contained in the human body. They can take over the world with it unless they are stopped in time. I'm afraid it's up to you, Agent 69 . . .'

Agent 69, his face wooden to indicate the seriousness of the situation, held the pose while the camera in extreme close up scanned the rugged jaw, the manly brow, the passionate nostrils, the fearless eye, then pulled back to reveal the compleat hero, undeniably handsome, slightly sadistic, perfectly groomed, vaguely epicine. Mamma's boy.

He dropped his left eyebrow one sixty-fourth of an inch to indicate he had taken on A Foreign Power single handed.

When life becomes unbearable, when the world is too much with me, I have the faculty of being able to switch off into sleep. This I did, untroubled by dreams. When I awoke it was to horrendous screams uttered by a beautiful nude young lady being slashed to death in Technicolor by a mysterious assassin whose back was to the camera.

In the row in front of me was a young couple. They were clasped together convulsively, perhaps in fright. The girl seemed to moan with every murderous blow but as I rose to leave I could see she had her face buried in her companion's collar. Perhaps she was watching the screen out of the corner of her eye.

On the street it was dark. I felt fearful of returning to my room. The thought of Mrs. Peake frightened me, I don't know why. Pigeon breasted, luscious, perfectly mature (and a bit), willing, and perhaps eager, attractive in every way except one: a sense of purpose.

I was tempted to call her predatory, even rapacious. I began to fear some larger purpose. After all, what did an attractive widow in the low thirties want with an obviously middle-aged car washer. Granted that I was still robust and in good condition due to my work, and granted that my substantial if unathletic figure could inspire confidence, and granted that even my somewhat quizzical personality could have appeal, still, there must be younger, more apparently prosperous, more stylish and current men who would catch her eye?

What could be her purpose, discounting romance? And women always have a long range purpose especially in their romantic moods. Could she be a simple, ordinary every-day nymphomaniacal landlady mining the men to exhaustion in one establishment then moving on to the next, or was it more sinister than that? Perhaps she already had a life insurance policy on me and planned to ensnare me into drinking arsenic with my bedtime cocoa—a habit she intended to implant in me through her sexual wiles.

It was all very disturbing—especially this sort of fantasy which I put down to the bizarre and distressing experiences of the day.

I plunged into the Belvedere. In the absence of love, food must do.

The Belvedere is doomed. It has no gimmick. One dines not under Polynesian thatched roofs, nor under simulated hand-hewn beams, nor in plastic grottoes, nor in Viennese ballrooms under threateningly gay chandeliers, nor in Gay Nineties saloons. There are no straw hats or net stockings on the help; no rinky-dink pianos, no banjos, no powdered wigs, no flaming swords, no gipsy fiddlers, no singing waiters, no stencilled murals of Capri nor of Cambodian *wats*. No Muzak.

Crisp white napery, serviceable cutlery, substantial yet not inelegant china, honest food. Particularly fish. Attention must be paid to fish.

But disregard everything I have said about food. I have very little real interest in it. It is just one of the encumbrances I abandoned when I struck out for a freer life. I'm quite happy with a chunk of cheddar, some natural bread baked of stone ground flour, a handful of nuts, some fresh fruit and a glass of dechlorinated water.

No. The attraction of food for a slow, contemplative eater like myself is not in the stuffing of the gut but in the drama, in the imagination released by contact with such varied materials. Cutting through the taut skin of a sausage is surely akin to the first stroke of the scalpel. First penetration of Chicken Kiev is as full of danger and apprehension as the probing of a distended tumour. The delicate separation of the fillet from the trout skeleton is as skilled as the discovery of stones in the bile duct. Yes, a thoughtful eater can marshall and defeat phalanges of peas like a Napoleon; can extract *escargots* like the brain of a pharaoh; trepan a baked potato with the dexterity of an Aztec, peel a peach with the finesse of a skin grafter.

But on this occasion, after the shocks of the day, restoration of the physical man was necessary and I attacked the sirloin with the knife of vendetta, probed the baked potato (chives and sour cream) with an Inquisitorial fork, crunched the salad greens like the bones of infants, eyed the rose in its vase with the cold eye of a blood chemist and scalded the effete eclair with hasty cups of coffee. Ha, I thought, wait until I get into the swing of things. Walter and Desmond and Scaliger and Swingle, whoever he was, and that excrescence of a crossing-guard, I'll crush those sons-of-bitches like bugs.

I felt the need to soothe myself. I had several Triple Secs and would have had more but a party of salesmen at the next table made enjoyment impossible. They spoke intensely though not boisterously, as though they believed every word they were saying—except for a peculiar undefinable abstraction of human feeling as though they were playing some game and observing rules of sincerity.

'. . . seven units . . .'

'What! Seven units!'

'Yep. Seven units.'

'If you had offered me ten to one yesterday that Bob Clapham could sell seven units, I wouldn't have taken it.'

'My God! Seven units! The quota is three!'

'What the hell can they do with seven units down there?'

'They must be shoving them . . .'

'Ha, ha.'

'Har, har.'

'Ho, ho.'

'Bob has turned out to be quite a salesman.'

'Quite a salesman.'

'Seven units in one week.'

'Even the Old Man himself never managed more than five units . . .'

'When that Bob comes in on Friday take a good look at him.'

'Yeah? Why?'

' 'Cause you'll be looking at your next Area Manager.'

'Yeah. Anyone who can unload seven units . . .'

'Seven units. Fantastic!'

I had to get out. I took a good look at them as I left. In their early thirties. All looking very much alike. Like dentists. It seems to me that business men are looking more and more like dentists. Not that I have anything special against business men. Some of my best friends used to be business men. But they're getting in everywhere, nowadays.

Six

I had no intention of visiting the Castle. As I walked slowly home, trying not to think of Mrs. Peake, I thought I would call the Lawyer. What was his name? Swingle. Yes. Charles B. Swingle. I would say, 'Put it on the block. Get rid of it. The market? What do I care about the market? Take what you can get. Call Walt Disney. There's a realist for you. Perhaps he can see a money-making potential in a sixty-year-old fake castle. Stuff it with gnomes and charge admission. All the modern conveniences, too. Civic Duty? Well, approach the Mayor then. Perhaps you can unload it on him for a Home For Improvident Whores. Ah. I've hurt your feelings. Insulted you, have I? I do have this tendency to call a spade a spade. And I don't improve upon acquaintance, my enemies tell me. Would you care to turn over the estate to a solicitor of my choice? Your apology accepted. Perhaps you could sell the Castle to a parking lot operator? Raze the old mausoleum to the ground? No, I have no sentiment. No sense of tradition. Why should I have? Moses Muddiman founded his fortune as a crooked lightning-rod salesman. No, not crooked lightning rods. Crooked salesman. Uncle Moses. He'd wait for a thunderstorm then burn down a barn. Do a land office business in lightning rods the next day. So, get on the ball, Swingle. Put your shoulder to the wheel, nose to the grindstone and give it the old college try.'

So I strolled home in a leisurely fashion, endeavouring to put out of my mind the affair of Penelope and the police and trying to smile away the anxiety I felt about being waylaid on the way to my room by Mrs. Peake.

As I approached home, I saw a shadow withdraw from the curtains of Mrs. Peake's room which was at the front of the house but I thought nothing of it, only that she might be lurking in the hallway as I entered.

The hallway was empty but my door was ajar.

I felt a sudden suicidal gaiety. This happens not only at critical moments when in wine but also when one is on rock bottom. It signifies an upturn in spirit or, more accurately, the flowering of that what-have-I-got-to-lose spirit.

I expected that Mrs. Peake would make for the door as soon as I entered in order to maintain an appearance of chance encounter, of casualness. I did not expect to find her, as I did, standing on a chair in her bare feet, fiddling with the curtains. She was wearing a flimsy, filmy sort of negligée which did her great justice for, in her strained, arm-raised attitude, it clung closely about her. She was light boned but well fleshed—a voluptuous combination suggesting monumentality until she could be seen in proper scale. Then she appeared as quite a small woman with attributes impressively massed for the maximum of womanly effect.

I could see instantly that to-night we were not about to play the game of After You My Dear Gaston in the doorway and my gaiety deliquesced into resentful panic.

I say resentful for, as she turned towards me, she brushed away a strand of hair from her cheek. That utterly feminine gesture struck me with such peculiar force that I could not help thinking how strangely vulnerable we are to scents unconsciously smelled, to gestures whose anciently implanted values still stimulate us. Shapes of limbs, styles of motion, mysterious subliminal exhalations, apparently normal and innocuous attitudes and expressions are all weighted with idiosyncratic sexual burdens and rule us, from the womb, with terrifying force.

'Oh, you frightened me!' she said in the calmest manner possible. 'It's dreadful how filthy things get around here. I don't suppose these curtains of yours have been changed since months before I came.'

She clutched with serene modesty at her robe managing, almost, to dislodge one choice breast.

The correct procedure in the circumstance would have been to fling her to the bed, rip away her flimsy covering and ravish that late blooming flesh with all the force and endurance at my command. But Man has long fallen. The Apple has been polished so often and to such glittering reflectivity that I could plainly see an enormous and clear awareness in her expression. In the light of her calculation and my defensiveness it was obvious to me that this ravishment, although technically possible, could not spiritually take place. A rape, with both actors participating in cold blood, was unthinkable.

She pawed the air with her bare, delicate foot as though stranded seventeen feet above the floor. In doing so, all but three-sixteenths of an inch of leg emerged from her gown. 'Oh dear,' she said for emphasis, in case my attention had wandered.

She held out her hand—not exactly to me but in another one of those vaguely provocative but irresistible gestures.

I responded automatically. I held up my hands and she made the little hop, of about two inches, into them, like a child.

Those fruity breasts against my wrists gave me such a shock that my arms were immobilised and I held her there, a foot above and before me, for a half second before I wheeled, took one, two, three paces deposited her in the hallway and shut and locked the door before, she quite realised what had happened.

I turned and saw her slippers beside the chair. I picked them up, unlocked the door, dropped them at her feet just as her smile turned to cat-swallowed-sour-canary.

I locked the door and without even beginning to think, threw up the window and stepped out into the yard. I had to talk to Joe Bezoar. I made for the phone booth at Jack Dandy's cigar store on the corner.

'Yeah?'

'Arcadian Hotel? Joe Bezoar, please.'

'Sorry, Joe never answers the phone.'

'Well, give him a ring, anyway.'

'O.K., but it won't do any good.'

The night clerk may have rung Joe's room but I'm doubtful that the room phones work. The Arcadian isn't a flop house but it's astonishingly cheap for regulars like Joe and luxuriously expensive on a hot-pillow basis.

'No, he doesn't answer,' the clerk said after a plausible interval.

'Do me a favour. Go up and rouse him. Tell him it's a matter of life and death.'

'Now I *know* he won't talk to you. He says there isn't a thing you can do about life and death. He told me that just the other day. And he says that nothing important has ever been said on the phone.'

That sounded like Joe, all right. It had the ring of truth to it. Or, at least, half truth.

'I've got to get through to him.'

'I might as well tell you that he took a gallon of Catawba up with him a couple of hours ago. I don't think it's going to do any good.'

'Just try this, will you? Tell him it's Timothy Badger. Got that? Tim Badger. And I've got a joke for him. About the Philosopher and the Prostitute.'

'What's that? The Philosopher and the Prostitute? Yeah. Yeah, that's about his taste. A bit pretentious. That might do it. Okay. I'll give it a try. Hang on.'

The line went dead for five minutes then there was a click and a confused murmur. I thought I heard, 'That's it. Lean against the wall . . .'

'Tim.'

'Joe, I've got to talk to you.'

'Shoot.'

'I think there's a plot.'

'There usually is.'

'You see, I inherited this castle to-day.'

'Nice.'

'I don't want you to think I've gone paranoid or anything like that.'

'I never think that of anyone.'

He sounded so calm and sensible and yet I knew he was drunk. That's the trouble with Joe. It's that cheap domestic wine he guzzles by the gallon, until he blacks out. But I was desperate. I really couldn't call Joe a friend but who else did I have to talk to? I kept talking.

'I know all that Freudian crap about repressed homosexuality leading to paranoia . . .'

'It does? Live and learn . . .'

'No. Nothing to do with me. But everyone's gone crazy. Sex mad. Do you know the Police jumped me to-day? And for— guess—walking down the street with a five-year-old girl!'

'Young.'

'I'm serious. It happened. So I went to the show. They were holding a regular Bacchanal.'

'Burlesque house?'

'No. Just a cinema.'

'Back row?'

'Almost.'

'That's what it's for. Didn't your mother tell you?'

'But I tell you those kids practically had a douche bag hanging from the balcony.'

'So they're old-fashioned types.'

'And Mrs. Peake damned near attacked me when I came in to-night.'

There was a strangled guggle from the other end.

'A man isn't safe in his own home. Are you still with me, Joe? Joe? Joe?'

'Ah!'

'I tell you, that woman's up to something. It's not natural. Do you think she knew about the Castle?'

'Does a title come with it? Are you a Prince or a Duke or something like that?'

'No, of course not. It's just one of those half-arsed, made-up imitation castles that millionaires used to build. You know the one: Muddiman's Castle. My uncle. He bought himself a "Sir" by pimping for some feeble-minded Duke in Europe. At least, that was the story in the family. But that doesn't mean anything. The knighthood, I mean.'

'Too bad. I understand castles are draughty. You'd be better off without the stately home and with a title. Prince Badger. No. Lord Timothy Badger. Not so good. Duke Badger? No. Doesn't sound right. Stick with the castle.'

'They're out to get me. I don't know who. I feel it. It's an old trick. Get the victim entangled in some sort of sexual jam . . . any sort . . . and his name's mud in court. You know—the idea that if one is a bit off in the sex department he can't be sound in any other category.'

'Stick with the castle,' Joe Bezoar murmured. 'That's it. Stick with the castle. Pull up the drawbridge. Flood the moat. Fight 'em off with boiling oil.'

His voice kept getting fainter and fainter, like a radio fade-out.

'Boiling oil and arquebuses. Pikes and poignards. Culverins and demi-culverins . . .'

There was more that I could not hear, then a muffled crash. Silence. 'Joe! Joe, are you all right?'

I heard some sounds as though of struggle and after a moment the desk clerk came on.

'I think you've had your dime's worth, Mister. Joe's passed out.'

'Get him to bed, will you? He hasn't injured himself, has he?'

'No fear. He falls down like this four times a week.'

As I hung up the phone I realised that my case was even more serious than I had suggested to Joe Bezoar. I hadn't had a chance to mention Scaliger who, probably, represented the most sinister element in my oppressive day. It seemed quite possible that when I left him so abruptly he had immediately had the police follow me with instructions to get me on any pretext. The matter of Penelope would seem like a God-given opportunity to them and only the miraculous coincidence of being acquainted with Penelope's mother had saved me there. And Mrs. Peake's bold endeavours, both coming and going, suggested a certain desperation, an urgency, to involve me, to keep me, perhaps, out of the Castle.

This train of thought seemed obsessive, even to me. Yet, I could tick off on my fingers the equally peculiar obsessions others had had in me since early morning. Mrs. Peake's erotic interests appeared particularly strange at breakfast time. Scaliger's incredible tolerance of my insults, rebuffs and food fantasies suggested desperate overriding designs. The ferocity of the Police indicated more than normal self-righteousness. Mrs. Peake's midnight lurking was astonishing. But why on this day, of all days, must there be this convergence of coincidence, if it were coincidence. Especially the day I have news of inheriting the Castle? By any form of deductive, inductive or transcendental logic there was obviously something rotten in Denmark and perhaps even in my Elsinore.

And Joe Bezoar, dead drunk, had put his finger on it. Stick with the Castle. There was something funny about the Castle. It was changing my life already and twenty-four hours hadn't passed. Everyone wanted to deflect me from the Castle so it was obvious I must go to it immediately, I certainly could not stand in a public phone booth all night and I did not dare return to my room while a light showed in the house. Mrs. Peake was probably waiting for me with a meat axe.

It was late but I could still go and look at the Castle from the outside. It was probably locked up. Perhaps sealed by the government inheritance tax people. But I could get the lay of the land and perhaps confirm myself in my resolution to consult with

94

the lawyer to-morrow and go through any social, legal, govern-
mental forms and conformities to rid myself of the burden of the
Castle.

It was a good night for walking. Although it was nearly summer the air was clear, hard and cold due to an Arctic high that
had slipped over the city. I felt buoyant, suddenly. One shouldn't
underestimate the effect of atmospherics on the human spirit.
The moon was full, too, and perhaps its manic effect was operat-
ive. I felt sharkishly gay. Cars shooshed by, glittering in the
moonlight, impersonal, metallic. A night for bringing girl friends
home bleeding from the abortionist. For returning from parties,
quarrelling side by side, staring straight ahead at the blurring
road, neither quite sober and trying to assess the blame, if any,
associated with saying, 'That's a lot of shit, Mr. McMurty,' and
then repeating it, shouting it into that shellbacked Presbyterian's
hearing aid. A night for cruising with a trunkful of burglar tools.
A night for lurking in hard shadows, waiting to see who brings
your sweetheart from where she has been, ha, ha! washing
her hair at her girl-friend's. A night for sleeping with clenched
teeth.

Stick with the Castle! Would this prove the first time that Joe
Bezoar guessed wrong? It felt against all my instincts to trap myself in the Castle. And yet, Joe's attitudes and judgments had an
attraction for me. I first became aware of Joe when I worked at
Grabstein's Five Minute Car Wash. We were both working at
the drying end, and, at the time, were putting the finishing
touches on a new Cadillac convertible. I finished the bumper
and looked up. Harry Sprockett had his hand on the door
handle.

'For Christ's sake, Tim Badger! What the hell are you doing
here?'

'Hi, Harry.'

I spoke with a noticeable lack of enthusiasm for I have never
been keen on reunions with old school chums who by now were all
accountants, investment brokers or proprietors of small businesses

producing plastic toilet seats, mill work, etc. Harry Sprockett was a sort of speculator's speculator or, in plain English, a crook. Backbone Of The Economy.

'What is all this?' he demanded, at the top of his voice because of the sprayers and blowers back up the line. 'I thought you were a college graduate.'

I polished the Cadillac's tail light with an unnecessary flourish. 'Yes.'

'But didn't I hear that they threw you out?' he asked with suspicion.

'Yes. Collingwood. But I finished up at Wittwater U.'

'Don't tell me you took a degree in car washing. Or are you still doing research?'

'I taught school,' I said defensively. And I had, for a few months.

'By now you should have been a principal or superintendent— even a janitor makes plenty of money these days. What happened?'

Harry was always a bully. Perhaps not a bully. That's unfair. It was just that he always talked faster and oftener than anyone else and so he never had to answer a question. The answerer of questions is always on the defensive. Questions hurt. In this instance I felt a growing embarrassment. 'I had nothing against kids,' I muttered and, without thinking, I wrung out my soggy cloth, the water spattering widely on the concrete floor.

Sprockett sprang back, glaring alternately at his highly polished but bespattered shoes and at me.

'Well,' he said with elaborate calm, 'same old Terrible Tim Badger. Still don't know your arse from a hole in the ground. I can never forget the night I set you up with Miriam Schumacher. Lord! What she told me . . .'

Although I had been only a wide-eyed boy my humiliation even now, nearly thirty years later, flushed down to my boots. Something about getting entangled in Miriam's garter under the impression that she had elastic in the leg of her drawers. I still feel it is incredible that anyone would restrict the circulation in the leg with round garters, even in those days.

Bezoar saved me.

'Hey, Mister,' he said to Sprockett, 'your front fender is going to fall off in a couple of miles. Corrosion. Road salt.'

He picked at a seam in the metal, shook his head sadly and gave the Cadillac's tyre a kick. There is something about a tyre kick that implies not only contempt but a material deprecation, as though there was a suspicion that the tyres were filled with cream cheese or that some vital working part were missing.

Sprockett flung a panicky glance towards the front of the car and a look of hatred at Joe Bezoar but for once said nothing, for the Manager came charging up, shouting, 'Get that car on the road. The whole line is held up!'

So Sprockett got into his car but as he did so he said, 'Someone has to look after creatures like you, Badger. Next time you're in the charity ward of the Lunatic Asylum, give me a call. I'll do what I can.'

'If you're not in jail, like two years ago,' I muttered. Perhaps he heard me.

Ever since, I have had a tentative respect for Joe's judgment, especially since I learned that he feels there is something psychically wrong with politicians. It may only be a matter of the stopped clock being correct twice a day. In any event, I kept Joe's opinion in mind as I scanned the monstrous anachronism rising before me.

Perhaps I would be able to discover some useful purpose for which the Castle could be used. A home for mentally retarded children? No. It would save the taxpayer's money but would simply neutralise me. I would find myself in the role of keeping social and psychiatric workers out of the pool-rooms with little gain to the children, as usual.

Make it a centre, a world-wide symposium for the best brains in the humanities, sciences, arts. Indulge in polite, universal generalities and gain sure-fire international respectability. Have one's

G

name linked with such great scientists as Herr Laszlo Bottfink, who runs the world famous poison gas laboratory, or Professor Kruppdorf, famous for his philosophy of annihilation, or Nokomis Bongolo, Father of his Country and proprietor of a numbered Swiss bank account in the sum of six and a half million dollars. No. A sophisticate like myself would probably corrupt these idealists. A closer inspection of the Castle might suggest solutions.

From Dinsdorf Road and Heller Street the towers of the Castle could be seen floating above the trees in a gay, romantic, yet spooky atmosphere. Each of the four towers was of a different height. I could remember that one rose from an octagonal base, one from a square base, one from a round, the fourth from a base of twelve or fifteen sides. All were tiered with machicolated galleries, buttressed, flounced and turreted, and sometimes they excreted tiny ancillary towers near the top, yielding secondary pinnacles, conically roofed, steeply soaring. The effect was totally eccentric, light-hearted, ascending, and cried for pennants and though one might catch sight of these towers in the centre of the city and smile in amusement there was usually a compensating feeling of the ridiculous.

As I neared the Castle the towers disappeared behind the tree-tops and I was soon confronted by the sheer south wall. This rose abruptly from Dinsdorf Road, a grey mass without break except for a few slit windows near the top which was battlemented and from whose protection I was later to see tanks approaching. From this great blank face which suggested an inaccessible Norman keep, a twelve foot battlemented wall ran east and west to Wardour and to Anatole Streets then climbed steeply north and turned at Huggins Street to meet at the gateway in the centre of the block.

As I climbed precipitous Anatole Street I felt a growing excitement due, perhaps, to my close approach to the Castle or possibly to the effect the unwelcome excitements of the day were having upon me. I began to suffer certain borborygmal indications which suggested I should immediately seek the comfort of a comfort station, but the nearest was half a mile away in a restaurant which might be closed at this hour. I hesitated at the entrance of the Castle. It looked darkly and privately inviting, in the circumstances, for it was composed of two squat towers, rounded and crenellated in an eleventh-century design, which were joined above a passageway from which, if I remembered rightly, was suspended a portcullis. This entrance-way was approached over a heavy drawbridge which spanned a very shallow ditch of twenty or thirty yards length, dug to give a suggestion of sense to the drawbridge. I crossed the bridge and entered the passageway.

No, I thought, I may for some reason come this way again tomorrow to check inventories regarding the estate or for God knows what reasons lawyers may have. I passed dark doorways on both sides of the passage and resisted the temptation.

The garden, I thought. Good for the roses.

But the courtyard was paved and bordered by lawns. More walls separated the courtyard from the gardens.

Why should I be skulking around my own property, I asked myself. I shall use the proper facilities, presuming the place is still occupied.

I scanned the dark façade. The brilliant moon backlighting the towers threw only dense shadow for me to peer into. There seemed to be no lights in the Chambordian windows. The monstrous pile had an unwelcoming air. I plunged into the darkness of a Palladian portico and held my fist suspended above the door's panel. It was the sort of door one should knock on with the head of a cane.

I shall rouse some slavey who will take ten minutes to answer the door and will need another ten minutes to convince him to let me in to use the facilities, I thought. And if there is no one on guard here, I shall be wasting my time.

I felt the door knob. It turned. The door yielded. Ha! A tight watch, indeed! I could walk out with every stick of furniture. Something must be done about this.

The entrance hall was vaguely lit by moonlight reflected from the Great Hall. I recollected that on the left was an immense cloakroom with an adjoining washroom. I felt inside the doorway for the light switch. It was where it should be.

When I emerged I tiptoed into the Great Hall. Timbered, carpeted, festooned, lead windowed. Lumps of furniture crouched ambiguously in the half light.

No. I refuse to get into this now, I told myself. Time enough for that to-morrow. But it is so far from home. Still, technically, this is my home, now. At least, mine, if not home. The thing to do is to shut the mind. Settle down. Rest. Avoid Mrs. Peake. Arlette Peake. Banish her from your consciousness. Look the place over to-morrow. Call the lawyer, Mr. What's-his-name, Jr. Get the matter off your hands. In the meantime, beddie-bye. A nervous, light sleep, perhaps, but up at first light and prepared for any staff showing up, none the wiser.

There were remnants of a fire in the fireplace, which meant occupancy. A modest warmth radiated to the sofa in front of it. Yes, I would bed down here. I was already drowsy. I removed my jacket and slung it over my shoulders, up to my ears, and burrowed my face into the back of the sofa. I seemed to detect the odour of stale cigar butts which always inspires in my mind visions of urinous old men with stained white walrus moustaches. Perhaps it was the ancient, club-like, wainscotted, leather furnished atmosphere of the Great Hall. And was there a fragrance of brandy? Not likely. Not in that ecclesiastical gloom of oak hammer beams and vaulted, groined ceilings.

Thus, inauspiciously, I took possession of Moses' Castle. And thus, often, do extreme consequences ensue from trivial beginnings: an extra drink, a frontier stumbled across, a shot, a corpse, a guard reinforced by a platoon, counter-reinforcement by a regiment, by a brigade, by an army, by a coalition, by half a world, backed by the grave. Or, a hint of spring in the air, a look, the response of a smile, countered by a meeting, provoked by a touch of hands, escalation to the cheek, to the thigh, a quickened

breath, twins, a weedy lawn, vitamins, ungrateful offspring, fore-
closure, the poorhouse. I wanted only to use the w.c.

I slept, fleeing with leaden feet, pursued by Mrs. Peake. As I
fled I smiled weakly back over my shoulder at her. Probably due
to the way my head was jammed into the corner of the sofa.
Then the world exploded under my feet in a blinding yellow
flash.

Seven

It is an error to say that when one is violently awakened one is disoriented. In my case I know it to be untrue. When I dreamed that the world had exploded under my feet and awakened to find myself draped half over the end of the sofa I knew exactly what the situation was. There, staring down at me were Constables Walter Black and Desmond Stollery, and Desmond was fondling a night stick, slapping it into the palm of his hand as though dying to use it again. I could see immediately that he had whaled me on the sole of the foot with it: an unnecessarily cruel method of stirring sleeping bums off park benches. And there, hovering in the background, was old Shrubsole, the butler.

However, instantly oriented as I was, physical reconstitution was another matter and I struggled to my feet with considerable awkwardness.

It was too much.

'Walter.'

I nodded a sixteenth of an inch.

'Desmond.'

I nodded another sixty-fourth.

It was much too much. I ran my fingers through my hair. Walter and Desmond stared at me blankly, not daring to think. It was much, much too much, even for them.

'We had this call,' Walter volunteered.

'. . . an intruder reported . . .'

Old Shrubsole was sliding furtively around behind me to pick up a tray holding the heel of a bottle of brandy, a soda syphon and a plate of biscuits. Beside it was an ashtray with a massive cigar butt.

'Stand . . . right . . . where . . . you . . . are!' I commanded in a quiet, diamond edged voice. He froze.

'. . . only doing our duty,' said Walter.

'Attacking innocent householders with nightsticks,' I managed to mutter.

'We thought it was a drunken bum who had wandered in and flopped. An excess of zeal. I hope you will consider it only an excess of zeal . . .' Walter pleaded.

'You'll probably want to frisk me, eh, Desmond,' I suggested with deliberate cruelty.

Walter quickly interposed, trying to prevent escalation, 'It's a regrettable mistake, sir. I hope you'll consider it that way. We both hope so, sir.'

Expressions were fluttering across Desmond's face like wind through summer wheat. Hatred, horror and a hysterical smirk chased each other. 'You realise,' I said, 'though I hate to use the word, that you are doomed. Doomed!'

Desmond began shaking his head and he didn't stop until his partner finally dragged him out.

'A man's Castle is his home,' I said. 'You can't get away with it, breaking in without a warrant, clobbering him in his sleep without investigation. Think how that is going to sound at an inquiry. The Commissioners will love you. And so will the newspapers. Very queer business it's going to sound, if you'll excuse the word. Poor Desmond can't control himself. Can't leave me alone. Well, you never can tell . . .'

Somewhere close to this point Desmond's mind must have snapped. Perhaps snapped is not quite the correct expression. Corroded is more accurate. Later, I came to think of Desmond's mind as a fairly simple system of pneumatic tubes between two stations. At one end was Desmond as he visualised himself and at the other was the world of authority echoing approval as his mother's voice, his sergeant's, the Prime Minister's, Moses',

Jehovah's, Billy Graham's or Hitler's. And I had supplied that final drop of corrosive acid that had eaten through the tubes, deflating the whole system.

Every morning, whether Desmond knew it or not, he probably sent out and received unconscious messages like this:

'There. Pooped right on time. Set for the day.'

Thoop.

This little message is sucked down the pneumatic tube, undeviating, to Authority Central. Back, without hesitation, the response: 'Good boy. Mama is pleased.' *Thoop.*

Then, 'Scrape, scrape. See, I'm shaving. Lips thin, severe. Eye blue, cold, level.' Into the message carrier. *Thoop.*

Response: 'Manly.' *Thoop.*

Message: 'Taught that son-of-a-bitch of a drunk to get tough with me. Got him right between neck and shoulder. A dandy. And no bruise. Didn't know what hit him.' *Thoop.*

Response: 'Correct. Correct.' *Thoop.*

Message: 'Ought to wipe out that whole rotten district. Cordon it off. Search and check records. Pot. Horse. Perversion. Especially the perverts. Run them into a stockade. Maybe even . . .' *Thoop.*

Response: 'Maybe even what?' *Thoop.*

Message: 'You know . . .' *Thoop.*

Response: 'Absolutely right. We know . . .' *Thoop.*

Until yesterday.

Message: 'Wow! Yowie! Got a pervert. Smack! Crack!' *Thoop.*

Response: 'Get 'im! Get 'im!' *Thoop.*

Message: 'Help, help! A mistake. He's rich, powerful and known to the mother of the victim.' *Thoop.*

Response: 'We're right behind you. You have a good, correct record.' *Thoop.*

Message: '*No.* Oh, no! My God, no! Impossible. I am accused. I! Oh God, no! I shall kill him . . . In the circumstances it is right to shoot him, isn't it?' *Thoop.*

Response: ?

Message: 'What? I didn't get the message. What is it?' *Thoop*.

Response: ?

Message: 'I always search them like that. What if he had a knife strapped to the inside of his thigh?' *Thoop*.

Response: ?

Message: 'Why don't you answer me. You know I'm a respectable married man. A quiet obedient wife. A quiet obedient daughter. I've never tried anything strange. Except that once. Except that once. With my own wife. And I didn't go through with it. Anyway, I was only fooling. To see what her reaction would be. Why don't you answer me. I'm innocent. It's all a mistake. It's a frame-up. I'm innocent. Innocent, I tell you. Innocent.'

No answer. No responding *Thoop*. The pressure dies in the system. There are only phantom echoes as Desmond shrieks down the channel that he has depended upon for so long. No answers any more. The system has failed him. He is on his own. Free. He has the freedom to be terrified as he has terrified others. The freedom of a victim to lash out in mindless reaction against the echo of his own desperate protests.

But Shrubsole, behind my back, was demanding my attention. He was certainly fidgeting uncomfortably about the tray of brandy and soda. He was broadcasting guilty vibrations.

I waved the policemen away and Walter Black led his partner Desmond out of the room. I whirled on Shrubsole. He was in the act of flipping the cigar butt out of the ashtray and into the fireplace. It was of a Churchillian size, thick as a ditch-digger's thumb. Since he had been keeping an eye on me he had to flip it backwards and it landed on the hearth. I gave him a chilly glance. Lord of the Manor. No word needed but I supplied one anyway.

'Nightcap,' I said.

'Sir?' he responded humbly, and with great pains, great creakings and gratings of joints he bent and picked up the cigar butt and replaced it in the tray. I examined the cigar band; it looked familiar. It was a Habana Miraflores de Santiago. Holmes, even Watson, could have easily guessed it to be in the luxury class from the way the ash had lain uncrumpled in the tray.

'Prosperous guests,' I ventured, thinking I must check on Uncle's brand of cigar.

'The lawyers for the estate, the excise men—for death duties, internal revenue officers, public trustees. We've had a torrent of people since poor Sir Moses died, sir.'

What! Had the internal revenue been drinking my brandy! It was mine. It had been mine for six months. Damned if I'd stand for it. But it was probably Shrubsole living it up without supervision.

But I didn't go into it. Old Shrubsole looked so old, so fragile and servile that I let it go for the moment. My God, I thought, he must be hundreds of years old!

As a child both he and Uncle Moses had seemed incredibly ancient to me but, to a child, even an eighteen-year-old seems quite mature and an inhabitant of another world. At eighteen, when I had last seen him, he had seemed to me to be in the Old Age category. Now, a generation later, I added twenty-five or thirty years to my old impression and got the distinct feeling that Shrubsole could be no less than a hundred years old.

Still, his spine hadn't collapsed and he held his head fairly erect. But he still had his servile habit of casting his eyes elsewhere as though he were talking to you on the phone. I suppose it was his way of denying the real existence of his masters. I must re-member to re-read Buckminster's *The Servile Mind* where he deals with that unique and mutual vulnerability of master and servant, employer and employee, owner and slave, politician and electorate, demagogue and poor white trash, torturer and victim. A fascinating though repellent symbiosis, fragile and independent of apparent power.

Old Shrubsole, I thought, has reached that ageless stage of ageing in which there is little change until that last fatal upset of equilibrium precipitates total dissolution. He could be any age. A hundred and forty. He had the enlarged, flaccid ears of the aged. His dentures were grey and without pretension to naturalness. He was bald but for a slight, babyish fuzz on his cranium which now, undisguised, showed a concavity in profile. His lip was long and he seemed to cock his head slightly sideways to favour his better ear but he had no real trouble hearing and he wore no glasses though the whites of his eyes had gone quite yellow.

Though he was of average height I judged him to weigh only about a hundred and twenty pounds. Perhaps this was the secret of his longevity. And his skin, though slack, had a healthy colour, slightly tinged with pink. His walk suggested the infirmity of age, not because it was uncertain or feeble but because he wore his shoes a size or two too large and this gave him somewhat of a shambling gait even though he moved quickly enough.

I sized him up as he stood before me, guilty and fretting about the brandy bottle. He had a jacket over his pyjama coat and was unshaven. No doubt he could have wished to appear to better advantage. Considering his age and his vulnerable appearance I began to have gentler feelings. Phrases like "Old Retainer" and "Faithful Old Shrubsole" flitted through my mind, Capitals and all. I visualised pensioning him off; setting him up in a sunny little cottage in some small quiet village—perhaps his home town.

'What's your home town, Shrubsole?' I asked gently.

'Toronto, sir.'

So the rose-covered cottage was out.

'Whereabouts in Toronto?'

'Cutler Street, sir.'

Cutler Street! The worst sort of rat-infested slum, torn down years ago. But his sort probably made retirement plans when they began work.

'And how long have you worked for my Uncle?'

'Forty-seven years, sir.'

'You haven't changed a bit, Shrubsole,' I lied, mostly because

107

of the shock of his statement. Forty-seven years of slavery for a mean old son-of-a-bitch like Uncle Moses! I couldn't comprehend it.

'You've filled out since you were a boy, sir.'

I scanned him seriously but his remark seemed without malice. Still, I wasn't positively sure. He had maintained his half-servile, half-reserved expression. With less interest I asked, 'And how old are you now, Shrubsole?'

'Seventy-seven, sir.'

Thank God he did not show that smug attitude some of the aged exhibit on expressing the exact degree of their decrepitude. I felt a faint disappointment; I don't know why. Perhaps because I had presumed him to be older—something closer to Uncle Moses' age—but here he was, a man of seventy-seven looking exactly like a man of seventy-seven. Carrying on even though his lifelong master is dead. Without the imagination to get out of his servitude. Good for nothing else.

Perhaps my disappointment was deeper than I recognised. As an individualist, I fancy that everyone has another, deeper, secret life that he would live if circumstances permitted; that he would blossom like the rose once the everyday pressures were off; that a sweeter, more beautiful personality exists in everyone and that it needs nurture and freedom to grow. History has proved, time and again, that slavery, sometimes hidden and agreed-to, has been the acceptable norm but I am always dismayed when I meet it in the flesh. So I changed the subject.

'I'll have some breakfast, Shrubsole. Stir up the cook, if you will.'

'I'm sorry, sir. We have no cook at the moment. If you will allow me to prepare bacon and eggs. I do believe I have an extra egg . . . If you have the patience. I have only my hot plate nowadays. The gas has been turned off.'

'Hot plate? What's the matter with the kitchen? No maid around?'

'Oh no, sir. Mr. Swingle closed up the place immediately.
108

Dismissed me on the spot. Kept me on as watchman at a reduced rate, since I knew the old place. You see, sir, I have only my little room . . .'

'Dismissed you! Why, that's illegal, I believe. That's Swingle, the lawyer, of Cutter, Mandrake and Swingle? By God, he can't do that to my staff. You're rehired, Shrubsole, at your old salary. And call Swingle. Tell him to get up here immediately; that I've taken possession. We'll see what Old Man Swingle has to say for himself. Yes. Bacon and eggs will be fine. And flush the toilet in the cloakroom as you go by, Shrubsole.'

'Yes, sir. And thank you, sir. The thought of re-establishing myself in new quarters after all these years . . .'

'Yes, the idea is ridiculous, Shrubsole. Preposterous.'

As he shambled off I felt much less certain than I sounded about keeping him on. What use could this ancient retainer be to me? It might be only a matter of weeks before I disposed of the Castle, then he would have to go, too.

Would I then have to furnish him with a life pension? See him through his last illness? Arrange his affairs upon the onset of senility? Why should I? Uncle Moses had been the recipient of his services all these years, not I. I had simply opened my mouth unnecessarily and precipitately as I so often do. Any business man worth his salt would have hemmed and hummed and thought fast about the future, and given him a pat on the back. But, by God, Swingle wasn't going to run things a moment longer. Of that I was certain.

I looked around me. I could see that a firm hand would be needed. Dust sheets covered most of the furniture but everything from floors to limp hanging banners was filthy. It looked like the accumulation of six years rather than of six months of dust.

I found I was beginning to feel proprietorial, keen, even aggressive. There was a challenge here. Just because I was inexperienced at the job of being wealthy did not mean I was going to let myself be taken advantage of. No. I'd have to keep a hawk-like eye on things. I had no intention of piddling away my inheritance. I should dispose of it in some way that would make a permanent impact upon the community, upon society as a whole if possible. In the meantime, I might just as well be comfortable.

I threw some newspapers and kindling into the fireplace and it caught from embers buried in the ashes. I added several billets and soon was enjoying a cheerful blaze. Although it was not actually cold I found myself spreading my hands before the flames and turning and toasting my backsides. Under my nose while in this position was a curious, deep, wedge-shaped gouge in the parquetry flooring.

I knew that gouge. It was more than thirty-five years old; and it embarrassed me.

I retreated to the sofa, which was the only clean seat in the room. In this position I was forced to face the fireplace, scene of my humiliation. The fireplace was enormous, the mantel eight feet from the floor.

'Big enough to roast an ox,' Uncle Moses had bragged, gesturing towards the fireplace with a lordly, white, workless hand.

'A small ox,' my father murmured.

'A whole ox,' Uncle Moses had insisted.

'I don't see a spit,' my father said, making a big point of stooping and peering into the cavernous fireplace.

'I said "could". *Could!*' Uncle Moses almost shouted.

'. . . have to be crazy to cook an ox in your living-room,' my father muttered, and turned away in apparent disgust.

I say 'apparent' because in later life I realised that my father set out deliberately to irritate Uncle Moses on these semi-annual visits. Since these visits were begging expeditions instigated by my mother and reflecting on my father's abilities and status as head of the family, he naturally resented the position into which Mother thrust him and so made it hard for Uncle Moses to patronise him and make his enforced contribution to our exchequer; made it possible for him to maintain a façade of independence and integrity; and if a donation were made, put him under no obligation.

During these exchanges Mother turned her most prissy, tolerant smile on her brother as though to say, 'Humour him. Poor man, he's had a hard time. And remember, he's a wounded war hero and may never get over it.' But, when unobserved by her brother, she turned the gentlest but most minatory of smiles upon my father which implied, 'Just wait until I get you home, my lad'.

The situation was made more complex by Uncle Moses' tendency to brag about his wealth, his accomplishments and status. But this satisfaction must have been sorely tempered by the realisation that the loftier he soared in status the more difficult it would be later to plead hard times when Mother put the bite on him.

So there was always a considerable tension among the grown-ups which disturbed me. Although I did not thoroughly comprehend the situation at the time I had enough sense to sidle away from them and go wandering down the panelled corridors to search for hidden passageways, to inspect the esoteric furnishings of the Castle.

Among the objects which fascinated me—besides the standing suits of armour—were the swords, spears, halberds and other murderous instruments arranged decoratively on the walls. And above the mantelpiece of the Great Hall, crossed below a smoky escutcheon of what seemed to be a unicorn buggering a stag, were the most compelling pieces of all—a battle-axe and a broadsword. And the battle-axe galvanised me.

It may be that I had seen some illustration in *Chums Boys Annual*—perhaps about the siege of Acre or some lethal Viking foray. In any event, there above me was a real battle-axe and behind me were adults in some unreal squabble, paying no attention to me—even forgetting to admonish me as I ran my fingers along the polished furniture. And I was wearing running shoes, as we used to call them in those days, the kind with the round rubber reinforcing patch at the ankle bone, except that it never did coincide with my anatomy.

After eyeing my parents and my uncle bickering quietly like distant crows and curling my toes easily on the sweaty insoles of my running shoes, I took action. The mantelpiece of dull greyish uninteresting marble was carved in a most eclectic design. Thin Ionic half pillars supported on their capitals pedestals from which rose a sort of Grecian funerary stele topped by the helmeted head of an anonymous goddess behind which rose sprays of acanthus leaves supporting the mantel itself. From these, great fat swags sagged across to a boar's head in the centre of the hearth's breast. The whole mass of decoration afforded dozens of foot- and hand-holds for a small boy and it took me only an instant to climb the eight or nine feet to the mantelpiece which turned out to be uncomfortably narrow.

I reached down the battle-axe, which proved to be astonishingly heavy, perhaps half my weight. I had removed it from its pegs but now had little room to manœuvre. I wanted to raise it above my head to get the heft of it but it was an almost impossible task, considering our respective weights and the confines. I braced the end of the haft against my skinny thigh and hoped with this support to heave it up overhead as though ready to bring it crashing down upon the helm of some treacherous, black-a-vised, infidel wretch, when I was jolted by a piercing scream.

I lost control of the battle-axe. It swung me around facing the room and threatened to topple me. My mother was screaming and making clawing gestures in the air. Uncle Moses darted, enraged and alarmed, towards the fireplace. My father eyed me with an interested glint in his eye, holding his straw hat with the blue and red band behind his back in both hands and flipping it gently up and down.

'Get down from there this instant, you young vandal,' my uncle roared. 'Get down, do you hear?'

'He's going to kill himself,' my mother shrieked.

'That's all right, Mother,' my father said soothingly, which sounded ambiguous to me even then.

This sudden shouting and shrieking which diverted my attention, which turned my head, which changed my balance, could have caused me to fall but I had sense enough to let the battle-axe go. It fell with a solid, unquivering thud into the parqueted floor, standing erect on the front corner of its blade and six inches from Uncle Moses' foot.

He went white. He sprang back, much too late. 'That boy is trying to murder me,' he said in an astonished voice, as though he believed it. '. . . in my own house. I won't stand for it. A man of my position, prominence, wealth. It's intolerable . . .'

He leaped forward, wrenched the battle-axe from the floor and raising it with both hands tried to prod me off the mantelpiece. Since, in regaining my balance, I had flattened myself against the wall, he could not reach me over the edge of the mantelshelf and I had no feeling even then that he was trying to harm me with the weapon. But my hand was close to the sword upon the wall and the most natural thing, it seemed to me, was to parry his thrust. So I seized the sword which, although nowhere near as heavy as the battle-axe, was unwieldy enough for a child and it came down in an essentially uncontrolled slashing arc and clanged against the handle of the battle-axe, very close to Uncle Moses' hand.

The battle-axe fell to the floor with a crash and Uncle Moses again sprang back, staring at his hand which he held close in front of his face as though he didn't quite believe it was still attached.

'I could have been maimed for life,' he muttered. 'This is a job for the Police.'

He suddenly screamed, '*Call the police. That boy's a maniac!*'

My father smiled, still flipping his boater up and down behind his back.

Mother wept and whined, 'Oh, he'll fall and kill himself. I know he will. Moses, do stop screaming. Tim, do something, for once. Get him down from there.'

'Timothy's all right,' my father said, smiling. 'Shows the proper instincts. Any seven-year-old boy who can defend himself against a rich and crafty middle-aged man with a battle-axe can't be all bad.'

'Moses, get a ladder. He'll break his leg for sure,' Mother whined.

'Shrubsole, get a ladder, immediately,' Uncle Moses roared.

'Don't bother with the ladder. He doesn't need it, any more than a cat in a tree. Can't you see he's just playing? Come away. Let him alone. He'll get down, all right, the same way he went up.'

And he finally managed to get them out of the room without really a great deal of difficulty for Mother wanted to soothe Uncle Moses and get him into a lending frame of mind. As their voices receded towards the library I could still hear Uncle Moses growling, 'Murderous young brute. He'll never get a penny out of me. I'll see to that. Not a penny. Never. No. Not if I'm dead and buried a thousand years. Never . . .'

Did I say this was a source of humiliation for me? Perhaps that is not quite accurate. It was humiliating only in so far as a child is abashed by puzzlement and frustration caused by the strange directions in which adults twist their attitudes. I had simply and spontaneously inspected the weapons, had been caught unawares by their weight, reacted playfully if unsmilingly to Uncle Moses' attack and had found the ensuing uproar incomprehensibly out of proportion.

If Uncle Moses had had any imagination or even simple sympathy for children he would have let me handle the weapons, unlocked his case of ancient pistols and blunderbusses, shown me the stairs up to the towers, the secret passageways, the meaning of the arrow windows, let me try on a helmet, peer through the murderous slits at the surrounding city. After all, adults aren't the only ones attracted to playthings.

Even as I gazed upon the scene of that early fiasco I felt a recurring curiosity. Those weapons would heft more realistically in my hand now. Now I could truly get the feel of a Crusader, armed, bloody minded. And, in fact, those weapons were now mine so other considerations need not enter the situation, other than reaching them.

I slipped off my shoes and, having tested the old hand-holds, climbed quickly on to the mantelpiece which I found to be even narrower than I remembered. It seemed to have shrunk and was certainly a better fit for a child than for a grown man of a hundred and ninety-five pounds. I inched cautiously towards the weapons but remembering their weight and tendency to over-balance one, I crouched down before them.

I had just raised the battle-axe off its pegs when I heard old Shrubsole shuffle in. I glanced down. He was about to place the tray on a table in front of the sofa but, not seeing me, he straightened up and wheeled in a slow circle until his eyes came to rest on my shoes standing in front of the fireplace. He raised his face and his eyes slid by mine with only a faint and fleeting flash of alarm. And yet I must have looked strangely formidable, perched high above him and in what could be construed to be a menacing attitude. He held the tray up, as though putting a barrier between us.

'Breakfast, sir,' he said.

'Shrubsole,' I commanded as though the situation were the most normal and ordinary in the world, 'put down that tray and take this battle-axe. I wish to examine it at leisure.'

He turned, placed the tray on the table, turned again and approached the fireplace. I brought the battle-axe down, to hand it to him but the end poked the wall behind me and threatened to throw me off balance and down from the mantelshelf. I was forced to release the axe in order to maintain my balance. The forward point of the axe embedded itself in the hardwood between Shrubsole's feet. He froze, staring at the handle which stood almost chest high in front of him.

My performance on the mantelshelf wasn't improving with the years.

'Awkward,' I said. I felt it was a brilliant thing to say in the circumstances. It could be taken as an accusation directed towards

Shrubsole for not catching the axe in time or directed towards myself for dropping it. It did not commit me to an apology nor actually suggest that one was due and yet was still ambiguous enough to satisfy or at least quiet any too strong sense of hazard arising from the incident. A typical master-servant relationship. I felt I had learned something from this instinctive remark.

'Take the sword,' I ordered, being careful to hand it to him handle first. He was trembling visibly but he took it and, having all the weapons at hand, seemed to accept the situation as nonmurderous.

Descending the mantel was harder than ascending. About four feet from the floor I missed my footing and ended up sprawled across the hearth. But Shrubsole had probably seen Uncle Moses in even more peculiar positions. He would accept lapses in dignity as part of the job.

I arose, wrenched the battle-axe from its billet and pretended to examine it closely but I was secretly hefting it, luxuriating in visions of stricken fields. I caught a glimpse of a legend on the blade of the axe, close to the handle. My heart leaped. I hoped I could decipher it. It might be an inscription in French, German, Arabic. I inspected it closely.

Made in Sheffield, England.

Another childhood fantasy exploded. I turned to breakfast.

'You've done the eggs in butter, with the lid on,' I said, astonished. 'I haven't had a decent egg in years.'

'Sir Moses insisted on this style, sir, as slightly more robust than poached.'

'Slightly more robust! Perfect. Perfect. I didn't think the old lunatic had that much judgment.'

Shrubsole looked pained.

'Oh, come off it, Shrubsole. You're not going to give me that "Speak no ill of the dead" nonsense, are you? That's how monsters perpetuate their monstrosities. Sometimes, in life, we don't have the power to resist them but in death, surely at last isn't it time to rear up on our hind legs?'

'But sir, I worked for Sir Moses for forty-seven years.'

'All the more reason to kick up your heels, Shrubsole.'

'Ah, at seventy-seven, sir, one hopes for a quiet, continuing life . . .'

'But knowing how peculiar Uncle Moses was twenty-five or thirty years ago, I am certain that he was more than a little bit daft, senile, paranoid, towards the end . . .'

'I know nothing about the technical side of the matter, sir, but although he wasn't his normal self, we mustn't forget he was an old man.'

This sounded very civilised and I was partially impressed. Mostly by the diplomatic way he had put it.

Eight

But it is no secret that Uncle Moses died a lunatic. More obscure is the matter of his alleged normality. I prefer to think that he was born lunatic, lived lunatic, died lunatic and nothing in the twenty or thirty times I met him during my first seventeen years did anything to dispel this notion.

By lunatic I do not mean those temporary disturbances now genteelly labelled mental illness or technically considered to be chemical imbalances. No. I mean those phenomenal aspects of character, behaviour, personality that seem to owe nothing of their inhuman tendencies to any traceable factor in immediate inheritance, environment, cultural tradition, education, toilet training, weaning, tonsilectomy or any other socio-scientific fad of the past four thousand years. By lunatic I mean those unexplained crippled areas of the personality which by some blanking-out process allow a man to devote his life to the manufacture of anal suppositories and in the end make him feel his life has been successful and well spent; a process that allows a commander to issue the order 'No quarter' although to-day it may be rephrased 'We are not equipped to handle prisoners on this exercise'; to raise the price of food on a starvation market; to send men to their death in order to have a border incident on hand at the conference table; to consider a column of figures of greater interest than a dance; to cheat a million children a million times on the weight of their penny candy in order to build a monument to themselves; to force the world into the gutter if they are unable to rise higher than the kerbstone; to laugh all the way to

118

the bank; to raise castles on dung hills; to reign as king of that castle.

They used to call it blood: it was probably example. From a noble family, noble sons: from a swinish tribe, swinish actions. It may be that the Old Timers had a point there. They noted that opposition of Good and Evil long before it was perverted into Spirit and Flesh by a handful of really powerful evil doers. Yes, all myth points to a different Mankind (and myths arise out of truth), a Mankind of a Golden Age living in upright generosity of spirit before some great Fall. So that myth of Eden is probably quite true in a literal and historic sense, taking into account the usual transference that occurs when, after the passage of time, some awkwardness of understanding arises and corners have to be smoothed by guess-work. Unquestionably, the Fall had to do literally and historically with Adam, a living Jew, stuffing Eve, a lively (according to her name) female, under an apple tree; conceiving Cain, conceiving Abel.

But who was Eve? In Adam's first encounter with her he suffers a broken rib. If she was a product of Adam's sleep, she was a nightmare.

Consider the scientific facts: Late traces of Neanderthal Man in Palestine and surrounding Middle East areas and undoubtedly overlapping modern man in time. Then from the Hebrews, who are sexually sophisticated enough to define degrees of rape in their Laws, comes an enormously strong, irrational and continuing article prohibiting intercourse and marriage with aliens and indicating by its strength an obsessive fear at its origins. Is there a connection? Is Eve the mindlessly 'lively' gambolling Neanderthal wench creating with Adam a classic Mendelian line of descent from Man and Monster—a peaceable Abel and a murderous Cain?

Is this what the Old Timers were screaming about: the easy, cloddish, irresponsible copulation with the half-animal Neanderthals producing brutish, tigerish, voracious offspring too deficient in sensitivity to be aware of their inherent animal cruelty? And

Cain, wandering through the world, perpetuates his half-human
self in quarter-animal offspring who, in turn reproduce themselves in eighths and sixteenths. So this brutish gene is in the
blood now and re-encounters of those bearing the strain strength-
en the monstrous stock so that a few hundred generations later
the mating of two apparently normal beings produces a sport of
incredible, unforeseen and inexplicable callousness and we suffer
mass murderers of easy digestion from the brutes of Assyria to the
ghouls of Mongolia; from that bloody minded national hero
Napoleon to that mindlessly bloody Hitler; from the murderously
wise Solomon to the wisely murderous Churchill; from the cannibalistic Stalin to the fratricidal Mao; from Boy Scout turned mad
sniper to Sunday School Superintendent turned Bluebeard, until
finally we get a weak combination like Uncle Moses, just ruthless
enough to seize a goodly portion of loot; just savage enough to
protect it from encroachers of his own ilk; just mindless enough
and lunatic enough to establish himself as Somebody by building
the Castle.

I could have said all this to Shrubsole but he would have
thought me, rather than Uncle Moses, the lunatic. I could have
brought in Dr. McKenna's work on the anagalidae, those small
extinct animals with hoofed rear legs and clawed front legs, the
ancestors of both mice and men, and their relationship to Uncle
Moses' rodent-like personality (perhaps he too would have had
mole-like blood paths through the skull base) but Shrubsole
would only have said, 'We all have our quirks, sir, and Sir
Moses . . . et cetera.' And I realised that, as a servant, Shrubsole
would have expected to be put upon by his master and would
have acted similarly if the roles had been reversed. This made me
want to jump up and down with rage so I calmed myself, and,
strolling about the Great Hall with a plate of bacon in one hand
and feeding myself the crisp strips with my fingers, I said, 'Look
at this, Shrubsole. Can you honestly stand there and tell me that
this is not the work of a lunatic?'

I swept the great expanse of the Hall with a triangle of toast held between greasy fingers. Shrubsole looked puzzled and offered me a napkin. 'Surely that is a sign of mental instability,' I stated, pointing to a series of hammer beams. 'Surely a groined ceiling in the twentieth century indicates, perhaps, calcification of certain capillaries in the medulla oblongata? Some Foundation should make a grant to look into that rather than spend millions and years on a Report On Why The Starving Are Hungry and then shipping out tombstones with regrets.

I thought I heard a distinct 'pat' on the floor beside me. Shrubsole immediately dragged an enormous brass urn to the centre of the room.

Klong! The metallic reverberations were horrifying.

'And it leaks!' I shrieked.

'Regrettably, sir.'

I became quite agitated for some reason, perhaps because it was *my* roof, even though I wanted no part of it. Even though in a matter of days I would have disposed of it, still, my roof was leaking. Yes. Right on top of me.

'Do you know what caused the decline of the aristocracy?' I exclaimed. 'No, not social change, not industrialisation, universal education, communications, in-breeding (the butler can be relied upon to ginger up the old stock, present company excepted). No. Not punitive taxation nor the rise of the middle class. No. Leaky roofs.

'Do you know what it costs to reroof a castle? A palace? A manor house, Shrubsole? Thousands. Hundreds of thousands. One leak and you're on the way to the poorhouse. Shut off the wing and in ten years it's a habitation for owls. You fall right through the floors into the dungeon. Windows are mysteriously smashed and never reglazed. The tenants flee to the city. They have noted the hole in the roof. The estate doesn't produce enough to pay the taxes. Credit is short. The usurers take over. The coronet is pawned—and proved gilt. So call that goddamned lawyer right away. I'm unloading this ruin.'

'I have already called him, sir. He'll be along immediately.'

'Good thinking. The roof. It's slate? Oh, God, that's terrible. Send a man up to replace one damaged slate and he cracks a dozen more. The whole roof is shot. As strong as the weakest slate. And you try to tell me my Uncle wasn't lunatic! A slate roof! My God!'

I was quite disturbed, almost panicky. I couldn't quite understand why I was in the grip of sheer emotional reaction. I tried to divert myself from the ruination of the roof.

'Look at those pictures,' I said, pointing to six enormous, murky oils in grotesque, gold leafed frames. 'You can't tell me that any sane person even sixty years ago would buy that sort of thing. This one: *The Daughters of Lot* by Monteverdi.'

I stepped back and surveyed it. I wanted to be fair. Lot lay sprawled at the foot of a marble statue (or perhaps it was Mrs. Lot in carved and salted Greek draperies) gesticulating drunkenly with a flagon of what looked like used crankcase oil under a glaze of mahogany coloured varnish. One daughter simpered and covered her nose in a Victorian gesture of modesty as the old man made a grab at a protuberant breast. A couple of other daughters frolicked with vine leaves in their hair while the Esso refinery went up in bloody flames and smoke in the background.

'Monteverdi,' I said. 'Wasn't he the madrigal chap?'

'School of Brindisi,' Shrubsole offered.

'A likely story. Never heard of it. Investigation would prove it a barber college, I'll bet, according to this example. And what's this?' I demanded, indicating a second monstrous painting. '*Knights Crushing Boxes*. Now, what the hell is that?'

I read the engraved metal plate on the frame: ' "*Knights Crushing Boxes*—Master of Schrobenhausen—Late 14th Cent." This has to be some sort of a joke—a satire—which is impossible in the circumstances. The Knights would have had The Master stuffed in a sausage casing before he finished the cartoon . . .'

'Sir Moses suggested it was an allegorical subject, sir.'

'Suggested!' I exclaimed. 'Shrubsole, you are priceless. Suggested! To suggest that Uncle Moses ever suggested anything is to suggest an impossibility. Now, if you had said, "insisted, demanded, protested, asserted, vociferated, screamed, yelled, hollered, bullyragged, bawled, whined, stated, bellowed, fulminated, bombilated, expostulated or snorted," I'd be of half a mind to believe you but, "suggested"—never.'

'Sir Moses was a man of many facets, sir.'

'I know two of them, both being sides of schizophrenia as I have been trying to tell you. As an illustration, look at this: Am I mistaken or do I see six toes on the Virgin?'

I indicated the monstrosity with a crisp rasher. Shrubsole scanned *Virgin Refusing Breast To Child Jesus*.

'A trick of the light perhaps, sir. The chiaroscuro . . . Frescobaldi's style . . .'

'Oh, come off it, Shrubsole. That picture's as queer as a cockroach. *Virgin Refusing Breast To Child Jesus*, indeed! In fact, there's something queer about all these pictures. Look at that.'

I pointed to *Demons Gnawing On Sinners* by Aardvarkius Grosskirch. A Boschian steal if I ever saw one. Naked sinners arrested in acts approaching lewdness and perversions beset by half-animal, half-insect monsters; crushed by weird machines, consumed, tortured in complicated devices but made obscure and almost unexaminable by a varnish of concentrated bouillon.

Then there was a complicated *Judith Letting Down The Head Of Holofernes* by Beckstein in which Judith hangs out of a tower window lowering the severed head on a slanting tray to a crowd of pikemen and archers, dogs and cattle, lords and ladies in what might be best described as an Egyptian style.

'Bring me my coffee,' I ordered. 'If these things don't prove Uncle Moses' lunacy . . . And if this doesn't take the cake . . .'

I indicated a *Descent From The Cross* by Jan Vanderjordan. Underneath the oxo surface could be discerned the usual crucifixion grouping. But the man up on the cross, with the corner of a sheet in his hand, was holding his arms up in horror while the group on the ground, excepting the Centurions, was reeling back in horror. Christ was sprawled in an upside down, broken-necked attitude on the ground. Obviously, they had dropped Him.

'Now, level with me, Shrubsole. Just examine these pictures as a group. What would you say the dimensions are? Nine by twelve? Or three by four metres? Nevertheless, all of exactly the same size, wouldn't you say?'

'I had never thought about it before, sir,' he stated, with every indication of not wanting to start thinking about it now, either.

'Do you think, over a period of a couple of hundred years that these pictures are supposed to span, that this coincidence in size is a coincidence?'

'I beg pardon, sir?'

'Isn't it obvious that he had these monstrosities made up to order, to fit the walls?'

'It was before my time, sir.'

'Who did he think he was kidding?' I demanded. 'Why, even an institutionalised Mongoloid finger painter would see through that stuff. *Virgin Refusing Breast To Child Jesus*, for Christ's sake! Those damned things were manufactured on an assembly line in some little factory in Eindhoven—or on the outskirts of Bergen op Zoom. Some apprentice whitewasher probably botched those toes.'

And, although I was ranting and glaring at the six-toed Hysteric and had worked up enough indignation to report her to the Children's Aid Society, something had begun to tickle me somewhere at the back of my mind. I felt a certain piquancy, a sort of smirky amusement beginning to intrude upon my irritation. Virgin Refusing Breast . . . yes . . . distinct possibilities. Foundation of Christian Society. Basis of Western Malaise. Homosexual Origins Of The Church, etc. Surely old Uncle Moses couldn't have meant . . . surely he didn't realise . . . surely . . . surely not . . .

It occurred to me that I didn't know Uncle Moses; that he could have been more than a pedlar of patented breakfast food; a money grubber of the meanest mortgaged mind.

But I had built up a certain momentum and found myself saying to Shrubsole: 'How could anyone maintain sanity in these surroundings? It's like living in an Anglican Church on Garrison Sunday. What do those banners mean?' I asked, pointing to flags, pennants and wall hangings high up.

'They've always been there,' Shrubsole informed me stolidly.

'Up until now,' I snapped. 'They'll be coming down. There are going to be changes made. Call that damned lawyer. Get him up here immediately.'

'I have already done so, sir.'

I marvelled at his patience. I had given him this order at least three times that morning yet neither by word nor gesture did he indicate that I was losing my mind, as he had every excuse to do.

I cannot say that I realised I was enjoying this exercise of power—playing master to his servant—and yet I was slipping quite comfortably into the role under cover of the sound and fury. Every demand, no matter how politely couched, is a blow. Every order is an injury imposed by power even though disguised as a request. Every manipulation, no matter how subtle, is sensed and remains a barbed arrow in the soul; and each such injury, though apparently not inflicted meaningly, provides the inflictor with his hidden if uncomprehended satisfactions and his victim with often unconscious agonies.

I now find it incredible that I did not immediately realise what was happening to me, especially since I had gone to such pains to place myself in an anonymous backwater of society where no apparent demands were made and no personal responses required. The cars appeared on the moving chain line, I washed my section of the car as it rolled mechanically by and at the end of the day collected my pay without further conditions—to return next day or not, as I chose; to escape the notice of the government by virtue of my inconsistent labours; to avoid the intrusive demands of the social departments of the municipality by reason of the money in my pocket.

But then, it is not in the nature of man to examine his satisfactions too closely. This examination he confines to the envied satisfactions of others.

'Come, Shrubsole,' I said. 'We are going to make an inspection. There must be more to this dump than meets the eye. Bring keys, if they're needed.'

'Very well, sir. The keys are in the kitchen. If you will excuse me.'

'I'll come with you. No use wasting time. I want to see everything. Cellar to garret.'

And I did see everything, almost, in a superficial way.

'If you will come this way, sir,' he said, touching a panel in the wall. A section of walnut panelling gaped suddenly. 'I remember that, as a boy, you were fascinated by the secret passage.'

We stepped into the passage which was actually the landing of a stairway and as I shut the door behind me a light went on automatically. We descended carpeted stairs in silence and Shrubsole, at the bottom, placed his hand on a handle jutting from what seemed to be a brick wall.

'As a boy you would have come this far. Sir Moses did not like it known that the passageway extended from top to bottom of the house.'

He released a lock and a section of the brick wall swung open. 'Unless you insist on seeing the very deepest cellars?'

I pushed the door closed again. I felt a boyish, intense excitement. I had the feeling that this passageway might come in handy. This possibility of silently slipping quickly and mysteriously to any floor of the house intrigued me; of appearing suddenly and unexpectedly; of people turning their heads and finding me there where, a second ago, there was no one.

But who?

I should be gone in a matter of days. A few weeks at the most when the inevitable details of settling the estate had been dealt with and the Castle put on the market.

I would be bringing Joe Bezoar up to see it, possibly, but I wouldn't be playing hide and seek with him. Still, this had no effect upon my excitement and I emerged into the deepest cellar like a conspirator. I was immediately disappointed.

It was a cellar very much like any other cellar but much larger. Concrete floor, concrete walls, even the ceiling was concrete. One end was strewn with boxes and barrels of an obviously considerable age. S.S. *Leviathan* via New York. Cunard Line, etc. The packaging of china and other imports of fifty or sixty years ago saved, possibly, for the move to the next castle?

'Someone has been pawing through this junk lately. Rats?'

'Internal revenue and the lawyers' men. Searching for assets, I believe.'

'Find any?'

'No, sir.'

'Strange,' I said, and I found myself scratching a concrete pillar with my fingernail as though to discover something beneath its surface.

'Sir?'

'This is concrete.'

'Yes, sir.'

'The whole thing is concrete!'

'Yes, sir.'

'I suppose I expected stone.'

'Concrete and steel, sir. Sir Moses once explained to me that it was cheaper and stronger than masonry and wooden joists. The walls are a veneer of stone. The complete plans are in the archives on the second floor.'

What can be expected of a furnace room? Steam boilers, water heaters, pumps, even a pile of discarded parts such as grates (when the boilers had been converted to oil) iron rods, mysterious metal casings. But an enormous coal bin full of sand? And several hundred filled sand bags? And a dozen great bales of burlap bags. I looked at Shrubsole.

'The time of The Bomb, sir.'

I returned my glance to the sandbags.

'He began to age rapidly about that time, sir. He seemed to

have no heart either for the shovelling or for holding the bag, and I must say, I saw no good in it.'

I began to see Shrubsole as a sort of zombie to Uncle Moses' ninny-hammer. The very idea of two old men trying so desperately to save their skins by filling sand bags so enraged me that I could have lashed the old cod if I'd had a cat-o'-nine-tails. I began to understand, too, something of the feelings of ancient despots who used their subjects so cruelly in spite of, or perhaps because of, their subservience. I prodded Shrubsole in the ribs.

'Let's go. Let's go.'

We passed a row of cubicles in concrete with great iron rings set in the floor and walls. They looked as though they had been designed for *The Man In The Iron Mask*, Hollywood circa 1932, then abandoned. Next was the wine cellar. It had been meant to furnish large entertainments and was still about a quarter full. A great number of cases of liquor, too, dating from the time they used wooden boxes.

I was attracted to the champagne; more, I suppose, because of its cachet than any interest I have in drinking. There seemed to be thousands of bottles. Mostly *brut*. I inspected several and chose a Chateau Pomme de Cheval which I thought I remembered drinking on a few of other people's festive occasions.

'I am not a drinking man, Shrubsole,' I said, lining up six bottles on the floor.

'No, sir.'

'In fact, I have lately been living a Spartan, if not completely ascetic life, and am uninstructed in the finer points of consumption . . .'

'You have made an excellent choice in this case, sir. One of Sir Moses' favourites. If I may venture—Sir Moses showed great discrimination, in his prime. His cigars were hand rolled especially for him in Havana. He had only to cable for bespoke shoes, made on his own last in London. He had Winnipeg Gold Eyes shipped direct from Gimli. And I still remember those perfect intimate little dinners in the Tower Room: champagne and oysters, fresh out of the barrel from Malpeque that afternoon . . .'

'How intimate?'

Shrubsole affected to involve himself in a discreet mortician's cough on to the back of his hand and this occupied him so obviously that he forgot the question.

'An old lecher,' I said. 'You won't be involved in that sort of thing for me. I'm against conspicuous consumption you see, and that lets out fancy women.'

I said this in reaction and resentment of the picture I conjured up of Uncle Moses breathing moistly into the bosom of a Gibson Girl, feverishly entangled in her corset strings, plying her with the aphrodisiac of his bank book while, hovering in the background with his oysters, his champagne, his cheeses, his gamecocks, Shrubsole pimped away unobtrusively.

This prostitution of Shrubsole to Uncle Moses' whims not only irritated but confused me. After all, for several years my life had been based on refusing to carry another man's pot whether that pot contained his brutal wars, his biased laws, his perverse philosophies or his bloody, greasy money. So I should have felt quite clearly about it, in spite of my sympathetic response to Shrubsole's position after forty-seven years with Uncle Moses. Anyone associated with one of Uncle Moses' kidney for that long wasn't being put upon. No. My irritation was due to my confusion and my confusion was due to my refusal to recognise the question that had now suddenly arisen: Was I now willing to have someone else carry *my* pot?

Nine

I was having trouble with the halyard. It was flopping wetly and lazily in the same drizzle that was soaking through my roof into the Great Hall and ponging into the great brass tub. The halyard had come loose from its cleat and was dangling just a few feet beyond my farthest reach. I was trying to snare it with the pennant I planned to fly from the Tower's staff. I was flipping the dusty, greasy oriflamme across the halyard in the hope of dragging it a few inches towards me when I heard the noise: a grinding, growling, spitting, farting, geary noise which seemed to emanate from a tiny sports car climbing the hill, turning the corner and wheeling again into my gate.

It stopped directly below me, a tinny, totally exposed two-seater that looked as though it had been designed by a kid too old for the soap box derby. It was a Lotus Seven, the sort of machine only madmen drive in the rain. Irritating to see go by noisily and, obviously, uncomfortably. Arousing the angry question. What the hell is that kid trying to prove in this traffic, on these roads, with that machine? And later, unbidden, come creeping visions of tramping on the gas, throwing it around the curves at the limit of adhesion, braking at the last split of a split second, squeezing through, using the road like a one-way street.

I whistled down shrilly, angrily.

'Who's calling?' I shouted.

He threw a thin ski-ing jacket on to the seat and looked up.

'Swingle,' he called up. 'And you'd be Timothy Badger.'

'Come up,' I ordered. I was shocked. Swingle. I had expected an older man. Grey. Cautious. Shrewd. Substantial. Obscurely feral. Frigid. Vaguely frightened about me and my reputation. But this Swingle I had not anticipated. He was surging up the stairs, two or three at a time. He arrived in seconds and he wasn't even breathing hard. I continued in my endeavours to ensnare the halyard.

'Good to see you settled in, Mr. Badger,' he said, sizing up the situation instantly. 'Could I help you with that.'

He was out on the sill before I could reply, clutching the eaves with one hand and stretching as far as he could reach along the Tower's masonry, eighty feet in space. There was a slight cracking noise and he hooked one foot up behind the beam supporting the roof of the tower and I saw him drop crumbled slate from his hand. When he eased himself to the floor again he was holding the halyard.

'Must see to that roof,' was his only comment and he began rummaging in his attaché case. I bent the pennant to the line and hoisted it to the top of the staff through a block complaining like a toothachy rat.

'A nice touch,' young Swingle observed. 'Give the old monument a bit of gaiety.'

I craned out of the opening. The pennant which may originally have been red or orange had, in the past forty years or so, faded to a greyish depressing yellow. It hung in the breezeless drizzle like an ancient and diseased scrotum.

Before I hung out this dismal burgee I had a feeling of gaiety, of pageantry, almost. Banners, trumpets, flags fluttering in the sun. I had chosen this particular pennant at random, more for the purpose of ensnaring the halyard than of actually flying it. I later found, through researches in Uncle Moses' library, that it corresponded, as closely as I could make out, to the ensign of the Idaho Cycle and Song Club, 1912. I had hoisted it simply to get it off my hands and to tackle Swingle with his disturbing youth.

'How were conditions in Portillo?' I asked, sizing up his deep tan and judging he would be much too much *in* still to be ski-ing in Austria.

'Excellent, excellent! You still ski?' he asked, looking up in astonishment.

That 'still' gave me a sinking feeling as always happens when I am suddenly reminded of my middle age.

'No longer,' I said. In fact, I had never skied. I have always thought it as mindless as bowling. Another aspect of the Age Of Masturbation. Up mechanically, down by gravity. A thrill a day keeps the mind at bay.

'By the way, what engine are you running in the Lotus?'

I thought he looked a little frightened at this. I was suspicious. Ordinarily, sports car enthusiasts do the Ancient Mariner on you. They seize you with tales of high-lift cam shafts, sludge blenders, magnetic diapasons, rocker arms, manifold whifflers, turbo-swags, induction scorbers, and over-sized centrifugal boglers.

'The 1340 c.c.,' he said hastily. 'Look, I must be in Court in fifteen minutes. Could I leave all this stuff with you? There's a handful of wills, an inventory of the estate, a couple of releases you'll have to sign—all the usual nonsense. I'll drop in later—this evening if you wish. Agreed?'

He gave me his winning, manly, manipulative smile, and thrust out his hand. I agreed. It would give me a chance to assess the situation, just in case anything were being slipped over me.

I'm not fond of lawyers.

Nor of politicians or bankers or barbers or dentists or merchants or teachers. Children are all right, generally, until they turn into fully-fledged consumers, which is happening earlier and earlier.

So I let him slip away and I surveyed my domain from my tower, which was the highest of the six and the only one which had an open gallery giving a full circle view of the city and much of the Castle grounds. I saw that the grounds were divided by walls into half a dozen compounds: one, the front courtyard and entrance gate: another comprising formal gardens: another sloped steeply downhill, heavily treed and in a state of nature: another obviously of a service function, filled with tool sheds and garages and adjoining a service entrance.

The horizon was limited, the atmosphere dank and grey. Still, I was at the high point and centre of a limited, visible world and a childhood rhyme began flitting through my mind unbidden:

I'm the king of the castle,
And you're the dirty rascal.

This we used to chant upon reaching a high point—the top of a fence, the higher branches of an apple tree, the ridge of a shed, the crest of a hill, defended against all comers. It was something of a challenge, to be chanted while jumping up and down, if possible. A taunt. But still with a sense of gaiety and accomplishment.

I'm the king of the castle,
And you're the dirty rascal.

The refrain went murmuring on, ricocheting against invisible surfaces of my mind. I felt anything but gay. In fact, I began to feel mighty depressed. It was quite inexplicable. I felt trapped between tears and rage. Instead of feeling like jumping up and down in triumph, I felt like stamping in fury.

I gave a little hop, experimentally.

I realised I was holding Swingle's attaché case. It had been years since I had carried such a case. I dropped it as though it were a fresh turd and recoiled in horror. I felt an enormous sense of relief. I smiled out upon the city-scape. The sun showed a sudden misty disc through the grey cloud.

'I'm the king of the castle,
And you're the dirty rascal!'

I shouted it across the roof-tops. I doubt if anyone heard but my spirits rose abruptly. In a more conversational tone I added, 'Yes, you'll hear from me. I've a little leverage now. You'll listen.'

To what?

I hadn't decided about that. It was just something I shouted at the city. I wasn't aware that I had changed my plans to get rid of the Castle.

I ran swiftly down the circular stone staircase that gave access to the tower. I re-entered Uncle Moses' suite and closed the unobtrusive panel which was the uppermost exit of the secret stairway. I hadn't stopped here on my way up from the cellars.

I had taken the six bottles of champagne, three between each of the four fingers of each hand, and carried them to the kitchen. 'Chill them, just in case,' I told Shrubsole.

In case of what? What did I mean by that? I must have meant something, even though I was unaware of it at the time. I must have had some celebratory idea in mind and it could have been related only to the inheritance of the Castle. This drives me to the conclusion that all my conscious attitudes were hypocritical, but my unconscious mind knew the truth and spoke. And perhaps it was that simple.

But that is in retrospect. In actual fact, I had no time nor inclination to examine the matter for I immediately added, 'And call Mrs. Peake, my landlady. See if she will accept the job of supervising the clean-up of The Castle. I have reason to believe she will come—strictly as a favour to me. Stress that with her, Shrubsole. As a favour to me.' And I gave him her telephone number.

This was an impulse that obscured the significance of my impulse to prepare for a celebration. But an impulse is only a series of lightning calculations which is why impulsive people are so irritating. They have conned you deliberately before you've had time to retreat to defensive positions.

By now, with millions and a castle at my command and the leverage of their authority, I judged that I could meet Mrs. Peake on equal terms. Before, I had resisted the juicy temptation out of sheer self-preservation. She'd have gobbled me up like a cannibal on the forty-first day of Lent.

But on second thought, all that business about lightning calculations is nonsense, otherwise young Charlie Mactier who lived next door years ago would be alive to-day rather than electrocuted by peeing on an electric cord with frayed insulation in his father's garage. But what did young Charlie know about insulation at that age? No. Impulses are impulses.

I wanted to see Mrs. Peake on my grounds rather than on hers. I wanted to see her because she had seemed so irresistibly meaty and toothsome the night before and I didn't want her to feel I had rejected her because she lacked attraction. In fact, I wanted to see her. In fact, I wanted to . . . In fact, I wanted her.

I hesitate to mention it in this circumstance and Ziggy F. and his Viennese Wombats could play a very shrill tune on their phallutes at this stage but, when I left Shrubsole in the kitchen with his instructions to call Mrs. Peake, I proceeded immediately to climb the secret staircase ascending through the centre of the house. This brought me, as before mentioned, to Uncle Moses' suite which I scarcely glanced at. It was onward and upward for me and I didn't stop until I got that damned, sleazy pennant flying at the pinnacle.

Now, on returning to Uncle Moses' suite, I gave it closer inspection.

The main room itself was large, and it was dominated by an enormous Jacobean four-poster. Or perhaps it was antique Spanish oak. Or Grand Rapids, 1900. This key piece did not stand out as much as one could expect because of the clutter of chests, presses, commodes, divans, tables, tabourets, mirrors, hangings, vases, peacock feathers, Morris chairs, bolsters, chaise-longues, fire tongs, besoms, carpets, candlesticks, chandeliers— in Roccoco, Buhl, Moroccan leather, Indian brass, Victorian mahogany, Tudor oak, Versailles gilt, Venetian crystal, Arabic inlay, Chinese lacquer, Birmingham iron and other imitations of imitations with some more graceless and cruder items which may have been genuine antiques which is to say, they had been abandoned to attics centuries ago by people of taste.

In other words the place looked as though it had started out in life as a pretentious *antique shoppe* and had found its natural level as a junk shop.

That bed, I thought, may be real. We've lost the touch for that sort of grotesquerie these days. Life is simpler since we lost our imagination. Them or Us. Freedom or Slavery. Slavery or Freedom. Peace or War. In or Out. Black or White. Ginsberg's Moribund Mother's Vagina or The Spiritually Damned.

(Hence my imitation bombs and their suggestion of alternatives.)

Still, it was depressing to see this shabby, grubby, dusty, obtrusive furniture looking as lifeless as stage props stored in a loft. I couldn't help thinking of the hours, years of work involved; of the patience, craft and vision ultimately dedicated to this ersatz castle, pipe dream of a madman.

That great bed, I thought, may have witnessed the amours, conceptions, births, deaths, adulteries of dukes and ends up in mid-continent, the property of a car washer and part-time mad bomber, nephew of a successful lightning rod salesman and breakfast-food entrepreneur.

A peculiar and probably womby experience, I thought, sleeping inside those velvet curtains. Something like an upper berth.

Six months' dust lay on the counterpane and I threw it off. Probably I would be sleeping in one of the Castle beds for the next few weeks so I thought I'd try this one for comfort. It proved a bit saggy towards the centre but quite soft and comfortable. I pulled the draperies closed on one side but the other was stuck. I tugged. Only when I felt a faint, sneeezy sifting of dust did I look up to see myself completely reflected in a mirror suspended over the great bed.

'Son of a gun!' I exclaimed aloud. And I had an answer, if I had asked the question, of why Uncle Moses had to protect himself within the fastness of a castle.

But that didn't seem to be the question. What, I asked myself as I stared at my recumbent reflection, could be the purpose of this peculiarly placed mirror? Surely it could only complicate an already graceless, not to say, awkward procedure?

However, I am a poor judge of this sort of thing. I've never had the heart for determined titillation. And besides, perhaps it was an innocent matter. Perhaps Uncle Moses was one of those eccentrics who insist upon sleeping in a position consonant with the magnetic lines of force; who each year adjusted his bed to the magnetic declination announced by the Dept. of Hydrographic Surveys so that these magnetic lines of force coursed harmonious'y through him from head to foot rather than interruptedly across his body.

On the other hand, it could have been simply a matter of style. At the time when playboys like Thaw were murdering philanderers like White over girls in red velvet swings, that sort of thing was *de rigeur*. No self-respecting man about town was without a mirrored *pied-à-terre*. And the installation of a bidet could cause a scandal. Perhaps Uncle was one of those gay dogs.

It makes one think, that mirror business. The psychologists should investigate that sort of thing. Now that I think about it, they probably have. There's something perverty about that gang. But if they've published a report on it, count me out. I wouldn't want to read it.

My uncomfortable night on the sofa had left me unrested. I must have dozed off while speculatively examining my image in the mirror above me. And I had one of those realer-than-real dreams.

I saw myself distantly, slightly blurred in the suspended mirror. I felt pinned down, trapped. Beside me, Mrs. Peake undulated like the sea, clad only in the filmiest of garments and in the act of turning towards me, about to envelope, encompass, overwhelm me. And yet, my vision was static in spite of the feeling of an on-going, continuing, smothering process by a fascinating, voluptuous, yet deadly dangerous monster. I awoke with a strangled shout to find that my right arm had gone to sleep.

'Timothy! Timothy Badger, you bad boy. You're hiding from me. Where are you?' I heard in the unmistakably firm tones of Mrs. Peake.

I thrashed about on the bed in blind protest only to find that I was in fact now awake. And I could hear her tripping in with her gay, light footstep.

'There you are, Timothy! You are a devil, teasing me like this,' she said in mock severity as she came to the side of the bed. She looked at me as though she could swallow me whole, without sauce. 'Oh, you've been napping. I am sorry. I've awakened you.'

'What . . . when . . . how . . .'

'Isn't this a lovely old bed,' she purred in tones of new velvet. 'I'd just adore sleeping in it. So cosy with the curtains and the light all shut out.'

She left off stroking the bed and hugged herself deliciously so that her balcony projected another six inches in my direction.

'It's certainly not my style,' I said firmly, and I tugged open the curtains on the left side and turned a meaningful glance to the ceiling.

'Oh, isn't that fascinating,' she whispered. She jounced the edge of the bed awkwardly as though preparatory to climbing in. The bed was very high, almost up to her diaphragm. 'Oh, I must see this!'

She gave an extra strong jounce and came tumbling in just as I went tumbling out on the other side in panic; as close to fright as I have ever come in my life. As I landed on the floor I could see reflected in the mirror Mrs. Peake flopping into the soft centre of the bed, legs flying up uncontrollably. Perhaps.

If I were placed on the witness stand I couldn't honestly swear that she was wearing her panties.

It may have been due to the poor lighting and the murky mirror; or to the giggly way she was kicking her legs; or to my imagination; or to wishful thinking; or to the remnants of my dream. But no. The hunted feeling, the brassy rush of the prowling woman is unmistakable.

And Father had warned me, just before he died. I was about sixteen at the time and not quite the perfect receptacle for receiving advice. 'Tim,' he said, 'You've got a whole free life ahead of you now. Remember that?'

THE FIREFLY HUNT

'I remember, Dad.'

Clearly.

About twelve years earlier we were at the Castle on a fine summer day. Mother had cornered Uncle Moses and was probably squeezing a few hundred dollars out of him. My father was strolling back and forth beside the parapet looking quite cool and handsome in brown and white shoes, cream-coloured flannel suit with stripes, boater with blue and red band which he said were the colours of the Holy Joe-Hand-In-The-Collection-Plate-Club. This sent me into wild convulsions of laughter so that Mother called out, 'Tim, what are you doing to the boy?' And turned away without waiting for an answer. The convulsive part was that each time I asked he would have another title: Searching For A Nigger In A Coal Mine Club. (It was socially acceptable to use a word like 'nigger' in those days.)

I suppose he was a bit of a dude. That happens with those who see no real role for themselves in life, from the idle rich to the displaced youth. Get yourself into a uniform and you'll be able to identify yourself the next time you meet yourself coming around the block. But he was amiable. He didn't seek me out, nor I him. We weren't pals but we liked each other. Perhaps more. Even as a small child I resented the tolerance the rest of the family exhibited towards him: 'Poor devil. The mustard gas at Ypres finished him.' Or: 'What can you expect? Weak chests always did run on the Badger side.' Or: 'When the chips are down, you really can't expect much from a rich man's son, once the money runs out.' etc.

So, while Mother carried on financial and diplomatic negotiations with her powerful brother, I ran from aperture to aperture of the battlemented parapet. Bang, Bang! repelling cowboys and Indians. I was probably playing the role of a Crusader or perhaps a Legionary in *Beau Geste*. And Father would halt in his leisurely pacing to point out the tallest building in town through Uncle Moses' telescope and say, 'Five point drop in the Market and that magnificent edifice will be as empty as a rats' nest in

December. All its millionaires in the bread line.' And another time he turned the telescope on the Official Residence and said, 'Lieutenant Governor's mansion. Nearly as large as the Castle. Seventy-six rooms and a State Ballroom. His wife won't let him sleep on the same floor, let alone the same room. What do you think of that for sheer power? No wonder Bismarck was frightened to death of women.'

I stared through the telescope trying to decide from which floor the Governor's wife had excluded him. I visualised her as twice as large as he—on about the scale of Mother and myself. I did not answer my father. I simply had a feeling. Lonesome.

And then a feeling began to develop that Indians were silently scaling the walls and they must be stopped or the Castle would fall to the bloody screams of the massacred. So I peered through the embrasure but I was too short to see anything although the embrasure widened abruptly on both sides and bottom through the depth of the battlement.

I hoisted myself on to the lip of the embrasure but, even lying on my stomach, I could not see over the edge and all the time those painted savages were groping silently and steadily upward. I hitched myself forward and began to slide down the steeply sloping angle of the embrasure. I tried to brace my hands and feet against the sides but they too opened like a funnel and the greater the pressure I exerted against them the more I seemed to force myself outward until my whole chest was hanging over space. No Indians. Just the street, sixty feet below.

Killed.

That was the word. Not dead or death. Killed. Sudden violence and a still body.

Cowboys and Indians.

No fear. No scream. Just astonishment and a sort of suspended belief as I began to slide with perceptibly increased speed. My hands lost their final contact with the stone and sprang away from my sides into a swan-dive attitude and I became air-borne. Suspended by the heel.

My father lowered me gently to the ground, head first. There were screams and a rush of feet. I scrambled erect, clutching my father's hand. His smile was tight but he smiled down at me.

'You've a whole free life ahead of you now. The old one is gone,' he said quietly.

'He could have been killed,' my mother screamed, grabbing me violently and burying my head in her skirt with incredible ferocity. Protective reaction. Get the idiot back where he'll be safe and out of sight.

'It's all right, Mother, he's safe.'

'I don't know how you can do this to me, Tim, as soon as my back is turned.'

She put her hands to her face to cough out a few sobs but had to relax her clutch upon me in order to do so. This saved me from suffocation and I retreated behind my father.

'No harm done, pet, none at all.'

'Just when I was arranging with Moses for his whole future . . .' Sobs.

'Well, he still has a future. Nothing to cry about.'

'It's not a future I'll underwrite,' Uncle Moses snarled. 'That boy's a ninnyhammer.'

'Tim's all right,' my father soothed. 'It's just that he has a lively imagination . . . an active curiosity.'

'Curiosity killed the cat. Now if he'd devote a little of that curiosity to his studies . . .'

'But Moses, he hasn't even started school.'

'Killed!' my mother shrieked. 'I try so hard to keep my little family together and in one instant . . . smash!'

'Now, now, Puss, your little family's still in one piece . . .'

But she flung away from him and distributed herself so dramatically on the edge of the parapet and with the volume turned so high that both men had to hasten to her side to calm her.

'I'm so exhausted by all this strain. I don't know how I can bear another minute. And no holiday for years. Not a proper one anyway. I swear I'll go mad. I can wear myself to a rag and no one cares.' Etc.

So she saved my life for the second time that day. Or, at least, my sensibilities. For although children of my age are not frightened of death and have a very real acceptance of its arbitrary character and their powerlessness in relation to it, they still have a high degree of social sensitivity.

She could never bear to lose centre stage and I could usually count upon her, when I got into a scrape, to steal the limelight from me with a fit of hysterics or martyrdom induced by the disgrace I had brought upon the family.

In the end, she managed to squeeze quite a few hundred dollars out of Uncle Moses, which she accepted grudgingly, to finance a trip to New York for her nerves.

Ten days of speakeasies, dinners, bathtub gin, cabarets, parties, musical comedies, genuine imported French wine with union labels printed in New Jersey, teas, theatre, and expensive room service set her health up to normal. But my father insisted upon an afternoon at the Metropolitan Museum and this so exacerbated her nerves and her fragile physical condition that when they came home he had to bring her breakfast in bed for three weeks.

'Yes,' I told my father as he lay dying, 'I remember that. I was just a little kid.'

And as I sprawled on the floor beside the four-poster watching Mrs. Peake jiggling and giggling on the yielding mattress, I remembered telling him that I remembered.

I remembered, too, his quick, light breathing. Something to do with fluid in his chest cavity and they drained it off periodically through great needles. But we never talked about that for my mother felt that not all diseases or injuries were respectable. So it was 'your father's war wound' or 'Tim's wound' or (outside the family) 'Mr. Badger's War Wound.'

No one ever died of cancer although many, women in particular, succumbed to tumours. Heart trouble was respectable. Venereal disease did not exist. T.B. was a disgrace and the social equivalent of a jail sentence. Women suffered, mainly, from headaches. Broken bones were clean and adventurous.

Not everyone believed in my father's War Wound. A missing leg would have cancelled all doubt but, as it was, weakness was suspected.

At sixteen I had no time for Death. I could see a progressive deterioration in my father but only old folks draw rational conclusions in such cases and are, in fact, somewhat precipitate about funerals. But I was dying of love.

' "A whole free life ahead of you", I said,' he repeated. 'You didn't know what I meant at the time?'

'Well, you saved my life. Thanks. I could start again. I could pretend to start again, like a baby?'

'Yes, that's some of it.'

He never hurt my feelings.

'You were too young but I couldn't resist telling you; hoping you'd remember. A boy can't change his life. He has to do what he's told but you'll understand now.'

I was in agony. I thought if I hurried I'd be able casually to bump into Victoria Clubb at the corner and walk her to the library.

'I meant not only that you started a fresh life but you started from scratch, free of all the old ties, old ideas, old directions that had you in a box. I had one chance when I came back from the War. Gassed, wounded, but alive when most of my friends from school and in the army were already dead. I could have done something. Taken up aviation—a new thing, an adventure—but I married your mother and that seemed like a new direction at the time. I suppose it always does. So while I was convalescing (and there seemed no hurry about that) I lived the life of a gentleman on the proceeds of my father's harness factory until the Peace showed it was over-expanded and the Army began hitching guns to trucks and horsepower came out of gas engines. By the time I decided the factory should be closed to save something from the decline, the factory had closed itself. Willy-nilly, I was a gentleman, which is to say I was without a job. Except as Secretary to the Annual Flower Show which took a year to do six weeks' work—just about the level of my business ability. But that was the right tone for your mother and she made up the extras by charging Uncle Moses for the privilege of being her brother.'

I must have been shifting from foot to foot as though needing to go to the toilet.

'I'll let you go, now. I thought I'd tell you while I was in the mood. I haven't much more time . . .' He tapped his chest.

'Gee, Dad, you look great,' I lied, but he shook his head.

'Perhaps I should have run off. Your mother would have managed. Perhaps better, alone. She never did much care for . . . Well, I let other people's ideas of life trap me. But you're free. Throw your life away if you want to. Above all, don't take to accountancy . . .'

And he waved me away, sadly.

I ran. I was in just the mood to throw my life away for Victoria Clubb. Save her life at the expense of mine, if need be. Hurl her from the path of a speeding train, automobile, runaway team, if one could be found. Yield her my lifebelt, place my body between her and the madman's bullet, repel the knife-wielding midnight marauder.

Only years later, a decade after he had drowned in his own fluid, and after I had married Myrtle, did I really know what he was talking about. Really. And it took me more years to act.

Now, with Mrs. Peake bouncing and giggling on the great four-poster, I was shaken. And my father's admonitions about a free life passed before my eyes like a drowning man's agonised visions. For I knew that if she managed to press one of her honey dew melons against my hand, if her dark hair flowed fragrantly over my face, even for an instant, if I caught the faintest, most subliminal of scents from her warm thighs, I was doomed, all my high purposes dissipated.

'Oh, I must sleep in this old bed. It's so romantic. Just once,' she cooed, writhing about in delight.

I must have looked very stiff at this for she went a bit arch.

'I'm not a servant, you know. I hope Shrubsole told you I'd come and help only on a friendly basis. I don't know how you can deny me a little favour like that. There are dozens and dozens of beds in the house.'

She threw me an exaggeratedly moony glance through the mirror. Then she pulled the pillow out from under her head and hugged it to her body almost forcing her breasts out of her bodice. And she was so careless about the way she was flinging her legs about that she reinforced my already high, not to say fervent, opinion about her haunches; and this so alarmed me that I leaped to my feet. I hadn't thought of her sleeping in the house. At least, not intensively.

'No, no. Yes. Help yourself. I mean, what about your rooming house? Won't you have to look after . . . I can't ask you, on a friendly basis, to neglect . . .'

'Oh, Marika will look after that,' she said carelessly. 'You could run me over in the afternoons to make sure she's doing her job. There must be a car around, some place. Bargain?'

She held out her hand to seal the bargain in such a warm, charming and candid manner that I almost took it before I realised how much of what sort of business was involved in the bargain. I yelped, 'My God, I'm hungry! It must be late. I must have slept the morning away. I hope Shrubsole has got some supplies in.'

'I came up to tell you that lunch was ready. I brought a few things along with me.'

I took off and she followed close behind.

Where the hall bannister turned abruptly down the stairway she almost caught up with me—enough to brush the top of my head as I passed below her. This was such a magnetic contact that I took off like a rocket, circled the Castle twice and landed one step below before she even noticed I had moved.

We had Spanish omelette, hot rolls, shrimp salad, a soft cheese —perhaps a boursault, and half a melon. Shrubsole brought in some champagne. I must say, Mrs. Peake had a delicate hand with the omelette.

I insisted on eating at the enormous table in the Great Hall although she thought it would be cosier in the breakfast room. She sat on my left, my sinister or vulnerable side, and Shrubsole served.

By the time we were half-way through the second bottle I began to feel quite jolly and Mrs. Peake seemed to have softened, to have become less aggressive. But she beamed upon me continually and with no less intensity than she beamed upon the omelette, the melon, the wine. In the end, I found I was beaming back at her.

That was how she gained control of my stomach.

Ten

Does that sound strange?

Consider a woman shopping for groceries.

She not only selects for herself and for her family but she antici-
pates the feel, texture, quality, savour of the food; its toothsome-
ness, juiciness, density, digestibility—all according to her own
standards. Then she prepares it, cuts it, pounds it, grinds it, but
above all, handles it and, finally, cooks it. All the while she
absorbs its qualities, its aromas, its acids, its salts, its pungencies.
Then she satisfies herself—note that—satisfies herself as to its
proper seasoning, tenderness, done-ness, crispness, density, liquid-
ity, fluffiness, butteriness, temperature. Then she apportions it
—lean and fat, bone and gristle, cabbage stalk and leaf, soup from
the bottom or the top of the pot. The half burned, the underdone,
the doughy, the stale, the stringy, the greasy, the over-salted, the
lumpy, the sour, the unripe, the wilted, are all apportioned
according to merit or favour with an arbitrariness that at times
seems like impartiality.

There is little for the family to do but chew, swallow and
chemically digest. It is no wonder that she, the cook, has no
appetite. Like a great bee she has processed and, in effect, pre-
digested the food for the whole family. In the child-rearing years
she can be put to the most incredible slavery from morning to
night, moiling, toiling, impregnated, leg veins bursting, ravished
and/or beaten at frequent and random hours, ragged, womb-
fallen, diseased, living in squalor and terror and on half rations
and yet she thrives. There is no killing her.

I am astonished that the psychologists haven't investigated

this. They have ignored the whole subject in favour of fantasies about stuffing your own mother when, all the time, right under their noses, three times a day, there are billions of clinical examples available for research. But not every doctor makes a psychologist, an analyst. Only those with a tendency to make rectal examinations without the rubber glove.

I particularly take exception to Dr. Groddeck's thesis that the swelling of women's abdomens after the climacteric is a wish fulfilment symbol of pregnancy. But at this time the children are grown and gone and now what is to happen to all that food off which she has been symbolically feeding? There is no longer anyone to pass it on to. It accumulates.

No, all that symbolic sex stuff is sadly out of date in spite of Ginsberg celebrating his mother's grey haired moribund vagina to the clash of Mickey Mouse cymbals. No. He thinks he's playing to the shocked suburban audience but they're smiling at a re-run of the Dick Van Dyke show on Channel 7. No. He can rattle around the world from Tibet to Timbuctoo; he can immolate himself in Buddhist gasoline or jerk himself off on the City Hall steps but I doubt if he'll ever drown that awful question—not of his dying mother's vagina but of his mother's chicken soup.

At lunch I had no intimation of these dangers or that they would grow. I did not realise that, having gained control of my stomach, an enormous feeling of omnipotence would develop in Mrs. Peake. I thought the hazard lay in the sting of her sexual spice. I would have been much better advised to flee the terrors of her cream sauces. Reflection has suggested to me that every plate placed before one is an ultimatum: Eat at the risk of my displeasure. (For a child, every displeasure of this sort is a small crucifixion.) And meals are at specified times, even if those times are established by oneself. They must be conformed to at the risk of disruption as well as displeasure to the cook. And even a servant's displeasure is uncomfortable.

So, on fleeing the great bed, I cut a rod for my own back. I

should have faced her, then and there, on her own ground. I
could have claimed impotence, though that might have been only
a challenge to her. Or disease. Or queerness. Or kinkiness. Yes.
Take a whip and beat the shit out of her. But that's not my nature.
I couldn't have brought it off. One stroke and I'd have been in
tears, kissing the welt on her voluptuous arse, etc. No. I think all
that is book stuff made up for those who know little about women
and aren't likely to learn. Or, if it's true, then I'm naïve and
sincerely hope to remain so.

No. The softness that I noted was not due to the champagne, as
I thought, but to the fact that she had nailed me down pain-
lessly with asparagus spears, had built a cocoon of omelette about
me. I was so foolishly lulled by the thought that I had taken the
edge off her aggression that I went so far as to pinch her gently.
She turned on me, not the look of coy delight that I might have
expected but the absorbed and impersonal glance of a child
licking an ice cream cone.

In this self-confident and accommodating mood I went directly
to the garage building in the walled service compound. I had in
mind running Mrs. Peake back to her rooming house to check
on Marika, the slavey. Surely Uncle Moses had a car of some
sort.

The garage was locked but for a door that led to the second
floor to what were obviously long-disused servants' quarters. One
room seemed to be occupied and I took it to be Shrubsole's. It
was austere, depersonalised, but for the portrait of a child that
seemed vaguely familiar, and a shelf of paperback detective
novels. I glanced into most of the rooms down that hallway and
all were deep in dust. Just to lift a sheet was to precipitate ava-
lanches and cataracts of dry powder.

Some quick and very simple arithmetic showed me how easily
and quickly whole cities vanish from memory to be dug up a
thousand years later, ten, twenty or thirty feet deep in the earth.
And this was a weathertight building. Does this explain the shape
of the Pyramids? The resolve that the dust shall slide downward

rather than accumulate on top. Is this the origin of religion—
the determination never to be buried—survival—eternity? The
idea is free. I won't pass the plate for it.

I found a stairway down into the garage. Uncle Moses had a
car all right. He had about twelve of them and obviously never
turned them in. A Buick, about 1915, without brakes on the
front wheels and with the touring top hanging in tatters. An old
Locomobile, probably early '20s, with four wheel brakes. A
Daimler limousine from about 1912, give or take a dozen years
since it probably looked antique on the day of its purchase. There
was a wicked looking 1930 Cord Phaeton and a 1932 Cadillac V16
as well as a '22 Mercer two-seater which might have been the
Runabout. There was also a Winton Electric and a Rolls Royce
of about '36 vintage, the one with the high radiator with the
Goddess Of The Radiator Cap standing about shoulder high to
me.

That would be the one he used to the last—whenever that
would be. Perhaps it hadn't been run for half a dozen years.
The tyres were down but it looked in good repair. No mice in
the upholstery, no broken windows, no great puddle of oil under
the engine.

Why not? I asked myself. Under-powered for these days, and
the Mafia have taken to tooling around in bullet-proof models,
but the police are still deferential at the sight of a Rolls. They
smell not only of money but of Old Money which is the kind that
wasn't stolen in this generation. Worth a tug at the forelock, any
day. Yes, and when I threw the whole business on the market
and established a Trust For Trusting Widows with the proceeds
I'd be able to say, Yes, I could have had a Rolls Royce but I
threw it all up, on a matter of principle.

I wouldn't do this out of a sense of inverted snobbery but it
would certainly indicate that my attitude was not one of sour
grapes. For the most difficult thing in the world seems to be the
acceptance of critical truth. No matter what he says, the politician is suspected of self-serving or behind-the-scenes manipula-

tion. The sick are suspected of exaggerating their symptoms until the day of their funeral. The wealthy have no altruism and their philanthropy amounts to nothing more than tax dodges. The cripple's attitude is warped by his condition so that all that can be believed is his smile and he smiles only because he doesn't know any better. Only science is accepted at face value and gigantic programmes of crashing simple-mindedness and moony lunacy are accepted as high points in human development.

Consider that ultimate in sappiness—that famous aphorism of Einstein's: The Lord is subtle but he isn't simply mean. Excepting the 'the' there isn't a word of this statement that makes the least supportable sense even for a congenital Lourdes prayer. Why, even the dullest-witted theologian of the Hot Stove School in Shadrack, Tennessee could come up with sounder profundities than that, between squirts on the stove lid.

But your Public, your Man In The Street, refuses to see it this way. Even when that cuddly, fuzzy-wuzzy-haired little genius admits to the greatest blunder in the annals of historic stupidity no one listens. They think he is joking and, anyway, they haven't time for they are busy harrying drop-outs because of the length of their hair, and longing for the days of the lash.

Which is to say that actions speak louder than words and I'd be better off to drive the Rolls for a while and then give it up, rather than pretend to ignore it altogether as though it didn't meet my standards. And my curiosity about the mythological sealed-for-life gearbox and other exotic, if commercial, legends would be satisfied.

So I pressed the button marked 'Kitchen' on the house phone in the garage and Shrubsole answered, 'Sir?'

I admit to a certain satisfaction on hearing this Pavlovian response. Obviously, only the Master had a right to use the house phone. But I felt embarrassed, too, though I astonished myself by getting over this awkwardness quite quickly and easily.

'Shrubsole,' I said, 'how long is it since the Rolls was driven?'

'It was kept serviced until Sir Moses died, sir. I imagine that only the battery needs charging or perhaps replacement. I shall call the service department.'

'Who drove the old gentleman when he went out?'

'I did, sir. The car is in very good condition, sir.'

'Very good, Shrubsole. Carry on.'

Carry on! For Christ's sake!

They had the Rolls running, gassed, washed and dusted out that very afternoon.

In the meantime, I went behind the garage to inspect the stack of gas tanks I'd seen from the tower. There were seventy-two of them. Long cylinders of the type used to handle oxygen, acetylene, etc. Weeds had grown up about them and had died. Dirt had blown in windrows against them. A mystery. Lying on their sides, three deep, for several years apparently. Certainly not forgotten there by a welder after casual repairs. Shrubsole would know. I returned to the garage phone.

'The gas tanks, Shrubsole. Seventy-two of them. What are they for?'

'For hydrogen, sir.'

'Hydrogen?'

'For Sir Moses' balloon.'

'Oh.'

'The *Chronicle* is on the telephone, sir. Would you talk to them?'

'No!'

'They are insistent about your plans for the Castle, sir.'

The newspapers had not been kind to me. *Mad Bomber Strikes Again! ! ! Eccentric Anarchist Mails Bomb to P.M.! ! ! Reign of Terror. Sneak Attack by Mad Car Washer! ! !* But if I rebuffed them they would exercise their god-given right to manufacture news if there were none to report: *Mad Bomber Turns Recluse. Eccentric Heir to Muddiman Fortune Retires to Grim Fortress: Refuses to Discuss Secret Plans. Acme International Chemicals & Explosives Refuse to Fill Order from Mad Bomber* (if such an order is ever placed).

So I must not arouse hostility while trying to unload the historic pile. Something in the humanitarian line would do it.

'Shrubsole, you may tell them I am converting the Castle into a home for unwed mothers. And their boy friends. A humanitarian approach. Rational. At a time like this a girl needs all the love and support, et cetera. Have you got that, Shrubsole?'

'Girls, and their boy friends, sir? Explicitly?'

'Yes. A progressive and commendable approach, don't you think?'

'Very broadminded, sir, I'm sure.'

'After all, the damage has been done. Who gains by deprivation, eh? No one except those looking for a whipping boy, or girl, as the case may be. And this way we may get some quite nice responsible families, when they get to know each other, or avoid some disastrous unions. No, I can think of no more useful role for the Castle.'

'You wouldn't consider: "Plans for the future use of the Castle are under consideration by Mr. Badger and will probably tend towards a humanitarian function"? Just a suggestion, sir.'

'Was that spontaneous, Shrubsole?'

'Sir?'

'You read that somewhere. A bit pat. A bit on the public relations side . . .'

'I handled many inquiries, solicitations and importunities for Sir Moses, some from sources that could not be antagonised.'

'What does that mean?'

'Sir Moses would tell me to tell them to bugger off, and I had to translate.'

'I'll speak for myself, although, in this case, not directly. Plans are firm. No use shillyshallying at this point.'

'Very well, sir. There may be repercussions.'

'I would hope so!'

Balloons!

I was half-way back to the Castle before I realised that Uncle Moses' balloon must be one of those free-flight models—as big as a house. And why he would want to go ballooning at the age of ninety-odd was a very strange matter to contemplate. He must have been mad as a rattlesnake. And a careless match near the tanks would send the Castle into an orbit about the size of Haley's Comet's, as well as solving all my current problems.

And if the publicity did not turn up a customer, yes, why not turn the old mausoleum into a refuge for unlucky children? Take the pressure off them. Throw them all in together. Give them a sense of companionship, of community, which they have probably never had before. And an opportunity, perhaps, to shop around for a more suitable mate rather than be stuck for life with a chance, momentary, and unlucky impulse. After all, they are all potential fathers and mothers who, most likely, would be hard put to it to prove specific paternity—one baby being much like another. And the father's role, biologically, being only about as important as that of a pollinating bee, is not much of a basis for a lifetime of social and temperamental disaster.

The more I thought of the scheme, the more useful it seemed to me. Nothing involved but the alleviation of human misery and distress. An unchallengeable chunk of altruism. With a sensitive staff and some practical instruction on the Swedish style they might even, in the end, be able to distinguish between a genital twitch and an advertising goose: no mean accomplishment nowadays considering the barrage of garbagy intimidation hurled against the poor kids by industries, market researchers, Bible thumpers, retailers, psychologists, professors, doctors, pharmacists, teachers, communicators, pornographers, dope pedlars, generals, folk singers, abortionists, parents, publishers and politicians.

All screaming about how the kids are alienated from society, big S, when they are only trying to stay human and resist the enormous pressure to be deformed into the image of their makers; to refuse to co-operate in the old Jekyll-Hyde transformation into the solid citizen who looks like the unbandaged mummy of a zombie dedicating himself to Science and the Genetic Warfare Branch of Acme International Pluperfect Peace Products Division, Inc. where he counts the radioactive turds of chromosomatically disoriented body lice in the interest of human betterment. On the moon.

It is almost funny the way it is pretended that a youngster cannot recognise the higher wisdom of a Lawyer, a Politician, a Banker, a Merchant ('The balances of deceit are in his hand: he loveth to oppress.' Hosea: Chap. something, Verse something else). It's like spelling dirty words in front of eighteen-year-olds.

But they're not so dumb. They may even organise. Not as cats' paws for someone else's hot chestnut game but as a co-operative society of some sort. Within society. An enormous benign tumour. Spreading, taking over, dissolving the connecting tissue of a whole (hah!) civilisation.

There'd be the money to do it. And the Castle as headquarters. And perhaps hire McLuhan to give a few hints and lectures on retribalisation. And everyone would lie around doing only the absolute minimum of necessary work and if someone came running up waving a sheaf of papers and screaming, 'I've discovered that a compound containing one asymetric carbon atom can exist in two isometric forms called enantiomers . . .' he would be seized and sung to by relays of lovely girls, every time he opened his mouth, until he couldn't hear himself think; and if he showed signs of concern with the crystalline structure of giant molecules in sterioisomeric polymers he would be attacked gently but firmly by one or more of the more febrile of his singing companions. In this way anti-social behaviour might be diverted.

Yes, the Castle could accommodate hundreds, perhaps thousands, of perfectly sound young people able to live a life of intelligent virtue in their own society. And if money were needed to live within the larger society, enough for simple needs could be raised by singing groups on street corners; and if there were no money for instruments a few sticks could be knocked together for rhythm; and if no sticks were available in the city-scape (and there is often nothing really usable in the city-scape) then the human voice and the clap of hands would do very well.

I was delighted with the vision of a simple New Jerusalem established in my phony Castle. I was so delighted that I stood in the courtyard, half-way between the garage and The Castle, with the drizzle slowly seeping through my clothes. And although I was smiling to myself at the vision of the young girls and young men living in a sort of state of temporal grace I kept coming back to a remembrance of Mrs. Peake's nape; a delicate stem supporting abundant hair piled up rather carelessly with fragile wisps at the hairline and small attractively whorled ears. I could have eaten that morsel of her raw, without salt. As an appetiser. Without even another bottle of champagne which I didn't need since I was still feeling quite soft about the edges due to the magnum and a half I'd had for lunch.

Yet a cloud kept darkening my vision. I didn't know what it was. A Faustian truth, I told myself. 'Joy demands sorrow: sorrow demands joy.' 'No joy without sorrow.' Something like that. No. Nonsense. No joy without joy. That would be nearer the truth. That other is sheer Christianity. Rise from your lover's bed determined to put your foot unerringly into the pot. No. It was something else bothering me, something hanging in the back of my mind; in the corner of my eye; behind my back.

I retraced my steps. Went into the garage. Looked closely again at the Rolls. Nothing. I faced the telephone. Nothing. I picked up the receiver and held it to my ear, cocking my head as I usually do when waiting for the other party to answer.

Out of the top right-hand corner of my eye I read a label: Muddiman, Moses M. 282.4456.621. Written with a thick felt marking pen. The label was on a carton, a brown corrugated paper shipping carton not much larger than a shoe box but a bit squarer. Printed on the side of the carton was the legend: *Hecla-Holyrood Crematorium.*

I hung up the phone.

The carton was comparatively light. I broke open the paper sealing tape. A plain black pottery jar—urn, I suppose—lay inside. I picked it up, feeling nothing. I held it up, as calm as
156

though wondering whether to buy a jar of Scotch or of native marmalade.

I shook it.

Nothing.

Probably just fine, bone coloured powder with a few melted gold fillings.

Uncle Moses.

Since I was holding the jar in a sort of classical pose, contemplative, I tried, 'Alas, poor Yorick.'

Nothing. Not even chop-fallen. Not even a grave. No memorial except the Castle. Muddiman's Folly. Forgotten by all save his lawyers and it was all just business to them. Natural. Even the mighty fall quickly into obscurity. Alf Landon—remember? The Match King—was his name Kruger? And millions upon millions smiled every day at the motorman in the Toonerville Trolley comic strip. Remember his name?

I recalled reading lately that the value of the elements making up the human body had risen, mostly because of inflation, from the traditional ninety-eight cents to approximately three ninety-five, according to a scientist at Acme International Chemicals.

This did not cheer me. Nor did it particularly depress me. I did feel a bit annoyed. I didn't relish the thought of Uncle Moses sitting on my garage shelf through all eternity. And I had no inclination to scatter him. I didn't want a fragment of os coccyx in my eye.

I tucked him under my arm and went back to the Castle. There I placed him on the mantelshelf of the Great Hall until I could think of something to do with him.

A mistake.

Eleven

I made my way up the secret staircase reflecting upon Uncle Moses' fate: stuck there on his own mantelpiece like a left-over jam pot. For hundreds—thousands—of years millions of men of inflated importance had been imposing themselves upon the landscape, then going to their expensive graves after a lifetime of mean endeavours. The pyramids endure, but for how long? Gravestones erode in a generation and those enormous sepulchres, the cathedrals, disintegrate stone by stone before our eyes. Now, within six months of his death and after all the money, planning, ingenuity, secrecy, time and effort he put into the Castle, Uncle Moses lay in his unlabelled black unglazed pot.

I sighed. The bubbles had gone out of my champagne. My instinct would have been to go running through the house like an overgrown child, eager to investigate every corner, wide-eyed. Now I trudged up the carpet-silent stairs with a sense of neglected duty. I started to slide back the panel giving access to Uncle Moses' room when I heard singing. I peered through the narrow gap. Mrs. Peake was singing *Ain't Misbehavin'*. Rather, she was humming it softly, with a snatch of the lyrics here and there.

I watched her fit a pillow case on to a pillow which she held under her chin. She used the firm manipulations of a woman dressing a child. But when it came to plumping up the pillows on the bed, she buffeted them like a lover mock-struggling with her beloved. And she placed two of them, side by side, at the head of the great four-poster.

Her endeavours had brought a warm dewy flush to her skin and her hair was beginning to unpin with wisps crossing her brow and dropping in front of her ears. She brushed them away with that ineffably feminine gesture of the wrist. I had never seen her look more lovely, more unconsciously magnetic.

Now, if ever there was an appropriate time, this was the moment to tumble her, already slightly warmed, into the great four-poster. However, even though the path of folly may be, all things considered, the only wise way to go with women, I quailed. I had discerned the tiger's stripes amid the lush jungle foliage.

I noticed for the first time that Mrs. Peake's feet had begun to toe out. This phenomenon, which may or may not be called Bunyard's Syndrome, gives a clue to the whole personality. It makes its reappearance when the will, suppressed in childhood, is freed in middle age, especially in women. After a few decades spent in manipulating husbands, children, lovers, store clerks, they feel that there is nothing that will not bend to their will. Outwardly most signs contra-indicate this. Vaccillation is very marked and is interpreted by the uninitiated as uncertainty. Ordering from a menu is like a skirmish with irresolute guerrillas in dense jungle.

But . . .

The difficulty is not that of choice. A woman with her feet turning out is not torn between the lobster and the fillet. She wants both—or all of the menu—but since this is impossible to encompass and she is too shrewd to make this an immediate demand she resorts to confusion. Hence, the extra serving of snails that no one seemed to order; the mushrooms that just happen to arrive when she has actually (ha!) no appetite.

Yes, when the feet turn outward, beware. You are practically surrounded. She's capable of walking around you on both sides at once. It's a syndrome that is on the increase. A sign of the times. Look at the fashion models. Standing astride, one foot going each way. A warning. To the male.

Half an hour earlier, in my folly and fettle, I'd have said upon glimpsing Mrs. Peake in this rosy condition: 'I don't give a damn if she does swallow me whole. I'll dance her such a Jonah's jig that, in the end, she will be more than happy to disgorge me.'

But that takes stamina, and recklessness that is almost saintly. I've had the stamina, in other days, but now in the forties, it's so easy to forget to be troublesome. Occasionally I've even thought of giving up that business of sending out the clocks.

On second thought, folly is not foolproof. Even in my prime, during The War, I was stopped dead in my tracks by Muriel Hemming. I felt I could be comfortable with Muriel. She had been brought up very strictly in a good family which meant that her parents had placed an extremely high value upon sin. By speaking in hushed tones of ordinary human peccadillos and malfeasances, they had aroused in her an insatiable curiosity. When tempted she fell like a ton of fermented apples.

By the time I met her she had had several abortions, had gone through about a dozen lovers and hundreds of pick-ups, specialising in airmen; allegedly had dabbled in fraternal incest and was rumoured, in incredulous tones, even to have slept with a Negro. She hadn't tried dope. It wasn't really fashionable in those days. Only doctors were favoured with a ready supply and, then as now, formed the core of addiction. An addict then was still called a dope fiend.

So Muriel was as swift a little girl as any I could hope to be acquainted with, short of a complete pro. And there was no need to shilly-shally. Muriel was direct, demanding and, I thought, crude. So folly was the order of the day. I felt that there was no boundary over which I could stumble, to anyone's embarrassment.

I had gone to the kitchen for refreshment leaving her lying like one of Van Dongen's brutally lascivious but vulnerable looking nudes. I was exhausted.

'What are you doing? Don't leave me, don't leave me,' she moaned.

'Hang on, Moo,' (I called her Moo—not the least of my follies), 'be with you in a minute. Just making a sandwich . . .'

160

It was one of those sultry summer nights and I was stark. I stood over her offering her half of the sandwich.

She stretched up a languid hand, then withdrew it as though burned. 'That's meat,' she said accusingly. 'That's cold roast beef. It must be after one. What time is it?'

I looked at my watch.

'Two-thirty,' I said. 'What's the matter? Don't you like cold beef?'

'It's Friday now,' she said. 'It's against my religion. You know that. What are you trying to do to me? What are you? Some kind of Protestant bigot?'

She was quite irritated to think that I had brought her to the verge of sin. In fact, she was enraged. I laughed. She became even more furious though I said nothing. And she threw me out. There were some things she just wouldn't bring herself to do.

Of course, Muriel was quite wrong about my bigotry. If I have any religion it is akin to the Murungs'. They say they once had a fine religion written on banana leaves but a cow ate them. I once went to St. Swithin's where they had a complete religion written down on the finest, thinnest Bible paper but at the age of ten I read it.

I had a feeling now about Mrs. Peake. She had a slightly religious look that intimidated me. She seemed the type of woman to have a religion with an extremely low centre of gravity, probably located somewhere in the vicinity of the pelvic floor. A female sort of religion whose principal tenet is, 'I want everything that it's humanly possible to get, plus ten per cent', and is basically the same through the ages no matter in which style the men hang the crêpe.

So when Mrs. Peake began vacuuming the draperies around the old four-poster I took advantage of the racket to close the secret panel when the click would go unnoticed. I decided I'd tackle Mrs. Peake when I had my morale restored and had recovered my sense of humour, although this is a two-edged weapon. It is the unexpected element in humour that irritates women. It

L

catches them unawares by going behind their façade which is bad manners, but since it is an intrusion, and intrusions are, in a manner of speaking, right up women's alley then a pretty fair size emotional tension is created. Since any emotion if intense enough can be mistaken for love, this is the most convenient interpretation which explains the profoundly thoughtful expression on the face of the wife of the Life Of The Party.

But one does not always want to be loved.

With this instantaneous though elaborate sleight-of-mind feat I managed to talk myself out of approaching Mrs. Peake.

So I went down the secret stairway to the second floor and back up by the ordinary stairs. The third floor was a disappointment. Nothing but bedrooms and dozens of bathrooms with marble showers and basin tops, tiled tubs and gold plated faucets. But in spite of these gildings the bathrooms had a public toilet effect, with all that ceramic and stone. No towels, toothbrushes, lotions or lingerie hanging about. Lacking the woman's touch.

In a storeroom I did have a piece of luck. I found a fold-up cot, covered by a cloth and I carried this to the Tower Room where I planned to sleep. The Tower Room was full of couches, chaise-longues, love seats, sofas, divans, etc., but nothing for real sleeping. I'd get Mrs. Peake to make it up later.

There was an attic which I ignored. Full of rafters, beams, king posts and queen posts (I'm not kidding. I was a mortgage inspector once) and chimney stacks in brick although they were finished as stone on the outside. And dust, inches thick, with hundreds of footprints in it as though a battle had surged across it lately. It seemed mysterious because there was nothing there and no sign of anything being there at any time. Not even old bits of broken furniture, old steamer trunks. Nothing.

The second floor was another matter.

Besides the big nearly vacant ballroom there was the usual clutch of ante-rooms, sitting-rooms, a music-room and furnished wide hallways leading off the gallery that hung at one end of the Great Hall. From my childhood I remembered that there was some spot in one of the hallways or rooms where one could stand and hear everything going on in the Great Hall below. I wasn't sure whether there was actually some acoustic phenomenon or whether, as a child, I had strained to believe that some miraculous distortion had occurred in the law of nature. I'd have to ask Shrubsole about the Whispering Gallery.

The rest of the second floor was a rat's nest. There were about a dozen rooms filled with a variety of collections that a jackdaw would have blushed at.

A very large room was filled with guns. Racks of blunderbusses, horse pistols, flintlocks, smoothbores, rifles, revolvers, automatics, carbines, shotguns, lever-action repeaters, bolt actions— even an old gangsterish Thompson sub-machine gun. I examined a Luger. I slipped out the magazine. It was loaded. I picked up a dusty Smith and Wesson .38. It was loaded too. Most of the modern guns seemed to be loaded including an M 1 carbine and a repeating Winchester 12 gauge.

I opened some drawers and found them stuffed with cleaning equipment, some silencers and ammunition—all comparatively fresh. Very strange. As though Uncle Moses were preparing for a siege. The old guns were battered and rusty, the modern ones had been oiled in recent memory.

It was a brutal looking room. I've never seen a truly graceful or elegant gun. I suppose it's not the nature of the machine. Meant for nothing but destruction. Repellent. Perhaps some sexual hostility in there, somewhere. Must look that up. Never knew anyone keen on guns who didn't have an inhuman, tigerish streak in him somewhere.

I backed out the door, feeling threatened.

Next door it was worse.

Hundreds, perhaps a thousand shallow drawers lined the walls. Each was numbered. I pulled one out at random.

Bugs.

Platoons, squadrons, regiments, phalanxes of bugs mounted on glass-bottomed trays. I pulled out a dozen more drawers around

163

the room. Nothing but bugs, beetles, cockroaches and other comforts to the sleepless. I felt as though I'd just been sentenced to life in a provincial Mexican jail. I left that room precipitately with resolves about fumigation cricketing through my brain.

The next room was full of buttons. What can be said about buttons? Even that ancient guardian of respectability, the fly button, has had its day. Anyone who could bring himself to collect buttons must have a very low fascination point indeed.

Fortunately, the next room was full of old Waterford glass. I'm more one for rough, dark, earthy pottery but at least this wasn't complete junk. It was of some use. Or perhaps I'm wrong. Perhaps I have no taste. There seems to have been little in our family: witness one large, fake castle on the city's skyline. And my mother bought everything by label. If it was expensive it was good enough for her. And my father was a bit of a dude; a dandy. It's a wonder I've retained any sense of proportion—and I think I have—at least in relation to staying human. Which may return to fashion any day now.

But after the glass was a room full of old match boxes. A memorial sacred to the memory of the old Swedish Match Trust. Absorbing. As a stainless steel blotter.

Oh God! More beetles, cockroaches, arthropods, arachnids, myriapods and other creepy, crawly, nitty, scratchy, buzzy, twitchy and improbable looking earwigs infesting a room across the hall.

Another room, empty but for a rosette of swords, points in, upon a wall. A samurai model looked best to me. A lot more human than the guns. One thing about a sword: when you kill a man you mean it. You mean to stick it through his guts, his heart, his liver and lights. It's a meaningful action. It may be mean, treacherous, cowardly, murderous but it's meaningful. It's not a matter of statistics. You'd know you had killed a man or wounded him. You'd feel it at the time, both of you. No yards or miles of air space between you; no simple abolition of a distant silhouette; no blasting of map co-ordinates; no spreading

164

thin of guilt. Orders from above cannot strengthen a reluctant arm.

In other rooms there was a great deal of travel junk: assegais, fragments of eerie looking Australian bark painting, several intricately carved panels of wood from New Ireland or thereabouts, commercial looking ivory from Japan, a shrunken head that looked real and some ridiculously obscene Peruvian pottery. There were thousands of objects, all undustable and giving the rooms the dead and threatening air of those anthropological galleries at the British Museum full of brutal manikins with gaping vaginas or partially suffused penises; idols seeming steeped in blood and, I hope, maligning a continent, as perhaps the brush cut gives a tone to some aspects of our days.

But the biggest collection was of breakfast food boxes with Uncle Moses' Health Meal packages predominating. God, that was terrible stuff. Cut coarse and, when cooked, having the approximate texture of builder's sand. It scraped you raw-clean, from pylorus to sphincter. The notion that duty and pain were synonymous still clutched the bowels of the older generation when I was a boy. In my case it was more complicated than that. My mother felt that since we had to eat breakfast food it might just as well be her brother's. Since he was prospering on our trade there could be no compunction about battening on him. A three cent profit might justify a three hundred dollar touch.

'It's your Uncle's Health Meal,' she would say at the first sign of misery. 'I'm sure he wouldn't put anything into it that would hurt you.'

A fifty-fifty proportion of brown sugar helped, but that just covered the problem of swallowing.

There were half a dozen more rooms full of junk including a variety of old commercial labels going as far back as about 1670, the date on a tobacco wrapper. One scrap book showed some of his advertisements for Health Meal, written by himself in the crassest of terms—Eat, Enjoy, Evacuate. If he were in his prime to-day he would probably be running an advertising agency and

165

writing ads for dog foods, denture stickum, laxatives, toilet paper, mouth deodorisers and other TV staples.

At first glance it may seem that a detail such as the proportion of brown sugar to Health Meal that I used for breakfast is an item of monumental insignificance. Nothing could be further from the truth. Everything I have to say is of the utmost and most urgent significance. A glance from a window. A remote, vagrant sensation from a generation ago. Nothing, not even the vaguest gesture, the slightest action in the past is unrelated to the present. Even though we may have forgotten it or never heard of it, the Mongol victory at Liegnitz has more enduring effect upon international affairs to-day than the bomb. How do we handle the fright of a fright? Or antique public relations: 'One of the causes of the revolution was the character of Philip II. He was personally without reproach in most important respects, devoted to the Catholic Church, frugal in his habits, fully conscious of his duties as a ruler and capable of an enormous amount of work.'

No. I cannot drink a cup of tea without . . . Well, there you are. Tea. And we pretend that all the kids need is a haircut and feel hurt when they reject our brand of hallucination for theirs.

The incredibly banal fragmentary proofs of my uncle's recent existence oppressed me like a grievous physical burden so when Mrs. Peake came looking for me to announce that the Rolls was now in working order, I said, 'Fine. I'll drive you over to the house. You can check on your slavey.'

'Oh no. It isn't necessary to-day. There is so much to do here.'

With a minimum of persuasion to overcome her feminine, ritualistic protests I induced her to come along with me. On the way out I picked up one of Uncle Moses' old black Homburgs. It fitted me and I thought I looked properly dignified for a town excursion in a Rolls. It gave the expedition a period look that I thought fitting.

Mrs. Peake's appearance seemed appropriate, too. Wearing a short fur jacket she displayed quite chunky proportions. In fact, the jacket was so boxy and showed such a lack of style sense that she could easily have been taken for someone born to wealth, to whom current trends don't matter a damn.

Driving the Rolls was like steering a coasting truck and I had the distinct sensation of being transported in a particularly stuffy, mobile, leather upholstered men's club during one of those crepuscular, disembodied moments of sensation when one is dozing off just before the head drops and one awakens with a jerk. So I felt that a stimulus was needed and, since it was now rush hour and approaching traffic was creeping forward in three solid lines, I decided on a left turn. This may seem perverse but it was actually more in the nature of an experiment in social psychology.

There was a traffic light and a policeman was in the intersection waving the cars on—as though it would help. I signalled for a left turn. He waved me away, pointing to the No Left Turn sign. I crept forward and managed to block the innermost lane of oncoming traffic. The policeman looked uncertain. I remained firm, dignified. There is nothing like a display of controlled firmness during an aggression. It creates a sense of righteousness.

For all he knew, I could have been a diplomat. And if he stopped me to give me a ticket, his intersection could be in a shambles for an hour. He yielded. With his outstretched arm he blocked the oncoming traffic and waved me through with only a barely perceptible display of impatience. No one honked. I felt the experiment showed significant results. I proceeded calmly.

A few blocks later I glanced casually in Mrs. Peake's direction. She had murmured, 'There's no left turn here, Timothy.' Now she was gazing at me with, if not increased respect, then a new wariness.

This is more like it, I thought. A few more occasions to display the firm hand, the controlled unpanicky mind, the arbitrary direction, and there would be some hope of negotiating a tender entente that would not immediately degenerate into a holocaust.

I left Mrs. Peake at the rooming house saying I would pick up Joe Bezoar. I had none but altruistic motives in this. I wished only to indulge an acquaintance, a fellow worker, now that I had at hand the momentary resources of a rich man's wine cellar.

I smiled to myself as I drove. Actually, I had all along been crying wolf to myself about Mrs. Peake. There was nothing wrong with Mrs. Peake even though I kept telling myself she was a ravening, hot-pantsed monster. She was fine for me. Perfect. Beautiful in a mature, womanly way; organised (I hate a ditherer) and apparently sensible and energetic. But I knew myself.

I have always had a tendency to fall in love; and with a thump. Nothing can stop me once I decide to fall in love. I am quite capable, to-morrow, of falling in love with Catherine the Great. It will be useless to tell me that she is long dead, consumed lovers like salted peanuts, had dropsical ankles and a rugged man's physiognomy, suffered from all diseases including bubonic, women's vanities and men's strengths and on top of that was much too smart for me. This would not deter me.

On the other hand, I should very likely fall out of love with her within six or eight days. This is due to lack of moral training in youth. All was right with the moral world if my mother felt comfortably indulged. My father looked upon the world with mingled horror, amusement and contempt. Neither had a system to impose upon me. This left me free to examine—a great danger to any society. This is why it is always pretended that those who don't subscribe to the local morals are degenerate when in truth the opposite is usually the case and moral anarchists like St. Francis can go out and lick lepers' wounds without regard to social outrage.

So, too, with Mrs. Peake. I saw no reason to throw Mrs. Peake upon the social junkpile just because she was of a certain age. I saw no reason why I should, because of middle-age, hanker after the twitch of a Playboy Bunny's synthetic tail.

I could see the first wisps of grey in her hair and the tell-tale crease before the ear. There was a certain firmness about the mouth that indicated a limit to the folly she could tolerate. And,

168

undoubtedly, in summer those fine breasts, not quite so high as ten years ago, would be sweaty underneath. And perhaps those generous thighs would chafe in humid weather. No matter. I was in love with her. Unquestionably. And I planned not to fall out of love.

This time I was keeping distance until that first madness wore off: that peculiar insanity during which I was quite capable of finding myself snuffling delightedly in her armpit. During this period of truce she would come to respect the fact that I was not completely manipulatable and I would spare us both the spectacle of myself nibbling at any exposed skin, fondling the shape of the air she had just vacated, rolling over like Rover, sitting up, playing dead and slavering like a hungry mongrel. Without this excessive initial reaction an even balance could be achieved that could go on indefinitely, even into age. And Mrs. Peake looked as though she would stand up to it, having come this far practically unscathed.

I recognised, theoretically, that this was one of those excessive dreams of moderation that only the true extremist indulges in. I recognised this danger, yes, but I had incentive to moderate my usual behaviour. Yes, I was going to be moderate this time even if it killed me.

I had never been in Joe Bezoar's hotel before.

Hotel!

A small structure near the Market built about the year 1847 as a morgue for cholera victims off the Irish immigrant boats. And it had gone down since. The Arcadian Hotel. Rooms by day or week. Maid service—which meant weekly inspection of the rooms for suicides.

But Joe's room had been refurnished in about 1921, by the look of it. It was graced by an iron bedstead enamelled in brown and chipped at head and foot to the metal. There was a dresser with a poxy mirror in the secondary stage, and a fragment of hopsacking that may have begun life as carpeting. Hanging from the ceiling was a frosted light fixture of the type seen in my youthful schoolrooms and casting the fulvous glow of a dying dynamo. The telephone was of the vintage that had a little writing shelf underneath it. There may have been a window. If so, it could only have looked out on to the chimney of a crematorium.

Everything was neat. I will say that. There was a neat line of wine bottles against one wall. Fortified domestic wine, the standby of the wino. But there was a film over everything that suggested the steam of ten generations of diseased whores condensed upon the furniture then carefully rubbed to a dull cataractic patina.

'Let's go. Let's go,' I urged. 'The stricken cries of extracted corks are in the wind. Come along, Joe.'

'Have you seen them? Where did they go?'

Did he mean elephants, snakes, scorpions lurking amid empty bottles?

'Damn it, where are my socks?'

'You've got them on.'

He was wearing a pair with the toes out of one foot and the heel out of the other.

'No, no. The other pair . . .' And he went fumbling under the bed to emerge with another balled up pair. He thrust his hand into one sock. The heel was missing. He pulled it on, over the sock with the hole in the toe. The other sock was lacking a toe but the heel was intact so he pulled it over the sock he was wearing that had a hole in the heel.

Clever, I thought. I'd never had got around to a solution like that.

Ordinarily, I'd have thought like anyone else: The filthy slob, why doesn't he buy a decent pair of socks instead of one of those jugs of rot-gut. But I was in a determinedly partisan mood. Joe was down and I was up, and I was full of the equaliser of good will as well as clenched teeth philanthropy. A Gladstone among fallen women.

He put on a pair of shoes that were cracked but clean, if not polished. He tied on a tie whose colour scheme was inspired perhaps by the mouldering dressings thrown behind a field hospital.

He stood up and pulled on a jacket that remotely matched his trousers in tone. He had obviously bought the outfit from grave robbers. There was no other explanation.

He felt his face as though he had forgotten whether or not he had shaved. He had half a dozen nicks to prove it.

He gave me the first and only smile I was to see on his face. Or perhaps it wasn't a smile. Perhaps his mouth was dry.

'O.K. Badger. Did you mention booze? Lead on.'

He looked quite neat, pressed, tidy, but a faint air of ancient, rancid human grease seeped from him. I thought he looked better on the car-wash line in rough, ragged, frankly dirty work-clothes. Now he looked like the majority stockholder in a small egg mending factory on the day before bankruptcy.

'Joe,' I said, 'your ship has come in, at least for a couple of weeks. Your troubles are temporarily over.'

But I had the feeling that someone else was speaking; that someone's mind, somewhere not too far off, had changed silently. I closed my eyes and for an instant conjured up a vision of myself walking by a bakery and inhaling the rich freshness. It enabled me to smile. A better smile than his, I hope.

Twelve

'So, you're in the chips now,' Joe Bezoar said as he flopped into the front seat. 'Castle, car . . . the works.'

He writhed on the seat as though suffering from one of the less delicate plagues of Egypt. I felt defensive.

'I'm going to wash my hands of it. Establish some sort of Foundation.'

'Christ! This is like sitting on broken rocks. What is this old heap? A Reo? Marmon? Pierce Arrow?'

He knew damned well it was a Rolls. And the older the Rolls, the more like a Rolls it looks. I detected envy.

'Of course, I'll retain some sort of administrative post—just to make sure the bureaucrats don't take over.'

'What have you got against bureaucrats?' he demanded. 'Throw out all the bureaucrats and you'd have to establish a Foundation to look after them.'

'I'd blow the sons-of-bitches up,' I muttered, as I wrenched the ancient vehicle around a bus. 'They're getting in everywhere; taking over everything. A million dollars are appropriated for the victims of automation or slum clearance and what happens? Fifty jobs for administrators at twenty thousand a year and what's left over for the victims? Advice on how to cope with a society the advisors daren't face even with a degree in Philanthropy, a post-graduate course in political bum-sucking and the goods on their Division Head in the form of photographs.'

'The wealthy have always hated the bureaucracy. Cramps their style with all those rules and regulations . . .'

'Who are you calling wealthy?' I demanded.

He tapped the walnut dashboard with a grubby finger and nodded sagely, and yet with some of the defensiveness of a cornered rat.

'A beggar, if his mind is honourable,
Is none the worse.'

Besides gratitude for saving me from Harry Sprockett's questions that time in the car-wash, this was the main reason I was interested in Joe Bezoar. He had the habit while working of dropping a quote, an aphorism, a bit of poetry, a fragment of philosophy that either seemed apt or was of some intrinsic interest. Often these fragments had a familiar ring.

'Shakespeare?' I would ask.

'From the Greek,' he would generally reply.

Now I suddenly saw that Joe Bezoar's quotations usually had a certain Calvinistic chill to them; a certain fun-killing sourness; an implication of fiddlers paid to the tune of the last drop of blood.

'Give every man his just deserts and who would 'scape whipping.' That sort of thing—said when you've caught someone white-handed, innocent.

Yes, I could see this now and I didn't like it. I realised that Joe always dropped his gems on the run between wiping a headlight and a fender.

A policeman's car would go through the wash.

'But who will watch the watcher,' said Joe Bezoar, with an insinuating jerk of his head towards the policeman.

Or, nursing a hangover, he would say, 'How did I come to find a flower of grief so painless.'

That's good, I would think. Flower of grief. Very good. Flower of Grief. By God, that's brilliant! Flower. Grief. Discovery of wine. They knew their stuff in those days, whenever that was. From the Sanskrit. Or perhaps Chinese. No. Greek, of course. The 'I'. Dead give-away.

I'd be standing there with my mouth open and someone would drive off with his back window unwiped and I'd have to catch up on a Chrysler sedan with thirteen chrome tail lights.

Driving home from the Market I could see Mrs. Peake in the rear view mirror sticking her nose into the tops of paper bags, sniffing reflectively and suspiciously as though fearful that some rancid bacon had been slipped over on her, or an over mouldy cheese, or a blue-rotten orange. She came up for air but seemed to find conditions even worse. Perhaps she thought the old unused car had become musty. Perhaps not. She opened a window, leaned back like a sulky duchess and observed, 'I understand, Mr. Bezoar, that you are staying with us at the Castle for some little time.'

'Yes'm,' Joe mumbled.

'I think that's terribly kind of Mr. Badger, don't you?'

'Mm.'

It was less than a mumble this time. A reflective groan.

'Not everyone remembers his old friends when he rises above them.'

'Arrr.'

'I'm sure we can make you comfortable,' Mrs. Peake observed, in the clinical tone of a surgeon contemplating a particularly painful operation upon a captured mass murderer.

'I ask nothing of anyone,' he muttered.

'Come, come, Joe,' I soothed. 'All is given freely. My house is yours as the Latins say. Figuratively. We might as well enjoy it in the few weeks I retain it before disposal.'

'Won't this heap go any faster?' he demanded and he licked his lips with a raw, scorbutic tongue. But we were already home.

Home. I helped Mrs. Peake carry her parcels through the front door as if into a suburban bungalow, through the Great Hall, past dining-room, breakfast-room, library, drawing-room, office, ante-rooms, music-room, etc. and down into the kitchen where Shrubsole was polishing silver. When I went back up Joe Bezoar was spitting into the ashes of the fireplace, staring at soot. He had followed us in, looking down at his feet, acknowledging nothing.

I was gracious. I played host. I set up the cooler full of ice and a trayful of generous goblets.

'Although this champagne has not been iced for the prescribed period it has been chilling in a special compartment of the refrigerator and Shrubsole advises me that it should be quite acceptable.'

I removed the bottle from the icer, swaddled it in linen and presented it to Bezoar who had approached warily.

'I'm not experienced at this sort of thing. Would you do the honours? A good year. One of the better vintages. I believe the label said 42 B.C.'

Bezoar only narrowed his eyes.

'You don't plan to drink that?'

'Of course. Delightful. Celebratory . . .'

I opened the bottle.

'Baby piss,' he snarled. 'I didn't come here to be insulted. I'm a grown man. You said you had a cellar full of booze . . .'

I remained determinedly affable. I could see that this rank bastard could easily turn into a real son-of-a-bitch and had probably been one all along. My normal reaction to his reaction would have been to become instantly enraged and to throw him out but I thought, in these surroundings I could only allow myself to become nettled, which I believe is in the correct genteel tradition.

'Ordinarily, Joe,' I said, 'your remarks would nettle me but this is an occasion. I said my house is yours and so it is, including the cellar. Follow me. And if you don't see what you want we shall order it for to-morrow.'

Bezoar was mollified enough to take a mouthful of champagne which was excellent; a brut of the highest rating as well as price. (I looked it up later.) He swallowed it as though straining seaweed through his teeth and followed me impatiently as I strolled down to the cellar carrying a full bubbly glass. I waved him towards the racks with a lordly gesture. He scurried in front of them like a starved rat at the cheese counter. He focused on the sherries, sampled a medium dry of not very high quality by drinking from the bottle. He nodded his head, picked up two more bottles and one of Bell's twenty-year-old Royal Reserve, and we headed back upstairs.

I now admitted to myself that, as a wino, Joe Bezoar would have been quite happy with a ninety-five cent bottle of Catawba, fortified to the Liquor Board limit with neutral grain spirits. He would have been happier in his fungoid, sepulchral chamber in the Arcadian Hotel grinding his teeth in solitude. And he would have been spared the necessity of envying me—in my presence.

But what could I do? I watched him fill his glass two-thirds full of sherry then add about an ounce of the expensive old Royal Reserve. He sipped away steadily at this concoction. Even though I am basically a non-drinker—as naïvely demonstrated by my preference for champagne—I was repelled by this exhibition of barbaric taste. Then I remembered that it was a local fact that the winos had developed this taste for Catawba because it provided More Bang For The Buck, if I may transpose the circumstance though not the philosophy. Perhaps I must admit to a certain stuffiness here. Perhaps Joe Bezoar was being no cruder than the martini drinker who imbibes one of the cheapest and coarsest of distillates flavoured with wormwood and pretends its preparation is a ritual of sophisticated significance.

It has been reported by eminent practitioners and investigators of Hibernian tippling that a goodly proportion of the populace has been born from one to three drinks under par. Joe Bezoar was probably one of these. When he had finished his second drink he said gruffly, 'Nice place you've got here.'

I fiddled with the stem of my glass, carried refreshments in for Mrs. Peake, built a crackling good fire in the fireplace and tried not to enrage myself against my guest even when he drew the spoon slowly through his lips and thrust it back into the pot of iced caviar.

'Nice place,' he said. 'You ought to keep it.'

176

'You said that before.'

'I meant it, too. Time you settled down. "The rightly happy must remain at home".'

'From the Greek?'

'Yep.'

'No. I don't think so,' I said, putting on a thoughtful frown. 'You're sure it isn't an old Lapp saying? They're migrating like lemmings all the time . . .'

'No. Greek.'

'I've got it now. Pontius Pilate's last words on Good Friday before he called in the Circassian dancing girls. Hosea, 79:4. Right?'

I said that 'right' with a bright nod of certainty that takes a considerable effort to contradict.

'Hosea?' he faltered. 'Are you sure?'

I knew I had him.

'Absolutely. Let's go along to the library and look it up.'

'No, no. I got that one from my old man and he was mostly wrong. Spent his whole life standing behind the British Woollens counter at Pennywise's Department Store then reading about man's inhumanity to man all night. We damned near starved to death . . .'

He drained his drink with a gulp and poured another gill of his miserable mixture. I could see he was one of those drunks who drink faster and faster as they get drunker.

'Is it any wonder,' he asked, 'that I went in for . . .'

But he was interrupted by the arrival of Chas. B. Swingle, Jr.

'Welcome, welcome,' I said. I'd have opened my arms to a cannibal. 'Have a drink. Champagne. Just opening another bottle. Sit down. We dine in a moment. Join us.'

'I'd be delighted. Very kind of you.'

He seemed sincere. And relieved. He had come in with a rush that tapered off to a falter as though unsure of his welcome. I poured him a bumper of the wine and he assured me it was not only as good but better than something similar he had tasted in

M   177

Varvenargues, vintage '65, or perhaps that was the year he had drunk it. But he seemed so worried as he drank that I felt he must have a galloping case of sprue, thrush or some equally malignant disorder. He rose from beside Bezoar and began to roam about restlessly, looking up at the crappy old paintings without interest, examining suits of armour, halberds, warming himself at the fire. He finally settled at the end of the table, about twenty feet downwind of Bezoar, who was scowling, naturally.

'Glad to see you're settled in already. No problems? Everything under control?'

I quaffed a goodly quaff of champagne. I seemed to have become gaily nervous and was drinking perhaps more quickly than was completely discreet. I smeared some goosy concoction on a cracker.

'All seems quite well, for the moment, Mr. Swingle. Have an olive. Some pâté. Smoked oyster. Dreadful things but perhaps to your taste? But do avoid the caviar. Bezoar has a proprietary interest in that little pot. However, I'm sure there must be a few more jars in Uncle Moses' pantry. I'll call Mrs. Peake . . .'

'No, no. A stick of celery . . .'

He bit into it with a crash.

'Good for the health,' I said.

'Yes.'

'Nerve tonic.'

'Yes. Oh. You don't like celery?'

'Noisy. Gives the illusion of eating. Eat a bushel of celery at a sitting and I guarantee the noise will drive you mad. It's a vegetarian form of torture they inflict upon any carnivores they corner.'

He examined the stick of celery as though it were a recent and exotic invention.

'I've had a few drinks,' he said. I recognised a probe.

'Good. They seem to have improved you. Removed that athletic edge. I find you much more acceptable now than this morning.'

178

He smiled a pearly, boyish smile.

'I was born with a terribly sweet tooth.'

More than a few drinks, I thought.

'But every time I wanted candy my mother gave me celery or a raw carrot or an apple. Didn't want me to ruin my teeth. I have perfect teeth. No fillings.'

He bared his teeth, edge to edge. They looked perfect. Any horse trader would have struck hands and led him off in an instant.

'Grand. Hurray for momma,' I said. Mrs. Peake had just brought in a bowl of olives or anchovies or some similar extraordinary fragments that one doesn't dare serve to the sober. 'Mrs. Peake, isn't that a grand set of teeth?'

She had been turning from the table when I put my hand on her arm to stop her. She gave Swingle a considered inspection.

'Lovely,' she said. 'I'm sure they're a great help in court.'

'Yes, a lawyer without a good sharkish set of teeth is lost,' I agreed.

'I didn't mean that,' she said.

She cast a splinter of a glance at her left shoulder and my hand. She wasn't taking chances on flushing shy game. I released her just slowly enough to indicate that it wasn't a completely casual contact.

Swingle laughed.

'Oh, they wouldn't let me loose in court. I'm a complete fool as a barrister. I'm just an errand boy on the Muddiman Estate. They have that absolutely tied up . . . Oh! There, you see, I've put my foot in it again!'

'Have you?' I said politely, not really caring. I seemed to be developing a less inhibited interest in Mrs. Peake. I turned and poured another glass for her. 'Tell Shrubsole to maintain the supply of wine, Mrs. Peake. It seems to be having a salutary effect.'

Over the rim of her glass she gave me a suddenly reflective look.

'Swingle,' I said, 'or do you mind if I call you Chas. Forget your troubles. Rejoice. More wine. Hold it, I'll open another. The Lord shall provide. Ask and ye shall receive. To him who hath shall be given. Right, Bezoar? From the Greek: Hosea 79:6.'

Bezoar, who had been guzzling away quietly though sneeringly at the other end of the table, looked for a moment as though he would argue, then sank back sourly for Swingle had thrown his celery in the fireplace and said, 'I'm off celery for life. To hell with it. And the judgeship too . . .'

'By all means swear off Judging. Judge not lest ye be judged: Hosea two or three hundred.'

'The family want to put me on the bench. They know I'll never be any good as a lawyer and a tame judge on the bench would be good for business. Steer the doubtful cases my way . . . that sort of thing . . .'

'A hardship. I can see you are being put upon. Drown it.'

I poured for him.

'I'm serious. My family has this weird dynastic complex. My great-grandfather was a puddler in an iron foundry, and my grandfather was one of those really crummy political hacks who got caught with his hand in the till. Dad was too close to him to make the bench so I'm it. I hate it.'

'Don't do it then.'

'They'll make me do it. You don't know them.'

'And I haven't the least desire. Don't cry into the wine. That's good stuff and deserves better. Here, let me bring it up to strength.'

'Is beef Stroganoff all right? It's quick and easy,' Mrs. Peake murmured in my left ear. She murmured it in a tone that suggested an assignation in the room next to Mme. Bovary's on the Rouen waterfront.

But I had had enough of being frightened.

I administered sacred rites: the laying on of hands. I massaged her back in the region of the shoulder blade, just where the brassière strap crosses, in the manner of a politician bringing a subordinate into close, friendly conference. I bent my head thoughtfully towards her.

Tim Badger, you hypocritical son-of-a-bitch, I said to myself. Who do you think you are, some creeping bank manager? Yes, you can back out now without the least difficulty. Just a simple, friendly gesture due to a few drinks, etc. But it just isn't good enough for anyone with a fragmentary residue of moral character. It would be more ethical to rip her clothes off and violate her in public, front, back and sideways, than to continue this pussy-footed shilly-shallying.

'Stroganoff would be delightful. I can count on you to furnish the best of everything. I am very fond of tenderloin.' And I slid my hand down her back very slowly, very definitely, very caressingly, the short distance to her waist. I bent close to her ear and muttered, 'I could eat you with a fork, Mrs. Peake.'

Did she turn towards me, look deep into my eyes, lay a gentle hand upon my arm, cast her eyes down modestly, wheel on me in final triumph, move discreetly away, blush, dilate her nostrils, press herself closer to me, flash urgent signals with her eyes, scan my face for reassuring truth, whip out a marriage licence, press a note of rendezvous into my fevered hand, silently move her thigh against mine, sweep me into her arms and rush me off to her enveloping four-poster?

No.

She gave me a cool, guarded look, raised her glass and emptied it and said, 'This wine is delicious. Don't spoil your appetite.'

And she turned to go.

'Never fear,' I assured her. 'I am ravenous. Wait. Let me fill your glass. Can't have you slaving over a hot stove without refreshment. I'll rush down with a refill every few minutes. Have Shrubsole chill a few more bottles.'

Hoo, hoo! I yelled, throwing my cap in the air and turning six or eight handsprings and running seven hundred times around the Y.M.C.A. track to cool my blood and moralise my thoughts. But it didn't work and I watched Mrs. Peake walk back towards the kitchen with a hip action as timeless and as enduringly fascinating as the sea's . . . She was pretty chunky in her low heels. Not over wide, just womanly.

Give me a woman, any time. Especially during these last ten years. Girls are beautiful and lively and they can be bought, awed, conned, impressed, intrigued, but it's not an honest transaction on either side. It's youthful skin that is being bargained for and consumed. Women are another matter. The product is time-tested in the market-place though the packaging may be a bit old-fashioned and subtler marketing techniques are in order, and occasional price wars. With the high standard of living, hormones and contraception women are refusing to turn into grandmothers and there's going to be a Woman Explosion. We're going to have a completely new natural resource that we hadn't suspected existed a few years ago. The politicians will be bolting for the back rooms like rabbits with weasels at their throats. The scientists will be staring glumly into test tubes and direfully predicting coarsening of the pores by the age of ninety-eight if women insist on acting human. But the women won't pay attention. By then they will have caught on to the half-men of science and the landscape will be crowded with women fleeing to the arms of lechers, nuts, lovers, pimps, gigolos, singers, actors, madmen, entertainers, anarchists, idealists, flat-earthers, U.F.O. watchers and anyone else with the imagination to encompass alternatives. And in due time, by a sort of natural process of Lysistratian selection they may breed out of the species the perverted tendency to explain man away in a stream of mindless electrons.

'No, you don't know them, Badger,' Swingle mourned. 'Night and day, work and play, they'll keep after me and in the end I'll give up.'

'Disqualify yourself,' I said airily. That seemed a simple, obvious solution.

'But how?'

'Oh, I don't know . . . Marry a tart.'

'What good would that do?'

'They might ostracise you.'

'No. And how could they tell, these days?'

This judicial remark indicated that he was already well along the primrose path to the bench, that last remaining outlet of un-examined, acceptable and total social aggression. I thought furiously.

'You have only one recourse.'

'Yes?' Eagerly.

'Politics.'

Complete deflation.

'They'd love that. Stem the upstart tide . . .'

'Labour. Socialist. Communist. Join a party. Defend agitators. Rights of Man.'

He quailed.

'That would do it,' he muttered. 'It would kill them. Me, too, maybe. I don't give a damn about all that tedious, subterranean jiggling.'

'A little adventurous thinking was all that was needed,' I boasted.

'All I really want to do is dig a garden. Yes, maybe run a market garden. With a little wife, not too pretty but not ugly, either. Just a nice person—without a lot of accomplishments that she's flourishing at you all the time but still with enough wits and capacity not to be needing mindless turmoil all the time. Just a nice quiet life. I don't want to spend my life dealing with rats. Doing the dirty work for criminal rats, corporation rats.'

'I guess you haven't heard the news.'

'What news?'

'The garden bit is out. Absolutely out of the question.'

'I don't understand. All I want to do is something useful, something non-destructive. Food in a starving world. A market garden is ideal.'

'You must be some sort of Rip Van Winkle, Chas. Where have you been for the last twenty-five years? Don't you know the soil everywhere is saturated with D.D.T., rat poison and a thousand other pesticides and pollutants to a mean depth of ninety-eight feet; that the fatty tissue of every American contains eleven parts per million of D.D.T.? And that's not counting fall-out, which we are trying desperately to forget. Do you know the visceral fat of the California Grebe contains up to sixteen hundred parts per million, and that it's even got into the Antarctic penguins? Are you going to go on feeding this poisonous stuff to innocent women and children just because you have a yen to grow carrots?'

'But what can I do? I don't want to drive that goddamned sports car any more. Have you ever followed a truck on a rainy day in one? I want to drive a Buick sedan and not prove anything and not listen to newscasters talking about war and then selling me miracle toothpaste. There's nothing wrong with my teeth, boo, hoo.'

'Don't blub yet,' I said. 'The situation is much worse than that.'

'Goddamn it I will, too, blub. It's a free country . . .' And he buried his face in his arms.

'You're right,' I said, placing a comforting hand on his shoulder. 'About the blubbing, that is. That's appropriate. That's human. That's pertinent.'

'All I want is to do something that means something, for a change. What can I do, Badger, what can I do?'

'I've been thinking about it for some time. Years. Palliatives are hopeless. There is only one thing to do at this stage.'

'I know I'm weak in some ways and not as sharp as the Firm wants me to be but I'm not really dumb. I'm strong physically. I'm capable. I want to do the right thing. But what can I do?'

He sounded terribly human but when, I thought, has that ever been a recommendation.

'For a start,' I said, 'you'd have to blow up every communication system in the world.'

Thirteen

Swingle leaped to his feet, upsetting a glass of wine.

'I knew it,' he shouted. 'You're mad. You've probably been sending real bombs all the time. No. You're not getting me in on this. No, sir!'

'Oh, for God's sake, Chazz, sit down,' I said wearily. It amused me to see that I had begun by calling him Swingle, then Charles, then Chas., now Chazz—whether out of contempt or because of the wine I could not say. It felt more like contempt at the moment.

'You're just like everyone else: looking for somewhere to place the blame and you don't even know what's wrong in the first place.'

'I know it's wrong to go around blowing people up,' he protested, refilling his glass with a trembling hand. 'Two wrongs don't make a right.'

'Really? Then what do a hundred wrongs make? What do a thousand, a million wrongs make? Or a billion?'

'I don't know,' he muttered, 'but I know they don't make a right.'

I hunched closer to him across the corner of the big table and I murmured in a conspiratorial whisper, 'I know what it makes; you know what it makes, Chazz; everyone knows what it makes. Why not admit it?'

'I don't know . . . Problems?'

'Oh, come off it, Chazz!'

'I don't know what you mean, really.'

'Why don't you say it?'

'What? What?' He actually sounded sincerely desperate.

'Death.'

He was truly exasperated now.

'What the hell has that to do with blowing up a—a—traffic light?'

I slammed my fist on the table, triumphant.

'Aha! Brilliant! A perfect example! A traffic light. A regular little Jim-Dandy life saver, eh? Regulating the flow of traffic and preventing autos from crashing into each other with consequent saving of life. Right?'

'Right.'

'Wrong. Couldn't be wronger. A traffic light is nothing more nor less than a death threat. Commands disobeyed on pain of death. Half of you go, half of you stop. Now, the stoppers go and the goers stop. Everyone under control, all of the time. Totally arbitrary. Run a red light—thirty dollars or thirty days. Either way, death of earning time or death of living time. But the significant thing is that there isn't a reason in the world to run lines of traffic head on into each other—except for the adversary system, and you know all about that, don't you, Chazz? That's the meaning of Law, isn't it? Prosecution–defence; plaintiff–defendant; winner–loser; executioner–victim. Our idea of Justice that we believe in so strongly that we'd smash the world for it.'

I was in great form. Words came trippingly on the tongue and I was striding back and forth between the fireplace and table, sawing the air with one hand and slopping my wine prodigally with the other. Bezoar was darting downcast glittering glances at me out of the corners of his eyes as though waiting for the moment my back was turned to slide a stiletto between my ribs. I could plainly see my mistake with Bezoar. My unqualified kindness had destroyed his world: a world of a snarl, a curse, a blow, a counter-blow, a graceless retreat, spitting spite. Kindness put him into a fury of frustration. He had no coin of repayment. He could only wipe out what he considered an indebtedness by a quarrel, by forcing a rejection. Yes, I knew his type now. Why didn't I know it before?

186

All this, and a warning to myself to watch for his sudden and apparently baseless attack, crossed my mind as I strode back and forth and spouted away, but it didn't stem my flow.

'Yes, we must have victims, corpses. Smashed mutilated evidence that we desperately need to tell us we are still alive. We rush avidly to accidents, swarm gaily about the scene of death, of funerals, but shun a birth which occurs in solitude, darkness and shame. Sure, you think I'm making it all up. Just a disappointed eccentric blowing his stack. But try and interest a doctor in keeping you healthy. He'll be so goddamned bored you'll turn into a blue icicle and he'll palm off a gross of placebos or tranquillisers on you as though you were a moustached, fifty-six-year-old spotting maiden aunt. And he'll blank out on you until you burst a blood vessel four inches south-west of the cerebellum or until that little nonsense of a wen has metastasised to a dozen inaccessible new sites and then watch how he shoves tubes up your arse, into your bladder, through your veins, up your nose and down your throat and in one ear and out the other. And if you still show signs of life he'll pump a few litres of chemicals into you just to show he's up to date and besides the names are cute: asstwisterol, dicarbofornicate and they have the reputation of Acme-International Chemical Trust behind them not to mention clinical results including half a million deformed babies, seven hundred thousand blind diabetics and three million impotent pancreatic cases. Or perhaps in friendly consultation with your neighbourhood mortician he will supply you with a substitute arsehole, epiglotis or medulla oblongata if he happened to mislay your original equipment somewhere in surgery while making notes for his new best-seller *Surgery For Fun And Profit*.'

Swingle was now looking at me in that stupid knowing way that implied I owed my doctor for at least three prostrate inspections. Bezoar was sucking away on his glass with fury and I feared lest he chew away the edge and swallow it in large jagged fragments. Trouble there. The prospect interested me but only in an offhand manner.

'No, the whiff of death is the big motivation in medicine. And the rest of us insist on poisoned air and murderous sludge in our drinking water, sewage in the old swimming hole, garbage blowing up our streets, assassination and mutilation in our automobiles, cancer in our cigarettes, perversion in our arts, slaughter in our international relations, ambush in civil conflicts . . .'

'I think you're exaggerating a bit,' Swingle murmured deferentially.

'Crap. Crap. Crap,' Joe Bezoar sneered in as offensive a manner as he could manage between gulps.

'Oh yes,' I said, slightly nettled, 'I can't wait until you come up with some such opposing idea as the increase in population. With statistics, of course. That would be a stroke of genius; present company excepted. Sign of creativity—life? Yes. Like lemmings. Forcing themselves into the sea. Mass international suicide. The only trouble is, these mass-maniacs want to take everyone with them and I'm not much of a traveller, myself, in that direction. But there's no sense in your trying to sidetrack me. I was talking about communications; and the wages of communications is death. That's my thesis . . .'

'In my professional judgment, you haven't yet presented a cogent brief,' Swingle murmured.

'You want to trap me in the winner–loser circuit again just when I'm trying to save your life, your soul, through a career in communication destruction. It's obvious you don't know the first thing about it so there is not much point in breaking the news about such matters as entropy to you; about the natural tendency for any communication to degenerate into garble and how we're determinedly accelerating the process. And I suppose I'll never convince you that news is simply death information? Heard any gospel lately—good news? Damned right you haven't. Two thousand enemy killed. Weekend toll seven hundred and sixty-eight. Border clash. Ship sunk. Train wreck. Sixty-four dead in fire. Planes shot down. Plot. Profits rise (get more of the other fellow's life than you give). G.N.P. up by seventeen billion (seventeen billion more worth of material to turn immediately into seventeen million worth of garbage that must be disposed of at great cost and degradation).'

And speaking of degradation: Joe Bezoar was following Mrs. Peake with sinister glances as she set the table and began to bring in the food. These glances were full of icy hostility but also of furious interest. The reason for these peculiar looks was quite incomprehensible to me but my blood seemed to grasp the situation and began to simmer. Still, I could not fault him for his interest. Mrs. Peake had donned an apron and the bow at the back fluttered engagingly with the play of her hips and the nipping-in of the waist only emphasised their gluteal generosity.

'Do the headlines ever say, "Miro Completes Another Painting!" Never. Do they say, "Miro Dies!" Of course. Immediately. Do they say, "Maiden Lady Of 37 Finally And Successfully Initiated Into Fascinations And Follies Of Love By Young Rascal"? No. Such signs of life are unmentionable since they are liable to prompt tribal celebratory orgies welcoming the not-so-young lady to womanhood but since our society's instincts are for death we say: Jail that young bugger. What does he mean by spreading joy, sensuality, pleasure, enjoyment, love, delight and sudden comprehension—all free and without tax? What does he mean by undermining our Way Of Life with its tried and true concepts of Duty, Dying For Country, Respect For Tradition, Religion, the Stainless and Spotless Virtue and Chastity of Our Women, Road Building Contracts, Slush Funds, Government Bonds, Inflation, Loyalty, the Twenty-Five Year Gold Watch, the Body And Fender Shop.'

'Do sit down and eat while it's hot,' Mrs. Peake murmured, discarding her apron and seating herself at my left with the patient air of a duchess during a butlers' strike.

'Damn all you know about communications,' Bezoar snarled. 'Eight to five you couldn't lick a postage stamp and get it on right side up.'

THE FIREFLY HUNT

I ignored him. I'll deal with the son-of-a-bitch later, I thought. Give him his last meal then, kerchunk, off with his head.

I began to notice that, whenever Mrs. Peake got within six feet of me, I succumbed to seragliotic visions, became swathed in diaphanous sensations, perfumes, warmths. The female moth exerts this effect upon males of its species for up to half a mile unless confined under an airtight bell jar. A woman's range is probably more than thirteen thousand miles, upwind. Research should be done upon this important topic. Is it any wonder that at a distance of feet and inches Mrs. Peake had pronounced and noticeable effects upon me?

I sat down and in the process managed to come within inhaling distance of her hair which so intoxicated me that in self-defence I pinched her quite smartly upon the sideward spread of her increasingly and incredibly voluptuous arse.

'Oh!' she exclaimed, half leaping from her seat. 'I seem to have forgotten the . . . Oh no. There it is.' And she sat down again without looking at me and proceeded to eat with all the dignity of a constipated duchess manipulating spaghetti on a tarnished fish fork.

I felt quite gay and a bit smug. A regular paterfamilias beaming on his little brood which in this case consisted of an alcoholic car washer, a lawyer betraying his father and his firm and a luscious, voracious widow bordering on the far edge of ripeness whom, in my slightly tipsy state, I saw as a luscious voracious widow bordering on the far edge of ripeness.

The pinch had not gone unnoticed but I didn't care. Swingle was staring at his plate in a flushed, guilty manner and he ate quickly and systematically. Bezoar was stirring about in the Stroganoff in the rebellious manner of a spoiled child. He kept muttering in snatches: 'Oh, for Christ's sake!' 'Never seen anything like it.' 'Can't stand it another minute.' Et cetera.

I arranged my napkin with a flourish or two and under cover of this deft cape work I grasped Mrs. Peake half-way up an unctuous thigh and applied firm but gentle amorous pressure.

190

'A succulent morsel of tenderloin,' I observed as I chewed judiciously on a bit of the beef.

Mrs. Peake genteelly dabbed her lips with her napkin and returned it to her lap, allowing herself however to caress me briefly but unambiguously somewhat higher on the thigh than I had fondled her.

'Oh God! If I only had my D.V.S. back,' Bezoar whined.

'D.V.S.?' I asked politely, in an endeavour to distract myself from my fair and formidable companion.

'Doctor of Veterinary Surgery. You don't think for chrissake that I'm just a lousy carwasher like the rest of you clots down there, do you? Why, my paper on botfly larvæ was a classic . . . is a classic still . . .' And he went on with some improbable tale about inventing an undetectable stimulant for race-horses on which he cleaned up hundreds of thousands—or at least several thousand before being betrayed by a double-crossing trainer, caught and defrocked (or perhaps it's fleeced, with veterinaries) and but for the grace of God and that goddamned trainer he might be a wealthy brandy hound rather than a miserable and starving wino.

I'd have dismissed all this as bibulous fantasy but for one detail. He gave an elaborate description of injecting his dope into some anal vein or other so the needle mark wouldn't show; and he outlined this savoury subject while sopping up sauce with a gobbet of roll so that I had to concede to myself that he must be as he claimed, to mouth this subject at table, or else be a mortician or medical student. Whatever his standing it only confirmed the fact that I must eventually throw him out.

Mrs. Peake left to bring in dessert and coffee. Bezoar followed her with malevolent eyes.

'She's stealing you blind,' he said.

'In one day?' I laughed.

'Rags to riches. Riches to rags. It's all very well for you wealthy people to laugh. You'll see. She'll pluck you like a chicken. Like a scrawny chicken,' he muttered with dour satisfaction.

'Whoopee! I hope I get something for all this dough she's going to haul off.'

'Mr. Badger isn't a wealthy man,' Swingle said quietly.

'Not really,' I agreed with a rich man's modesty. I felt that here was the spot to make some standard complaint about taxes but I wasn't fast enough.

'Not at all,' Swingle corrected, and he looked at me with a sort of near panic. 'Haven't you read the will? Haven't you signed the documents I left?'

'I'm afraid I've been quite busy. Checking the wine cellar and all that. May have neglected some small details . . .'

'But you know that Sir Moses only left the Castle to you in trust?'

'Did he? Well, that's perfectly satisfactory. A responsibility off my shoulders.'

'And only the residual income, after taxes, upkeep, management fees, et cetera . . .'

'I shan't starve, I'm sure.'

'You might. The residue of the estate was nowhere near what it was thought to be. Millions missing, according to the Internal Revenue.'

'My wants are modest.'

'Sir Moses' instructions were to establish the Castle as a museum to house his collections.'

'But it's hardly more than a rat's nest.'

I could see Swingle was dying. I felt like a torturer. He yielded his unwanted fragments of information with the greatest reluctance but under the most rigorous inner or professional necessity; probably the latter. I poured him more wine. He gulped it.

'And there will be a Curator appointed. In fact, he has already been appointed at a stipend of, I believe, thirty-five thousand a year?' The rising inflection demanded to know whether I found it as ridiculous as it seemed to him.

I did.

'To look after this jackdaw's treasury?'

'To break you. Daddy hates you, you know. And so do the other executors, Mr. Cutter and Mr. Mandrake. Both of the old school. All that bomb stuff enrages them. You ought to be horse-whipped and all that. When you awarded your medal to that madman who shot the automobile agency manager for welshing on his warranty, that finished them . . .'

'The poor chap didn't realise that commercial fraud is our way of life. I felt that innocence should be acknowledged occasionally, if not rewarded.'

'So, with improved facilities for display, washrooms for the public, creation of parking lots, burglar alarms, et cetera, I'm afraid the estate will run a deficit, indefinitely.'

'You mean?'

'I'm afraid so. Not a bean left for you. It's a shame . . .'

Bezoar began to laugh, silently but immoderately, his shoulders hunched and his face turned away. Or perhaps he was sobbing at my misfortune. A friend in need, indeed.

'Easy come, easy go,' coining this brilliant phrase with an insouciance I did not actually feel. In fact, I was feeling bafflement and a growing rage.

'A whole burden lifted from my shoulders. And my rent paid for life.'

'And harassment. You can expect they'll try to make it unlivable for you. As I see it, Daddy will try to force you into minimal rights of domicile. A broom closet, if he has his way. It's ambiguous. Several clauses open to interpretation as to when and how the museum is established but a court fight needs money. Do you have any?'

I fished in my pocket.

'Approximately forty-seven dollars.'

'Well, you see . . .'

I saw. I was being victimised, and so grossly that even this child of Justice who had been indoctrinated and inoculated with the virus of Hard-cases-make-bad-law could not quite stomach it.

N   193

To gain time to think or, perhaps, to avoid thinking about it altogether, I jumped back on my hobby horse.

'And we mustn't forget transportation. Now there's a particularly lethal branch of communications. I don't mean in terms of accidents, I mean in intent. We've made great strides, haven't we: supersonic planes, hundred and sixty mile an hour trains, four hundred horsepower family sedans. The basic effect is not to get you somewhere but to blur the environment, smear it, wipe it out; for we can't stand the sight of our surroundings and when traffic stalls we go mad—trapped facing ourselves in the cesspit of our own devising. Which accounts for war. If we can get to a foreign strand and mash it into a bloody hash of intolerability we can shift the blame, for we have finally found a scene worse than our own even though we have had to manufacture it at untold expense in treasure and blood. So there we are, stuck at a new low from which we must move out to new horrors if we are to make it, by contrast, a norm. So each war must get worse than the last and they must come faster. Entropy increases, chaos flourishes, and in a dying world our love affair with death is revealed, too late to make a scandal. Of course this is just common knowledge but we don't like to think about it because we'd have to weed out the survivor mentality of those who kill to give themselves a sense of life. And we don't want to do that for who could stand to contemplate life in a kindly world.'

At this point, Bezoar unseated me from my hobby horse.

'Talk, talk, talk,' he said. 'What a phony deal.' Then he mimmicked me: ' "My house is yours as they say in old May-hick-oh. All the booze you can drink, Bezoar, old boy. Your worries are over. Plenty for everyone." I've always thought you were a phony and this proves it. Riding high on a rumour . . .'

'No! It's not like that, at all. Have another drink, Bezoar. I'll get old Shrubsole to bring up a whole case, just for you. If it comes to that, I'll sign over my rights of domicile to you. I mean it. I meant it this afternoon.'

194

THE FIREFLY HUNT

I felt dismayed, anguished, apprehensive. He had touched me on my Achilles heel, with a gimlet. Anyone who is as critical of others as I am must be completely sincere; above the reproach of hypocrisy, pretension, phoniness. I felt panicky. There is no other explanation for making such a generous offer to Bezoar for he obviously lived by the soldier's philosophy: If you can't eat it, or fuck it, then shit on it.

In spite of my panic I still felt like slaughtering him but this sort of attack was new, unfamiliar. I wasn't prepared to cope with it immediately.

'Bull-shit,' he said, stretching it out slowly and offensively. 'You've got nothing to give. Or you'd have given it to that broad long ago.' And he jerked his thumb in the direction Mrs. Peake had gone, and he grinned like a lobotomised hyena.

'Be careful,' I warned, 'you can go too far.'

There was that smiling, murderous glee in the air that precedes catastrophe. I had considered saying, 'You are speaking of the woman I love,' but it seemed premature. I knew I'd be able to use that chestnut a bit later so I just said, 'You can go too far.' The sort of stereotype phrase that no one has ever paid any attention to yet is a marker on the road to disaster. I thought it only fair to mark this stage for Bezoar.

'I don't think so,' he said. 'All I'd need would be half an hour with that broad. I'd whip her into shape. Spare the rod and spoil the child . . .'

'From the Greek,' I said coldly, and it seemed time to add, 'Remember, you are speaking of the woman I love.'

'Yes, in ten minutes I'd have her kissing the rod; begging for mercy.'

'That's it! That's it!' I exclaimed. 'O. Henry's Law! "Any man who is excessively fond of dogs or horses is invariably cruel to women." So that's your trouble. Bedevil women so they don't know how to react, then claim they're troublesome, sexless, frigid, neurotic, eh? And you don't have to be a man. Not required in the circumstances. No, you'd rather pat a dog.' And I had an enormous vision of millions and billions of slavering dogs and mewling cats being stroked and petted and pampered; and millions and billions of wives and husbands, lovers and children pining, withering, committing suicide for want of caresses lavished upon brutes.

Bezoar paled. Rather, he went a dirty, sepulchral grey.

'I'll fix you,' he grated, and his face went taut and murderous. He poured himself another shaky drink. 'I'll shut your big mouth for you, for good, you crappy little mail-order hero.'

'Out,' I said and I reached across the table and slapped the drink out of his hand just as he was raising it to his lips. 'Out. You may be the champion billygoat futterer of the York County Association of Veterinary Perverts but here you are nothing. I've got your number.'

He wasn't exactly keen on losing his drink, especially in that particular way. He didn't even bother wiping the liquor off his face.

'I'm going to kill you, you goddamn' . . . uh . . . uh . . . *Snob*!'

He seized a bottle by the neck. With a quick, experienced blow he smashed the body of the bottle near the bottom, leaving the neck as a handle and four jagged glass daggers projecting towards me.

He crept around the table with a dead smile on his face and nothing in his eyes. Swingle leaped back out of the way, crying, 'I'm a witness. A credible witness. If he attacks you, you have a case. A clear tort.'

This was now more than an inane situation. I could tell it was deadly serious by the sudden lack of conversation. I backed away. I put out a hand towards Bezoar but it seemed undignified and useless against that jagged glass. I backed farther—and was trapped—against the fireplace. Bezoar crept on. Slowly. Enjoying it. I reached up. I felt a jar, a vase. I seized it. Uncle Moses' urn. No choice. I hurled it at Bezoar's head just as he decided to rush.

He dodged, slipped, dropped his weapon which shattered. The urn exploded against the table edge powdering rug, table, chair, floor with creamy ash.

I lunged towards Bezoar who uttered a cry of alarm and scrambled across the room, where he wrenched a broadsword from the hand of a fifteenth-century suit of armour. I halted. Retreated again, slowly. Bezoar hefted the great sword with a judicious, slaughterhouse look in his eye.

I can take a hint.

I plucked a halberd from the wall just as Bezoar began to close in and, with one motion, wheeled and chopped downward in his direction just as he raised the sword above his head. The head of the halberd bit into the floor inches from his foot. He fled, dropping the sword.

'I'll skewer you like kebabs of dead donkey,' I shouted, charging, harrying him out of the Great Hall, towards the front door and down the passage leading to the washroom.

He plunged into the washroom and slammed home the bolt. I flung the halberd, impaling the upper door panel on its spear point.

'You're in the right place, you turd,' I screamed through the door. 'Come out here and you're a dead man.'

And I hammered the door to terrify him further as I grinned with excitement.

That's war, I thought. That's what it's all about. Good guy lets the bad buy pull the wool over his eyes, suffering the illusion that everyone is basically good. Then, too late, it's defend yourself or die. Of course, bad guys fall out among themselves; gangster versus gangster, for control of the rackets, whether slot machines or nations. Good guys could never come to blows with good guys. In fact, good guys could never permit the conditions for a war to develop and yet here I have been through a small though comic war. Could it be that I am not actually a good guy? No. I've confused myself with wine and a trick of logic. I couldn't be a bad guy and still feel this tipsily amused to see Bezoar flee before my sham attack with the halberd. It certainly seemed like a sham attack, now.

'We must call the police. That man is dangerous. A bar fighter. You must prefer charges . . . A householder in your own home . . . He needs a lesson,' Swingle babbled, anxiously eyeing the passageway to the washroom as though expecting Bezoar to come riding out on a charger, lance level.

'Swingle,' I said, 'for a lawyer, you are singularly ignorant of the role of the police to-day. To them there is no difference between plaintiff and defendant. Their role is to involve everyone possible with the courts, indiscriminately. If anything, their real rapport is with the criminal rather than with the square, dumb, Honest John citizen.'

But I don't think he believed me and perhaps, stupefied as he was, he realised I was in that condition where I readily said things I would ordinarily only think.

Just at that point Mrs. Peake came in with the coffee.

'Good heavens! What's been happening here?'

She stared wide-eyed at the ashes, the fallen sword, the broken glass and pottery shards, and my footsteps through the ashes where I had pursued Bezoar. 'Someone spilled an ash tray,' I said soberly.

This set me giggling and I collapsed on the sofa beside Swingle, who recoiled in horror from my unseemly mirth.

'Uncle Moses' ash tray!'

Fourteen

'I know it's the fault of that dreadful Mr. Bezoar,' Mrs. Peake stated primly, bringing her luscious lips as close as she could physically manage to a thin line. I was in that charmed state where their voluptuous movement fascinated me. 'The moment I laid eyes on him, I knew nothing decent could be expected of him. I'll get the vacuum cleaner.'

'A little wine, first,' I suggested. 'Harmless to delicate tissue.'

She favoured me with a partial smile at this sally and hesitated. I poured.

'You mustn't be too hard on Bezoar. He's a hopeless case, you know. Calceolaria. He's finished . . .'

I didn't give a damn about Bezoar taking all the blame. I wanted to bring Mrs. Peake around to her old warm amorous self. I wanted her to forget Bezoar and remember me. I wanted to get closer to her; to put my arm around her waist, to nibble her delicate ear, breathe hotly into her bosom, et cetera.

'Oh. I didn't know. But is that any excuse for this sort of . . . untidiness?'

She drank her wine off quickly and turned away, unmollified. By the time she returned with the vacuum cleaner I had pitched the urn's shards into the fireplace, as well as some metallic lumps which may or may not have been gold or silver fillings. In a few minutes she had Uncle Moses off the furniture and floor and rug and sucked into the bag of the vacuum cleaner.

'I'll throw that out in the morning. That's enough housework for one day. Do you realise it is nearly eleven o'clock?' And she brushed back a wisp of hair with her wrist in that feminine gesture I find so endearing.

'Yes, that's quite enough of that. Quite, quite enough. We must get your mind off this drudgery and into a more . . . ah . . . creative area,' I said, removing the vacuum cleaner from her grasp and bringing myself into a position where we found ourselves leaning magnetically closer to each other. A sort of moment of truth was approaching when we would touch each other; when I would gently encircle her waist and we would turn towards the stairs together.

'You can't do that!' Swingle exclaimed.

'What! What's it to you?'

'It's sacrilege!'

'Sacrilege? What are you getting at, Chazz?'

What does he mean? I wondered. Is Mrs. Peake my long lost, non-existent sister and do I contemplate incest? That man can't hold his drinks and his discretion is not at its best even when he's sober.

'Sacrilege. You can't just throw your old Uncle Moses in the trash can. No. I won't stand for it. There's a statute against it. It's a criminal act. Respect for the dead. Indignity to a human body . . .'

'Human body! My eye! Why, even alive, you could hardly call Uncle Moses a human body. Ashes to ashes, dust to dust. Let's save him for use on an icy sidewalk this winter. If he saves a slip, a fall, a broken leg then perhaps he shall not have lived in vain.'

A leper.

They leaped back from me in horror. I had to look closely at my hand, which was resting on the handle of the vacuum cleaner, to make sure my fingers had not dropped off. Mrs. Peake was almost as bad as Swingle.

'Your Uncle Moses? How could you? How could you let me dust him off the table? How could you have me sweeping him up, like common dust, for ten minutes? Running the machine over. . .'

'Exactly. Common dust. Do you think it just goes away? Dis-

appears just because we don't want to think of it?' And I reached
back to melancholy youth for a feather to tickle her sensibilities
—to Omar's make-bait:
  '"And this delightful Herb whose tender Green
  Fledges the River's Lip on which we lean—
  Ah, lean upon it lightly! for who knows
  From what once lovely Lip it springs unseen!"'
'I think it's dreadful, shameless of you to talk that way,' she
said and she began to weep. 'Heartless.'
I made as if to comfort her but she turned away from me.
Swingle, of course, was a big help.
'The least you can do is give him a Christian burial. Even the
lowliest pauper is entitled to that.'
'You mean a rosewood and satin casket with silver handles and
four free Cadillac limousines included, and a eulogy by one of
God's Representatives on Earth who didn't know the old bastard
was alive but is sure he's immortal. Notices in all the papers.
Devil's Advocate please copy. Deceased looked so natural. Much
better than alive. And a cement box to protect the rosewood
finish and a wood box to protect the cement and a damp course
to keep out ground water for it wouldn't be seemly to show up at
the Last Trump with diluted embalming fluid, would it?'
'You're being difficult,' Swingle said reproachfully.
'You're being horrid,' Mrs. Peake sniffed.
'I don't know how I got the job. The old son-of-a-bitch practically cut me off without a cent—and I don't think he meant me
to have anything in the first place. It's only because everyone else
is dead and he lost count. Why, I couldn't even afford to mail
those ashes to the Dead Letter Office. How can I give anyone a
Christian funeral without even a roof over my head? Uncle
Moses was a monster. I'll underwrite a monster funeral. Any
ideas?'
I was incensed and I quaffed a gill more of the wine. Mrs.
Peake was perplexed.
'What does he mean by that?' she begged of Swingle.

'It's true, I'm afraid,' Swingle conceded. 'There was very much less in the estate than anyone expected and with the Castle in trust and the executors unsympathetic . . .'

'Crooked, you mean,' I snapped with a bitterness that surprised me. 'Your old man is out to swindle me and is probably going to succeed.'

Mrs. Peake put a gentle, soothing hand on my arm.

'Oh, I'm sorry. I didn't know. But there's always your old room. There's always my place . . .'

She said it with such a tender, mournful, cooing, dovelike air that I could have eaten her from her pretty little beak to the plump turn of her succulent drumstick.

'But I'm still King of The Castle—for to-night . . .'

'I'm sorry, but I just couldn't sleep in the same house with . . . with that . . .'

She pointed to the vacuum cleaner with more than distaste.

'All right. I'm elected. But not a Christian burial, An Age of Technology burial. You, Swingle, out to the Gardener's quarters and get a couple of shovels. You, Mrs. Peake, an additional magnum or two of wine and another cooler with ice. This promises to be hot work.'

We met, as I had instructed them, at the left hand of the front door where there was an unkempt flower bed which had at some time in the past been planted with tulips which now had dwindled to a few pallid blossoms and almost as few chlorotic leaves.

'Do you think it right?' Mrs. Peake asked plaintively. 'I mean, do you think it's really decent?'

'Completely,' I assured her and I twirled the bottle in the cooler between my palms in a mindless ritual for which I had no explanation. 'What could be more fitting than for Uncle Moses to stay in possession of the Castle—a permanent occupant? Mummified in the front hall is what those rich old boys really want but I've come along too late for that. Now, hold that flashlight steady and we'll get to work.'

Swingle, for all his youth, was not a great help. He seemed to have lost much of his co-ordination and from time to time would dig into the earth he had already excavated and deposit it in the most convenient position available—Uncle Moses' last resting place. He was sweating terribly but it couldn't have been with effort, for he spent most of his time at the wine cooler.

While I dug I endeavoured to allay Mrs. Peake's reservations about the funeral.

' "Count no man fortunate until his last day has been lived." From the Greek, I believe. Bunyardos Steatopygeous, or old B.S., for short. Uncle Moses had it lucky. Ninety-four years of wealth, accomplishment and give-nothing. Died comfortably, long after he was incapable of gnawing even baby bones. This should be an occasion for rejoicing. So rejoice. And you haven't had near enough wine. Don't worry, he's furnished with all the most modern of technical conveniences. Do you know that in the future—and it's happening even now—that almost everything will be done by the vacuum principle. You may think it's all electronics but that's just a simple on and off switching operation for other matters, such as vacuum.

'Do you know they have on the drawing boards great vacuum systems to suck smog off our cities? Municipal garbage disposal systems of vacuums in every house where, in the future, when grandpa begins to totter, you just stand him up against the vacuum outlet and *thoop!* sanitarily disposed of along with any other unwanted trash. So, Uncle Moses is in the forefront of a whole great movement. Education, for instance, is a vacuum system designed to suck out random sensibilities in the young and let abstract formulæ flow in to fill the vacuum. That's why we have such a horror of the drop-out—loose in society with a handful of non-commercial ideas, trampling cost-accounting underfoot in his ignorance; living primitively on dreams and ignorance with the aid of a bit of organic chemistry. Oh, there's no resisting the pull of a vacuum. Government turns on the switch and *thoop!* in flow the taxes. The communication media turn on

203

the propaganda switch and *thoop!* in are sucked the brains and resistant ideas under pain of sedition.'

Besides distracting Mrs. Peake with these ruminations I found I was enjoying myself tremendously. The dark of the night, the warmth of the work and the wine and the rich emanations from Mrs. Peake who was standing very close and above me as I dug, directing the light into the grave, all stimulated me tremendously. I felt gay, delighted, privileged. Who, after all, gets to bury his uncle in the dead of night entombed in a vacuum cleaner on Castle grounds aided by a voluptuous lamp holder?

I felt both vigorous and gentle. I wanted to bury my face in the Eastern perfumes of Mrs. Peake's gorgeous belly which was just at eye level from where I stood in the pit. I wanted to pull her feet from under her and ravish her in the raw earth.

'The flagon, Mrs. Peake,' I cried. 'And drink up. Good for man or beast. Take your choice.'

'Do I have to choose?' she murmured. 'I like both.'

Skyrockets. Roman candles.

My hand was on her instep and I leaned out of the grave enough so that my shoulder was against her knee. I dropped my head and turned it to the left and bit her on that unctuous pad of flesh at the back inner corner of the knee. Her nylons sprang a run and spurted down her leg and past my lips as though I had cut an artery.

'MM,' she said. Deep tones. I leaped back.

'You'll disgrace us both,' she breathed softly, giving Swingle the slightest of glances.

'All right,' I agreed. 'But after I finish this job. And I think Swingle will have to be put to bed by the look of it.'

At that moment Swingle, who had been leaning on his spade and inspecting invisible stars, toppled or, rather, slowly collapsed into the grave.

'Another foot to go. Put the old bastard below frost level, though why I should do him favours, I don't know.'

I heaved Swingle out of the hole and shovelled furiously. In a few minutes I had a hole big enough to inter a midget. Swingle didn't seem to mind that I was shovelling dirt on to his feet and legs. And I didn't seem to mind, either. I leaped out and flung the snaky hose attachment into the hole and dropped the vacuum cleaner on top. Then I began to refill the grave.

'Is that all?' Mrs. Peake asked in bothered tones.

'Perhaps I should leave the end of the cord on the outside. Plug him in on Sundays and holidays. Give the old miser a bit of a stirring up . . .'

'You're dreadful,' she giggled, and I could see that in her present state she meant both the dreadful and the giggle.

'I meant something like . . . a prayer?'

'Rust in peace,' I said. I bowed my head in a quick nod and continued shovelling. I finished off with a neat dwarf's mound.

We had a terrible time getting Swingle half-way to his feet and carrying him into the Hall. I laid him on the sofa, mud and all. He was pathetically grateful for my ministrations.

'You're good man for mad bomber. Best mad bomber I know. Not so many mad bombers bury uncle decent Christian . . . all that . . .'

His eyes seemed alert but his body no longer obeyed him. The sort of drinker who gives champagne a bad name.

Mrs. Peake and I found ourselves looking down on Swingle and holding hands. She squeezed my hand. I squeezed back. So there we were. On a squeezing basis if not friendship. A much more tolerable status without the enormous burdens and vulnerabilities of friendship.

'I must bathe,' she whispered, and squeezed my hand again.

'I'll throw a blanket over Swingle then I'll be waiting,' I whispered back and returned her pressure.

At that point there came a ruthless rapping on the door and the police broke in. Seven of them. Four in uniform.

'Inspector Claude,' I said. 'Come right in. But leave the door on its hinges if you don't mind.'

We had met before while he was trying to work up some sort of charge against me concerning the clocks.

'I have a search warrant for these premises,' he said grimly and he meant: 'I've got you at last.' He handed the warrant to me.

'All correct,' I said. 'What are you looking for?'

'We've found it,' he replied shortly.

'Half of everything found is mine. Proprietory rights,' I said.

'It's all yours and welcome to it,' Inspector Claude almost smiled. A bad sign.

'Get two men on those shovels immediately,' he ordered one of his subordinates. 'And bring the cameraman in here. There's a pike sticking into a door off the hallway. I'll want a record of that.'

'Oh dear!' Mrs. Peake was distressed.

'It's nothing. Have your bath. I'll handle this.'

I followed the inspector out to the flower bed with one of his plain-clothesmen dogging me almost in lockstep.

'Just what are you searching for, Inspector?'

'Would you care to tell us that, Mr. Badger? I'm sure it would be very interesting.'

He said it in an almost smirky but really disinterested manner as though he had me in a bag and the rest was just details. Usually, they say the dead-pan minimum. Just enough to get you to babble some sort of justification. Knowing this, I babbled.

'It was just an accident, Inspector, believe me. You see, we were having this orgy . . .' I indicated the wine coolers still standing on the grass and I turned up a bottle but it was empty. 'It was all part of my new religion, Badgerism. I hope you won't think it egotistical of me but all the great religious leaders have given their names to their religions—Mohammedanism, Christianity, Buddhism. Well, I won't go into the details but our central . . . ah . . . perhaps you would call it a fetish object is a vacuum cleaner which is the modern, technical symbol replacing the great Mother religions which take everyone to their bosom. So, to-day, we feel the vacuum cleaner symbolises that contemporary sucking in and elimination of all those troublesome elements such as compunction, qualms, conscience, regrets, sentiment, guilt, honour, virtue, chastity, probity, integrity, good faith, approbation, charity, love, et cetera. With all this nonsense stripped away life can go on unencumbered to its true purposes: fornication, greed, consumption, perversion, corruption, pettifogging, grovelling, plotting, betrayal, debasement, venality, brutality, delinquency, obduracy, crapulence, malevolence and, as you may agree, persecution. So, without proselytising, for which we seem to have no time at the rate your men are digging, I must inform you that you are about to commit an act of sacrilege if you dig up our vacuum cleaner and one for which you will be extremely sorry.'

He grudged me half of an infuriated smile which seemed to say, 'I've got you this time, you smart alecky son-of-a-bitch', and he actually said, 'Dig.'

'Dig!'

'Struck something, sir,' a constable said, prodding again. 'Something hard, something soft.'

'Careful,' admonished Inspector Claude. 'I don't want the evidence damaged.'

The constable scraped carefully for a time and then surfaced, somewhat embarrassed, which is to say he looked exactly as before, but more so.

'We seem to have struck a . . . machine . . . sir.'

Claude poked the flashlight into the hole. There was dead silence. 'Let's have it. There may be more.'

There was. The flexible hose.

'Dig,' he ordered furiously.

They dug to virgin clay.

'Would I lie to you, Inspector?' I asked, making a rug pedlar's gesture.

The photographer did not help. He got a perfectly posed picture of the inspector with his hand on the cleaner's handle.

'What about that pike in the door? Who's behind it?' he demanded of his minions.

'Locked on the inside, sir. No answer.'

'Lift it off the hinges.'

'Sir.'

They did. The room was empty and the window stood open. I was somewhat disappointed. I had planned to disavow Bezoar; pretend he was an intruder. Serve them both right.

Inspector Claude left without apology after his men had thoroughly inspected the Castle. Swingle added to his disgust when aroused by the activity. He tottered to his feet and muttered, 'I saw it all. I'm a witness. Member in good standing of the Bar Association. We'll sue.' And he flopped back on the sofa like an overturned turtle, eyes glazed.

Mrs. Peake, I thought. I shall find surcease from this insanity upon the generous bosom of Mrs. Peake. There is much to be said for the conspiratorial opposition of the boudoir, for participation in the tranquillity of domesticity, for enduring the toilsome mysteries of the feminine toilet. Better is a handful in quietness, than both hands full with travail and vexation of spirit: Elasticus 4:63.

Knowing that I was waiting, I felt that she would now become fertile with delays. The more urgent the deadline, the more apparent her tardiness, the more anxiously would she seize upon suddenly critical duties: a dab of scent behind the knee, an emollient to counteract the miraculously instantaneous appearance of a wrinkle, the rearrangement of cosmetic bottles upon a shelf. So I put in a few minutes examining the plans of the Castle in the office on the second floor. I sighed. If Internal Revenue could not find the missing hoard with a staff of experienced searchers, how could I hope to make the discovery? For the first time, I felt a pang of regret about it. I would have liked to roll Mrs. Peake in unlimited luxury for a week or a month or two. I stepped into the hall.

From the dark end of the corridor there was a flash and three

simultaneous sounds: the opening of a pop bottle, the snarl of a
bullet passing my face and the impact of the bullet in the panelling at my end of the corridor.

I found myself, with no apparent interval, standing behind the
door of the secret passage around the corner from the corridor
in which I had been shot at. My heart was beating furiously. It
didn't feel like fear. More like general excitement.

Someone is trying to kill me, I said to myself, realising at the
same time that this was not exactly a penetrating observation.
Yes, they have picked up a gun and silencer from the gun room
and have waited in ambush. That swine Bezoar. Out of the window
and called the cops and when that didn't work couldn't resist
the opportunity of chopping me down himself. I felt a surge of
rage and had my hand on the handle of the secret doorway when
I heard a swift, almost silent rush of running feet.

My assassin.

I heard slower footsteps returning, stopping close by as though
in calculation, then the creak of the stairs. The stalking tread of
my murderer.

He's gone stark raving, I told myself. Fortunately, it is only me
he is after. No need to arm myself for the rescue, and stage a
running, dodging, hiding duel among corridors and empty rooms.
After all, this isn't the movies.

The shock of that passing bullet had sobered me, mentally,
while leaving me physically quite shaken. For the first time in my
life I felt the need of a drink. Love makes the world go round?
Nonsense. It's booze, tobacco, pot, LSD, betel nut, cocoa leaves,
hashish, heroin, sadism, impotency-power syndromes, greed. But
Love? No. It's even more perishable than the governments
that owe their very lives to taxes and monopolies on booze and
tobacco. Yes, at that moment, sober as I was, I realised about
booze.

I sat down on the step. Something in the back of my mind was
bothering me. It didn't seem right that Bezoar would take the

o

trouble to go to the police, then come back after my life. Police weren't his style.

I heard footsteps again. A less urgent tread. On the other side of the panelling I heard, 'Timothy! Timothy Badger. Where are you, Timothy?'

Mrs. Peake had grown impatient. She was searching for me. She sounded like a mother calling her little boy in to dinner and it chilled me. I had a vision of her creeping down the corridor, enticing me, one hand hidden behind her back from which dangled a silenced pistol.

Impossible!

But no, I wouldn't come out. Bezoar might be lurking behind her in the dark shadows, waiting for her to flush me out then, *ffft!* A bloody corpse.

Not that I feared being dead or killed. As ideas these thoughts did not frighten me. The big thing was, I resented the possibility of someone else disposing of my life. This has always been my big resistance. Whether parent, teacher, politician, general, employer, policeman, bishop or even streetcar conductor—I had always highly resented their presumption that they had a mandate to direct or dispose of even a half-second of my life. This is what I was trying to avoid. Not the danger.

Or so I told myself at the time.

Perhaps it's that damned young Swingle, I wondered. Perhaps he isn't as drunk as he seems. Perhaps he reverted to Daddy's boy and decided to eliminate an awkwardness in the Moses Muddiman estate as a kindness to his father.

But no. He was with me all the time. From the fight to the funeral. Right up to the time the police dropped in. So he couldn't have called them.

I closed my eyes to visualise the sequence of events. I could see the light in Bezoar's washroom as we lugged Swingle in, and within a few minutes I was out again with the police and Bezoar's lighted window again registered. And it was closed. So he had fled between the time the police finished at Uncle Moses' graveside and the time they took the door off the hinges, probably as soon as he heard them go to work. So it wasn't Bezoar.

It was either Mrs. Peake or Shrubsole. Both had the opportunity. Shrubsole hadn't turned up after dinner. Mrs. Peake was in and out. And I doubted that Shrubsole was capable of running down the corridor after me.

So that was it. Mrs. Peake is out to murder me.

I felt like crying.

I writhed on the hard step.

Perhaps Shrubsole and Mrs. Peake were working together. A logical possibility. Motive? Unimaginable. She now knows I'm poor again and what has he to gain? Perhaps their devilment depends on me not being around to discover it. It could be only Uncle Moses' missing money.

Oh God! Betrayed. And I'd have sworn she loved me; that she couldn't wait to wed and bed me or bed and wed me or just bed me. But, on the other hand she probably couldn't wait to grab the loot. It's quite in order for a woman to have up to eight conflicting desires running at the same time. A problem arises only when a choice must be made between them.

I was excruciatingly uncomfortable, sitting on the steps with the edge of one striking me in the small of the back. I tried every position: back against the wall with one cheek on the step; lying full-length with the edges of three steps cutting into me; back against the secret door with my legs running up the stair.

It's a good thing, I thought, that there are no psychologists around to discover me in this posture: lurking in the secret passage of a fake castle, hiding from a mysterious and unknown assassin, who I think seeks to cut me off in my prime and who, if he finds the secret entrance, needs only to stick his pistol into the passage and, bang!

I found this ridiculous train of thought faintly amusing but it brought me to the fact that Uncle Moses had built this fantastic edifice, secret passage included, perhaps from a constant awareness, real or not, that he might at any moment have to dash for cover. All that unpacked electronic spying gear, burglar alarms, guns and live ammunition indicated more than senility. It may have been only the defensiveness of a looter protecting his loot; imputing his own motives to others, or it could have been a real physical threat. God knows, it is easy enough to make mortal enemies. So, the secret stairway may not have been for romantic purposes. It may have been a sort of unholy priest's hole.

I tried lying face down on the stairway with my head pillowed in my arms but this attitude, besides being cruelly uncomfortable with the edges of the steps gnawing into me, reminded me that it was an attitude of grief. I felt like crying over the loss of Mrs. Peake for I felt she was as good as dead to me. But frankly, I preferred it that way, rather than to find myself physically dead to her with a bullet in my brain.

What made it worse was the feeling I could be happy with her; that she could provide enough stimulation and inspiration to enable me to imagine that I was enjoying myself, which is the prime function of women, no matter what the biologists say. And, reminding myself of her fresh loss I remembered Lily, my first wife, and I began to hiccup and almost to cry and then to smile for I recalled one of her astonishing pronouncements: 'I'm going to have a baby.'

'No! How do you know? Have you been to the doctor?'

'I can feel him kick. Feel.'

'Nothing. Perhaps an undigested meat ball from dinner.'

'Oh Tim, don't fool. Isn't it exciting! There, he kicked again!'

I knew this to be impossible. She hadn't been pregnant six weeks earlier. It wasn't that she was a liar. She was simply adventurous with the truth. There was no child on the way but she probably wanted to find out how I reacted to the idea. The kicking was just an embellishment, to dress up the occasion.

'I see what you mean,' I said, 'but I think it's a stuffed olive. I'll check again.'

And I put my lips to her navel and called softly, 'Alfonso, if it's you, knock three times . . .'

She began to beat me about the head and shoulders with her fists. 'No, no. Not Alfonso. I'd never call him Alfonso . . .'

I had to bury my face in her fragrant flesh to protect myself against her blows. Or something.

I could have lived with Lily all my life. There was something not only alive but lively between us; but they killed her.

First, a runaway truck which may have had defective brakes or which may have been set off downhill by a mischievous child, according to the Acme-International Insurance officials. Then there was an error in the blood type at the transfusion. Mix up in records. Untraceable. Death by misadventure. And dozens of officials and witnesses standing around at the inquest trying to look innocent but sympathetic.

If she had lived I could never have become the Ishmaelite I am to-day. For instance when I said, 'I'm going to quit my job and punch the boss on the nose, not necessarily in that order,' she would say not, 'The rent is two months overdue,' nor: 'What about the payments on the refrigerator?' But: 'Oh dear. Mr. Johnstone is an important man. They'll give you ten days in jail. What will I do for love, all that time. Perhaps if we start right now we can get a little ahead and I'll be able to endure it.'

And of course I never punched anyone on the nose.

Myrtle was another matter.

I made a mistake there. I couldn't bear even to look at someone small and dark and lively so I settled for Myrtle, a large, lazy blonde. And she settled for me because it was more than time to settle.

And now, at last, the truth.

I had taken the car to the garage because of a wheezy carburettor. This meant I had to leave work early to get it in before the garage closed. In walking home I took a short cut across the back lawn and passed under the kitchen window.

No, it wasn't the milkman or the iceman. They hadn't a chance. Myrtle didn't exactly slaver over that aspect of life.

She was on the telephone. It sounded so tragic that I stopped and listened.

'Oh, Sally. I can't talk now. I feel so awful. Do you mind if I call you back? I've just come in and dinner isn't even started. I've been downtown all day and didn't spend a cent. There's absolutely nothing in the stores. And I didn't sleep a wink last night and my back is killing me and wouldn't you know it, I've got the curse and I suppose I'll have to jerk off the old son-of-a-bitch to-night . . .'

Old son of a bitch! So that's how she thought of me and spoke of me to her friends. Old son-of-a-bitch! And not yet forty. And she herself wouldn't see thirty-eight again. Old son-of-a-bitch! All I had to show for seventeen years of mindless schooling and another equal sentence of profitless work. Branch Manager of a small subsidiary distributing company with no prospect but merger with Acme-International Service Products. Old son-of-a-bitch!

I said nothing.

It wasn't too long after that that I sent out my first clock.

But these memories had so distressed me that I found myself lying on my back upside down on the stairs, my head against the secret panel, my shoulders on the first step, my heels hooked over the edge of the fifth. I had been thrashing around like a madman and now I could no longer stand the confinement, so I got up and released the catch on the secret panel and delivered myself into the dangerous world.

Fifteen

Do all roads lead to violence? Is war the outlet, the blown safety valve of a billion civilised domestic frictions? Is the insane asylum an antidote for awkward truths? Is the auto accident an Occidental running amok? Is the real purpose of the skyscraper to cast a dead and killing shadow upon its neighbours? Is surgery a matter of fun and profit? Is disagreement only an excuse for murder? Is the true state of man cannibalistic?

Yes, kill or be killed, I thought as I tucked a .38 Bankers Special into my belt. That's the message. Murder first, then send flowers. The fruits of ten thousand years of philosophy. They know exactly what they mean when they say 'make a killing in the market': someone loses something of his life.

Frightening.

I traded the Bankers Special for a really brutal .45 Colt Automatic. I turned off the gun room light and stepped out into the dark corridor. I waited. Nothing but silence and a murmur in the distance. I traced it in stockinged feet down the great staircase to the main floor and to the Hall. Swingle snoring.

I knew there was little use in scouring the darkened Castle. It would be laughably simple to evade me or, more likely, to ambush me. The thing to do was to check off the local inhabitants. The innocent would be in their proper places. The guilty I could expect to encounter in a blast of flame.

I have seen too many movies.

I would have liked to creep up on Mrs. Peake, sidling along, back plastered to the wall, hands spread out at hip level as though for balance, one holding a gun, and cast the corner of one eye around the door jamb to see ... but this proved impossible. There are side tables, chairs, floor lamps, picture frames, placed along most walls. I had to creep up to Mrs. Peake's lighted door in a direct fashion, gun in hand. This business of looking around door jambs, slowly, is insane.

I realised that I was sticking my nose in first and that if anyone were waiting for me I'd have it blown off long before my eye appeared to take in the situation. So I stuck my head in suddenly. Innocence.

Mrs. Peake was asleep. She had left a bedside light burning softly. She looked childishly small except for the generosity of a hip swelling the covers. Hair spread on the pillow, breathing imperceptible, lips slightly parted, the right side of her face was illuminated by the lamp.

It is impossible to imagine murder, violence, viciousness, greed, malice, deceit, in the face of a sleeper. The shock of its waking revelation is powerful enough to paralyse our reaction to it for a whole day and we are saved from retaliation by a night's sleep. There is always an element of sleeplessness in murder.

I knew, quite completely, that Mrs. Peake had never shot at me, had never conspired to kill me this evening, cared only to welcome me to her arms. I knew this in spite of any possible logical analysis indicating potential lures, traps and dangers. And yet, I did not go in to her. I had a dreadful feeling for my unprotected back.

An enormous error. The most enormous error in a life cluttered with error. So enormous as to be classed a sin.

I resisted the temptation to begin a new life in favour of defending the old.

I crept away.

I'd better settle with Shrubsole, I thought. There is only one reason why he wants to kill me. He knows where the loot is and he wants no busybodies on the scene.

I insinuated myself into the servants' quarters with the most elaborate and silent slitheriness since a crack of light showed under the old man's window blind. In the upper hallway I could hear nothing. He could have fallen asleep in his chair, I thought. His door was open. No movement, no sound.

I looked in.

He was in bed. I could see only his feet sticking up under the covers. Perhaps he had fallen asleep reading. He would have to do something to distract himself after trying to kill his employer.

I had become very nervous with all this creeping around and although it was to be the first time I had leaped into a room with a gun in my hand I felt myself feeling a sort of boredom about it, an 'Oh no, not again!' sort of feeling.

But I leaped in anyway, covering old Shrubsole with the automatic. Quite unnecessary. He was asleep, all right. Permanently. There was no mistaking that greeny-greyish look about the gills and the fixed eyes. A book lay open on his chest. I turned it over to look at the title, as though this were the most important matter at hand at the moment. It was *How to Make a Million in Real Estate* by Harry E. Sprockett. Hah! If that monster can write a book, anyone can, I thought.

I turned down the covers to make sure he hadn't been shot, then I pulled the sheet over his face. With reluctance I felt under the pillow for the gun. It wasn't there. Nor under the edge of the mattress nor in the closet nor the dresser drawers. His possessions seemed extremely few. The only item of interest I found was the picture I had thought vaguely familiar when I had glanced into the room earlier in the day. It was hidden under some shirts.

It was a strange thing to find hidden. It was of a schoolgirl in uniform. About fourteen-years-old with that half-questioning melancholy look suggesting emotional puzzlements, hidden longings, anxieties, guilts. It was this look that I vaguely recognised, not the plumpish, unwomanly girl herself. I placed the picture on the bureau and as I turned away I still had her in my peripheral vision. At this angle of increased perception I caught more clearly and recognised that expression. It was an expression seen in moments between thought and thought, between bouts of social animation, showing in Mrs. Peake's face.

She had to be Shrubsole's daughter. No need to carry the thought any further. The excitement of trying to kill me had been too much for the old duffer and he had retired to bed and suffered his heart attack. A random thought, to which I gave little attention, crossed my mind. If he had been ambushing me after midnight would he already be marble cold?

I threw this out in favour of thoughts of treachery and deceit. I was still vulnerable as well as exhausted. I seemed to feel a real, physical wound somewhere in my breast. I wanted to lie down, to plunge into the forgetfulness of sleep. But I didn't want to be killed while unconscious. That is no way to go. I'd rather go to her and bare my breast: 'Go ahead. Kill the man who loves you. Put a neat finish to your tawdry plans, whatever they are.' But even in my depressed state I refused to be eliminated in the interest of tidiness so I gathered an armful of cushions from the Hall, pulling some out from under Swingle's stupefied head, and retreated to the secret staircase. This time I installed myself at the top where I propped myself fairly comfortably against the secret panel.

Sitting miserably on the steps which were making an unmistakable impression upon my backside and nodding with fatigue I kept seeing scenes from the old movie *Battleship Potemkin* where the Cossacks are slaughtering women and children on the Odessa steps. Inhumanly brutal treatment of the Good Guys by the Bad Guys and, of course, perfectly justifying the eventual inhumanly brutal treatment of the Bad Guys by the Good Guys. And all this High Morality is established more firmly by the sight of an ancient, high, old-fashioned baby carriage careening down the steps unattended, past the bodies of slaughtered Mothers and Children. And it careens down and down thousands of steps with interspersed cuts of the Brutal Soldiers advancing in unbroken phalanx.

As the scene proceeded inexorably, I had found myself chuckling coldly for I had begun to realise that this enormous top-heavy baby carriage, by any laws of gravity, would have toppled at the first step. It was obviously being guided by wires for sentimental and exploitive effect and this immediately undercut any legitimate message the picture might have had.

I must have fallen asleep with this image in my mind for I dreamed I was plunging down the Odessa steps in the baby carriage which was guided by those unseen wires in the hands of unknown Directors and that at some moment not chosen by me would be precipitated out of the pram to plunge screaming and shattered into some unknown depths.

I was awakened either by the terror of my dreaming fall, by the fact that I had slid down one step, or by the flush of a toilet.

Still sprawled awkwardly on the stairs I heard Mrs. Peake beyond the panel stirring about between bedroom and bathroom. The rapid staccato of her heels indicated a certain briskness of temper. Other ominous signs of high temperament were a muted but explosive 'damn' and the slam of a door which I took to be the one leading to my designated room; the crash of the hall door, and a precipitate descent of the main stair.

I felt remotely grateful that I had been spared, during these last few years, a thousand unwelcome matrimonial blows: the midnight coughs, farts, sneezes, tosses and turnings; the morning's sleep-stunned stumblings, the mute poached eggs; the monopolised flushings and sloshings and the rear-guard of hair combings.

Still, when I heard her descend and I had rushed into the room to search for the gun, I felt a pang. I rummaged through her overnight case, then threw in her yesterday's lingerie and the cosmetics that were strewn about the bathroom. It was the mixed fragrance of yesterday's scent and womanly emanations on her garments that conjured up visions and odours of matrimonial mornings. Out, I thought.

But I found nothing in the room.

I went downstairs with her packed overnight case in one hand and the automatic in the other, although I did not expect to be killed in broad daylight. Recognition, in case of failure, ruled that out for the murderer.

Out, I thought.

Mrs. Peake was not in the kitchen although the coffee was on the stove. I sat down to wait, the gun on the table in front of me and her case in the middle of the floor. I had not long to wait.

She came in snivelling.

Out, I thought, hardening my heart.

'He's dead,' she said, reacting neither to the gun nor her packed case.

'Your father?'

She nodded mutely save for a slight hiccup.

'He was old,' I said.

'Not that old.'

'Very old for a murderer.'

'Why do you say horrid things like that at a time like this? For once, can't you . . .'

'Why do you and your father do horrid things like trying to kill me last night?'

'How did you find out he was my father?'

It was an accusation.

'Your photograph. Hidden under his shirts. A suspicious circumstance, that.'

'Not as suspicious as rifling through other people's possessions.'

But I wasn't going to be trapped into one of those female discussions.

'Where's the gun?'

'I wish you wouldn't be ridiculous at a time like this.'

'Out,' I said.

'What?'

'Out. Everybody out. If you think I'm going to have a gang of deceitful ambushers taking pot shots at me every five minutes, you're crazy. Finish your coffee, then out.'

I was feeling quite bitter. Mrs. Peake had continued sniffing and wrenching at her nose with her handkerchief until it was quite red and seemed to have become elongated; and her eyes had turned bloodshot with weeping and the lines beside her nose merged with the lines from the ends of her mouth and she managed to convey the impression that it was all my fault which made me want to kick her in her gorgeous pants all the harder, just to show her that this old reliable technique isn't dependable upon all occasions.

'I didn't think you were such a beast . . .'

'I didn't think you were such a schemer . . .'

'But I wasn't scheming against you. When Charlie found out where you were living, and I was looking for a rooming house to buy, anyway . . .'

'Charlie who?'

She realised she had said too much. She said nothing.

'Not Charlie *Scaliger*?'

I could see it was. I felt a rising fury. Her lover? Unthinkable. No. Not with that damned . . . I groped mentally for a word . . . fungoid . . . growth.

'There's something wrong with anyone who associates willingly with Charlie Scaliger. I know him from way back. Do you know what I've seen him do? Put a penny in a gum machine for a child who couldn't reach it, then palm one of the gumballs for himself and give the other to the kid. No. I can see that this is as low a plot as you could get into.'

'It's not a plot at all. Charlie is a brother-in-law of my dead husband and Daddy got him to trace you because that's one of his jobs—all that skip-tracing, bailiffing, dispossessing, bill collecting. And Daddy wasn't plotting against you. He wanted to bring you in because he thought it a shame that the executors were freezing you out . . .'

'And he knew I'd keep him on and he could ferret out the missing loot, is that it—while you kept me properly distracted?'

'It wasn't like that at all. Oh, Tim, you'd have had your share . . .'

'Gee, thanks. That's big of you. A share of my own money . . .'

'I didn't mean it that way. Oh, you're impossible. I really

liked you. I thought you were, really, a sort of idealist. Disenchanted maybe but not afraid to attack people so big that there's no profit in it. Right up to last night I thought you were, well, free and unfrightened but now I think you must be the madman who phones in bomb threats to the airlines.'

'Yes, and I thought you were a luscious, warm, spontaneous, womanly sort of woman and I find a plotter who won't even acknowledge her own father who, just by coincidence, tries to put a bullet through me after leading me on to the edge of the grave.'

'Timothy Badger, you've gone insane. I don't have to defend myself against that sort of accusation. I heard nothing last night and I was awake a long time. You're looking for an excuse to get rid of me. Well, I'm going . . .'

'Not with that holier-than-thou attitude, you're not.'

And I grabbed her by the wrist and led her upstairs to the hallway where I had been fired upon.

Almost at the end of the hall was a gouge in the panelling about a foot higher than my head. The bullet had ricocheted off the side panel into the end wall and the marks were even more impressive than I had thought they might be.

Frankly, seeing this path of destruction frightened me. It helped not at all to remind myself that on the highways, in the airways, in handling implements, machines we daily suffer a thousand hairbreadth 'scapes in the deadly imminent breach (not to mention the fact that we have been brutalised by the actual, reported and pictured casualties of our times). The intent here was too obvious.

I held both hands above my head to measure the size of the gap between the bullet's path and my forehead. Mrs. Peake seemed so disturbed by this that I attacked her.

'Don't tell me that once is an accident; twice a coincidence. With bullets, once is a funeral. So I'm clearing everyone out of this place. I'm not fond of coincidences.'

I gradually realised that I had been hearing a sound from down

222

the corridor as of drawers opening and closing and I rushed in that direction, thinking that Swingle, for some reason, was rummaging around in the collection. I meant to tell him to buzz off and take Mrs. Peake with him.

I plunged into the room where the beetles and moths were impaled and there, shuffling about in the lepidopteræ, was a stranger. Tall, slope-shouldered, weak chinned, bespectacled, blue-suited with tightly buttoned waistcoat, he looked like a senior clerk.

'See here,' I said, not quite shouting. 'How did you get in and what do you want?'

He scanned me mildly.

'Cloggpipe,' he announced—or something like that, 'the curator. I've taken charge and we might as well get it straight from the start that I'll tolerate no wandering about on the second floor among the collections. This goes for the front entrance, the reception room and the Hall which will be used to accommodate the Public. Clear?'

No defence like offence.

'Ah yes, I was expecting you, but not so soon. I must inform you that I am in residence here and have no intention of admitting anyone to my domicile without a Court order. Clear? This goes not only for the second floor but the grounds as well. Now if you will leave as expeditiously . . .'

At this point I took him by the elbow as though to usher him out but I had scarcely touched his sleeve before I found myself contemplating him from a crumpled position under a cabinet of Lampyridæ.

'I was warned you would be troublesome,' Cloggpipe said mildly as he pocketed the Colt that had fallen from my belt, 'but I've usually found that a firm hand brings about a clear understanding with persons suffering from a previous lack of discipline.'

'I can see you have extremely clear-cut ideas,' I observed, brushing fragments of crumpled insects from my coat. 'However,

I shall try to change them by an appeal to a higher authority. If you will await me here.'

'What's happened? Who is that man? Are you hurt?' Mrs. Peake demanded as I strode down the hall towards the gun room.

'Mortally hurt,' I said grimly, 'but I plan to sell my life dearly.'

I seized an old slide-action Mossberg twelve gauge from the wall and returned to the bug room with Mrs. Peake twittering Peace Resolutions at my elbow. Cloggpipe was standing in the centre of the room contemplating the shattered tray of fireflies on the floor, his hands clasped behind his back. I worked the slide action of the shotgun. Chick-chick. He turned his head towards me in a quick, birdlike way.

'I'm sure,' I said in conversational tones, 'that you have very clear ideas—judo ideas—about disarming an armed man. Would you care to try? I'd judge you have to cover about fifteen feet and I'd wager I could put two charges of buckshot into you in that time—especially since I'm eager for the excuse. No, don't raise your hands, although that is quite a conservative course to take in the circumstances. I'd like you to remove my gun from your pocket and drop it on the floor. No, not particularly slowly. It's entirely up to you whether you make me nervous. Frankly, I'd be delighted to kill you. After all you are an intruder. At this range, if you make a mistake, they'll be able to roll bowling balls through your thorax.'

This sounds completely insane, I thought as I heard myself speak. And yet I continued and I knew I meant every syllable for it seemed to me that my very existence as an independent person was at stake. To knuckle under to physical force was to carry a wound that would never heal. It was the story of any war. The plot is initiated for logical, if insanely logical, reasons. The lure of disproportionate loot is held out: glory for the natural-born idiot; unprosecuted murder for the natural-born psychopath. It is always a shock to discover the enemy is often willing to die and take you with him, to no one's advantage. Quite incomprehensible. Generals are always cheap-minded. This had obviously come

224

as a bit of a shock to Cloggpipe who may have taken the job more for the opportunity to harass me self-righteously than even for the money.

When I had run Cloggpipe out, with the assurance that I would shoot him on sight if he showed up again, I was still quite agitated.

'He attacked me in my own home. Hurled me through the air like a sack of oats. Perhaps I should have killed him immediately. As a lawyer, Swingle, tell me, would I have been justified? Do you think he is actually a Curator or is he just some thug your dear old Dad put in here to drive me out?'

'You'll kill someone eventually, the way you're handling that gun,' Swingle admonished me and he took it out of my hand and made mysterious and knowing adjustments to it.

'Why, this gun isn't even loaded!' he exclaimed.

'Do you think I'm a damned fool? Do you think I'd tempt myself with an infantile target like Cloggpipe—at the price of my neck, perhaps? A loaded gun carries heavy responsibilities with it. A piece of dark thread at the top of a midnight staircase suffices for a twit like Cloggpipe. Or, if he were to persist in this judo business, it is a simple matter to hire two judo experts.'

For some illogical reason, Mrs. Peake seemed to think my use of an unloaded gun was even more reprehensible than if it had been loaded and I bundled her off with Swingle to look after the arrangements for Shrubsole's funeral. She seemed almost glad to go but there was still a look in her eye that suggested she might return, when I had come to my senses, pluck me like a dandelion and tuck me firmly into her reticule.

My first instinct, now that I was alone, was to lock up the Castle tightly. I resisted it. I remembered the cunning of the Greeks who wanted to avoid another battle with the defeated but still formidable Persian host, yet still wanted to get them quickly out of the country. They put out the rumour that they were going to destroy the great pontoon bridge over the Hellespont and so trap the Persians. But a trap meant a desperate fight for all.

The Persians fled, the Greeks left the trap open. And so, I crept on stockinged feet silently up the secret stairway to the top of the house and, noisily shod, made a cursory, slow inspection of the house, top to bottom. If there had been anyone there, they left. I then locked the Castle tight.

There was no sense in scouring the Castle for the loot. Shrubsole had been at it for six months, and maybe for years before Uncle Moses died. The Revenue people had made a thorough search, as had the executors. That business about hiding things in the most obvious place would have occurred to everyone before this and all the obvious places would have been canvassed. Nevertheless, I spent most of the afternoon and evening scrutinising the Castle plans minutely and checking them against the actual construction. Every suspicious blank on the plans turned out to be solid masonry, so far as I could tell.

And what was I looking for? Uncle Moses, a shrewd man, would have kept this hidden portion of his wealth negotiable, would he not? But I am not a financially shrewd man so undoubtedly my thinking is idiotic. An anonymous Swiss bank account would be more his style or perhaps bonds in safety deposit boxes under assumed names. But the Revenue people would have taken that as far as they could go. And it is unlikely that he would have entrusted securities to some bricked-up chamber to be gnawed by rats and consumed by mildew.

I gave up in disgust to find it was almost dark and I was ravenously hungry. I rushed by cab to the nearest restaurant, which happened to be the Napoli. I found myself tearing rolls, snapping at shrimp like a barracuda, swilling minestrone, slashing through veal parmigiano, shovelling spumoni.

What has happened to me, I wondered? Why this wolfish appetite? Why does someone want to kill me? Why should people like Shrubsole and Mrs. Peake plot against me? What are the police doing on my neck? Is Swingle real? Why did I not see that Bezoar was a monster? What am I doing, searching for Uncle Moses' treasure, which may not exist? Is it all just one question, admitting of one answer? Have I suddenly gone money-mad over my non-existent legacy? Have I suddenly grown so much too big for my britches that the police and everyone else including Bezoar is out to kill me?

No.

It would be tempting to feel there was a Unified Field Theory capable of application to every human event and consequence but, since there isn't, we settle for European Paradox, Eastern Ambiguity, Northern Causality, Southern Tribality—all licences to not only bugger and beggar our neighbour but to butcher him. For, of the three billion inhabitants of this globe, there are three billion madmen lurking with sharpened butchers' knives behind the masks of accountants, barbers, mothers, Boy Scouts, nurses, bartenders, dentists, just waiting for the proper combination of circumstances, opportunity, pressure and excuse to leap upon child, wife, brother, neighbour, lover, foreigner, co-worker and wreak a bloody satisfaction in the name of whatever fad, disease or cause may be current.

In this way I convinced myself that there was no simple plot but, much worse, a universal, spontaneous reaction against me. I had lost my cover, as they say in spy stories. Before, without resources and classed as a simple, harmless eccentric, I was not worthy of notice. But with money attached, I became potentially powerful, dangerous and a worthy target, for there was now the possibility of loot of some sort for someone at my death.

Where before Bezoar could condescend to my lunatic prattle and pretension, he was now faced with my pretensions in action. And there is nothing more irritating than long-scorned pretension realised. It is for this reason that the *nouveau riche* are so bitterly resisted even though the old rich are brutal, crass, ignorant and spiritless and the upstarts may be gracious, tolerant, knowledge-able, kindly, generous and with a sense of style. The difficulty is in giving up a sense of superiority. This deprivation is never for-given, not even by such lowly crumbs as Bezoar.

Cutter, Mandrake and Swingle could be explained simply. My

clocks tended to blow up the established order which is to say—themselves—and damned if they'd give me any more ammunition. Young Swingle no more wanted to raise chickens in peace than I wanted to run the Castle. What he wanted to do was slaughter his old man, who was cramping his style. He wanted to be a modern, hip, swinging, sporty sort of lawyer with his picture in the papers and to hell with the gown and the Bar Association and the Conservative Club and keeping his nose clean, and political plums. I could probably count on him as a traitor in the enemy camp at least until his father had a stroke.

As for the police persecution. As I told Mrs. Peake, once is an accident, twice a coincidence, three times a plot. And when the waiter was resentful because I didn't order some of that rotten vinegary red Italian wine that goes with checked table cloths, I began to feel even more persecuted and to see myself the focus of a plot ranging from Scaliger to Shrubsole to lawyers I had never met and probably including even judges of the Probate Court. Unless my assassin were someone outside my acquaintance.

Who could have seen possibilities of damage to me when they spied on the burial of Uncle Moses' ashes? And when that failed, who would be inspired to violence? But perhaps the motive had nothing to do with Uncle Moses' inheritance. Perhaps it was sheer jealousy. Perhaps Mrs. Peake had a lover. Pray God, not Scaliger! In fact, it was highly unlikely that she had not.

This seemed very much more rational a probability than the existence of an enormously wide-ranging plot suddenly, within a day, springing into action against me. However, it seemed so plausible that it left me depressed. I felt more capable of coping with a universal plot than of competing in this shabby second-hand manner for Mrs. Peake's available affections.

I shuffled moodily home to the Castle, feeling that the spice had gone out of the situation. Yes, I should simply walk away from it. Do a Joseph Conrad. Ship aboard a tramp steamer, a slow one. Sulk through the seven seas. Every six months, from Singapore, from Valparaiso, from Archangel, from Port Moresby, send a registered letter to Cutter, Mandrake and Swingle saying, 'Am alive and well. Do nothing without consulting me.' Or: 'Hold you responsible for any action re Muddiman Estate in my absence.' Or: 'Am instigating legal and criminal charges against you for fraudulent actions re Muddiman Estate.'

Because of these gloomy speculations I did not notice that I was being followed until I was fifty yards from the gateway of the Castle. He was keeping to the shadows but hastening along as though to catch up with me. I increased my pace. So did he. He was still gaining. I broke into a run. All this without thought. I simply knew that it was my assassin. The thud of his racing feet echoed in my heart. As I dodged into the gateway I thought I heard the whine of a wild bullet from the silenced gun.

The courtyard was lit brightly by the front door lamps. If I made a run for the door I would be a perfect target for the whole length of the courtyard.

Sixteen

Doomed.

Wonderful how useful are some of the old-fashioned words. Much better than expressions such as 'I've had it', or 'this is it', or 'I'm finished'. But that was the extent of my thought in the situation. My reaction was as completely physical and unthinking as a rat fleeing a cat.

I hurled myself at the dark shadow that was the door of the gatehouse and it burst open under my weight. I leapt to the lever that controlled the portcullis and it released as if hair-triggered. The iron crash of its descent was followed by a baffled curse.

I looked out the gatehouse door for a moment to see a dimly silhouetted figure shaking the massive grid. I wasn't absolutely sure that I saw the barrel of a gun among all those bars but I couldn't take a chance. I closed the door and switched on the light. I had leapt upon that lever by memory alone and, now that I was no longer operating on blind reaction, I could not remember where the crank of the drawbridge windlass was situated. I did not have to use the crank which proved to be only an emergency unit. The drawbridge was operated by an electric motor. I had only to press a button and it whined into action. All King Arthur's modern conveniences.

I stuck my head out into the passage and pulled it back in a fraction of an instant and caught a glimpse of the silhouetted figure showing agitation as the drawbridge slowly rose, threatening to trap him between it and the portcullis. I heard an incoherent epithet of disgust and defeat. The drawbridge thudded home against the gateway and the motor shut itself off auto-

230

matically. Silence. I turned on the passageway light and stuck my head out again. No one. I cursed myself for not having turned on the light earlier. I could have identified my pursuer. But I did not curse very hard. Knowing my self-appointed executioner would have obliged me to take some sort of aggressive step to disarm, neutralise or exterminate him.

I felt thankful, too, for my Uncle Moses' eccentricity in building his Castle with drawbridge and portcullis for they had saved my life—except that, but for the Castle, my life would not have been endangered. I shook my head in confusion at the sight of the great wicker basket holding Uncle's balloon and walked slowly across the courtyard into the Castle.

There are those who will undoubtedly say that this whole incident was a primitive symbolic figment of my imagination; that I was anxious, nervous, disappointed, frustrated and sleepless; and that my refusal to emerge from the dark passage of the gateway into the brilliantly lit courtyard was only an illustration of my reluctance to engage with reality; that the gun . . .

But enough. Man or woman, boy or girl, dog or bitch, one gets out of the way of a speeding automobile whether it is considered a male or a female symbol. Fortunately, all that sort of nonsense is discredited nowadays and has been swept into the back eddy of literary criticism with all the rest of the intellectual fads.

I hung a variety of pots and pans in the stairway and against my door, tying them together into a hair-trigger alarm system with thread. I then retired to the great four-poster, which still radiated Mrs. Peake's fragrances, and slept the sleep of the righteous. But I felt no regret, not really, to be sleeping alone. I had had enough of emotion. Perhaps fright, love, terror, affection, horror, sensuality are all tunes played on the same string with only slight differences in the fingering.

In the morning I felt grateful to Uncle Moses and I began to appreciate one facet of his character a little more. I relished the quiet, the security of the great stone walls; the interposition of space between me and the murderous city. I could see Uncle

Moses had a point there—if that had been his point in building the Castle.

As I stood on the front steps, a cup of coffee in my hand, I surveyed the courtyard. All seemed well. The portcullis at the end of its tunnel was down, the drawbridge up, and I had left the light on. A good idea. That passageway in the dark could be a dangerous lurking place. The walls were secure. But in spite of this sense of peace and security I felt a disturbance, a sense of irritation, a desire to jump up and down in excitement. I could see nothing that threatened, yet something impinged upon my consciousness. The only unaccustomed thing was that the counterbalances of the drawbridge were now down, almost touching the ground. I strolled over to them.

They were made of circles of stone cemented together with an iron bar running through their core as though they had been added, one by one, until the correct weight was attained. They were about the size of oil barrels. I tried pushing one. It was incredibly heavy but, with an arbitrary persistence, I got one of them swinging enough to bump against the wall. There was a clink, as of chains rattling. A Trojan Horse sound. But I immediately realised that, under their enormous tension, the links of the supporting chain wouldn't be clinking.

The loot, I told myself. Uncle Moses' missing loot. Perfect. Hidden in this most obvious place where it couldn't be tampered with unless there were absolutely no one around and there was lots of time. It had to be coins—gold—to withstand the weather.

It was all so clear now, including why the Government couldn't trace any income from the hidden wealth. There hadn't been any. This had been Uncle Moses' portable nest egg. Something negotiable anywhere in the world. He could flee at any time and be wealthy still.

I found a heavy maul and a wedge in the tool shed and proceeded to split off the top disc of the counterweight. I can't say that I was expert and, besides, the weight kept swaying as I worked. I smashed a great chunk out of it and then decided it was no longer any use being delicate with it, and I attacked the top with fury, shattering it into a hundred fragments. Under the top disc it was quite hollow, the other lower discs being nothing but stone rings. I plunged a hand in over the edge and brought up a fistful of gold sovereigns on which Queen Victoria sulked fatly. Those I held in my hand were dated from about 1875 to 1898.

I felt no surprise.

I knew I had made a mistake.

I was now firmly trapped. If I let anyone into the Castle it would be evident to any eye that I had broken open Uncle Moses' treasury. Internal Revenue would be upon me. They would seize their share and turn the rest over to the executors of the estate. My find would mean nothing to me. I would rather throw it into the streets to the poor than dissipate it on a wretchedly incompetent government or hostile lawyers.

I had to get it out without discovery and get myself out, alive. That probably meant fleeing the country for an accounting would be demanded when the counterweights were examined.

I needed a magic carpet.

No.

I resisted the thought of the idea entering my mind. I put it entirely away from me. It was idiotic. Unthinkable. Senseless. Something a crazy, senile old man had dreamed up. A reflection of his greed, secrecy, paranoia.

And yet, for a short, silent, secret flight to safety, it was, in a way, a stroke of genius.

No. Strictly twittersville. I'd be damned if I'd sneak off in a balloon with gold coins for ballast. There must be another way.

Still, what could be quieter and less noticeable than drifting down the wind on a moonless night, landing in a deserted field, beside a road, burying the gold, letting the balloon drift away, God knows where, and retrieving the gold at leisure. There have been worse enterprises. Balloons played a large part in the siege of Paris, 1870.

I smiled fondly to myself, as though to an idiot, for even going to Uncle Moses' library and taking down the manual that had accompanied the balloon. It looked to be in Dutch with literally translated English notes. The diagrams were quite clear but I was not reassured by a description of a balloon landing as a partially controlled accident.

I began by filling the ballast bags with gold rather than sand, as recommended. This, I felt, did not really commit me to this harebrained scheme. The gold had to be carried in something, at some time, even by the Government or the executors, Cutter, Mandrake and Swingle. I weighed the bags, one by one, on a bathroom scale and the total weight was approximately one thousand pounds, worth about six hundred thousand dollars— and maybe twice as much in Oman.

Just to satisfy my curiosity, I checked with the manual and found that the balloon had been designed to carry this payload although the specifications laid it out as four passengers at seven hundred and fifty pounds; five hundred pounds for ballast and another couple of hundred for scientific equipment. This fictional payload obviously would carry both myself and the gold, based on hydrogen as the lifting agent with the highest efficiency. And the hydrogen tanks were lying there on the east lawn.

I was now thoroughly intrigued by the potential of the balloon. I wheeled the wicker basket out on the lawn and dumped it: the enormous envelope of the balloon itself, the peculiar gas valve operating something like an inverted toilet seat, the grapnel, rope ladder, trail rope, the enormous net, an instrument panel with assorted gauges, a radio and an aerial like a fishline with a sinker on the end.

I was fascinated by the challenge of turning this limp mass into a gigantic if insubstantial machine. I thought nothing of what I was actually doing in relation to Uncle Moses' gold: no more, I suppose, than a chemist working on poison gas; a ballistic expert working on phosphorus shells; an atomic scientist labouring away absorbedly to assure his great-grandchildren thirteen thumbs.

Spreading out the enormous envelope was the heaviest job. It weighed about five hundred pounds in spite of its fragility. And the big filling tit had to be properly centred. Then the tube from the gas tanks had to be inserted under it, a task that almost smothered me. Over all was stretched the net, and around its perimeter I attached the gold bags to hold down the balloon as it filled.

Another extremely difficult job was loosening the valves on the hydrogen tanks and by the time half a dozen of them had hissed into the balloon I was exhausted. I lay down on the grass, contemplating the squat mushroom rising under the net in huge orange and blue gores. I felt somewhat disoriented. I sat up. The sun seemed to be in the wrong place, going down the western sky. I had worked most of the day without food but, more important, in my absorption I had almost destroyed the secrecy of the project by letting the balloon rise in sight over the walls. And secrecy was of the utmost importance. What would be the point of a highly visible flight trailed by squad cars and sightseers, with a welcoming committee on landing composed of the Department of Transport and tax experts from the Succession Duties Branch.

So I ate, out of cans, lobster with mayonnaise and pork and beans washed down with champagne. And I put aside a few extra bottles of the wine, for champagne is the traditional drink of balloonists either because of the rising bubbles or the ballooning prices. Then I tuned in on the weather forecast: light winds and increasing cloudiness. Ideal for my purposes. The wind direction also seemed appropriate: west by perhaps a bit north as far as I could tell from the pennant flying from the tower. By laying a ruler on a road map I saw that this breeze would take me along the north shore of the Lake. I could, perhaps, choose a landing site north of Kingston in the sparsely populated, almost deserted, resort country. I might even have the gold cached, catch a bus and be back in town for breakfast.

At dusk I continued the inflation and towards midnight I almost panicked. The balloon, a giant now, was beginning to lift the ballast bags off the ground. I had forgotten that the weight of the basket, ring, grapnel, myself, etc., was still needed to balance the lift but I quickly flung an empty gas tank on to the edge of the net and this held until I could tether the balloon to the bumper of the Rolls. After that it was simply a matter of attaching the net ropes to the basket ring, the basket ropes to the ring toggles and load the ballast bags of gold aboard.

The last chore was to prepare half a dozen chicken sandwiches wrapped in a linen napkin, some olives, cheese, champagne and cooler. But something was missing. I had been working in my car-wash clothes. This would never do. There is a certain light-heartedness, a certain gaiety, a certain fair-weather atmosphere about ballooning that calls for Sunday-best clothes. Frills, bustles and parasols for the ladies; frock coats, silk hats, gloves for the men. And flags flying.

So I went in and changed into my tweeds and put on my favourite wool tie, hand woven in New Brunswick—a russet colour. But I thought I should have a hat.

I rummaged through Uncle Moses' wardrobe and passed up homburgs, opera hats, fedoras. A deerstalker, somewhat gnawed by moths, hung dispiritedly at the back of a closet. Exactly right. Top my tweeds with a suitably sporty and yet somewhat antique effect. I was ready to fly.

I clambered over the side of the wicker basket with a considerable difficulty due to the multiplicity of ropes and, I must confess, to a certain middle-aged lack of flexibility. I cut the rope tethering the balloon to the Rolls. With a despairing creak, the wicker basket settled slowly to the ground.

I stood in my balloon basket, on top of my fifty bags of gold, and felt, if not active chagrin, then a definite sense of anticlimax.

But I swiftly realised it was a technical matter. A change in the coefficient of lift with the cool of the night. Or something. In meaningful terms, the weight was too heavy for the balloon to lift. Something had to go. Normally, ballast. But ballast was too precious. I dropped the radio on to the lawn.

THE FIREFLY HUNT

There was a slight stirring, a feeling of insubstantiality. The
ascent was very slow and almost perpendicular for a dozen feet,
then the breeze from around the Castle caught us and we moved
towards the wall. For a moment I thought the basket would
crash but we passed over with a foot to spare. This was not what
I had expected. And once past the wall, the balloon did not gain
height. The downward slope from the Castle evidently creating a
downflow of air so that any rise due to buoyancy was cancelled
out by this sinking of the air. In addition, the flow of air around
the Castle seemed to create an eddy and little forward progress
was being made—less than a walking pace. There was a 'sproing-
sproing' sound from below and I realised that the trail rope was
passing over television aerials across the street from the Castle.
There was a slight jolt. We stopped. The basket tilted slightly.
The rope had caught, obviously, in someone's aerial. I felt despair.

I looked around, over the side of the basket to see exactly what
the trouble was. From the corner of the Castle wall came flashes
and the buzz of bees in the rigging. And just up the street I
thought I could make out the white painted door of a police
squad car. My lurking assassin. Desmond, the policeman, of
course.

Yes, in trying to ambush me, he had spied on the funeral of
Uncle Moses. He had kept out of sight after reporting the incident
to the police and skulked behind to kill me when that involvement
failed. Of course. Only those in uniform attempt to maintain
secrets nowadays, everyone else is brazen: murder your mother
and tell all about it on television; make buggery safe for the masses
through barefaced (if that is the word) public relations campaigns.
I must have touched a very raw nerve in Desmond and now here
he was shooting at me like a pigeon on a string.

All this flashed through my head in an instant as I cast off the
trail rope from its toggle and, since it was a thick heavy rope of
more than fifty pounds weight, the balloon shot upward smoothly
and swiftly. This is more like it, I thought.

The city receded like a reverse-zoom shot, became orderly.

237

Sounds were peculiarly clear, mostly the shush of traffic. There was no wind. I was riding along with it and though a flag in the rigging would have drooped I was being carried east at ten or twenty miles an hour.

This is the answer, I told myself excitedly. This is what Uncle Moses' money is for. Ballooning. As a way of life. A radical social revolution. Eliminate the automobile. Eliminate the home. Eliminate the job. Keep the career. Keep the family. Keep the Balloon. Keep the house.

Change the people!

I don't mean their characters. I mean, change them around.

It is an agreed fact that a steady diet of the same people or the same person is eventually indigestible. Our grief at the loss of a loved one through death or because of another attachment is mostly shock at the realisation that the loss is a blessed relief promising a change from the deadly monotony of mastered, appropriate responses; a chance for a new beginning.

There is no technical reason why marriage should be anything but a temporary condition. Contraception, abortion, education, economic resources, lessening sexual inhibition, universal skill, etc., all suggest greater and more frequent contact with our fellows.

Why should we not upon boredom, disillusion, friction, restriction, or over-use, hop into our balloon, drift gently and relaxedly on the wind for a hundred miles, set down in a chance community and walk into a congenial set-up—a house where the man has left just long enough ago for the occupant to need another companion.

And I don't mean this as a man's playground. There would be as many women as men in the air in their balloons. And as many male stay-at-homebodies as women, perhaps more.

If we must have computerisation perhaps this would be the way to use it—to match up this drifting yet constant tide of humanity; to see that no one was left out, for there would be responsibilities to the unattractive under which attention and indulgence they might become more attractive. The brutal concept of exclusivity would have to go in favour of one of common humanity.

The work of the world would get done, and it can all be done in a few hours a day; personal accumulation is another matter. There is no reason why a draughtsman, a chemist, an engineer, a teacher cannot teach, draw, design, analyse as well in one town as another; carry on experiments already begun.

To prevent destructive elements entering the system only a very few demerits would be considered—unkindness, exploitation, coercion. Anyone involved in such indulgences might find themselves confined to drifting in the sub-arctic air currents. And, since the computers would indicate the need to be filled, and since it would all be part of the system, there would be no shame, no self-consciousness or ignominy involved in these social relations.

This train of thought was broken by the realisation that I had turned up my coat collar and had been inspired in this idea of arctic ostracism because of the cold. The city was spread out directly beneath me and the dark country and the lighter tones of the lake were visible for miles about.

I'm rising fast, I thought. I must be ten, twelve, fifteen thousand feet up. Besides the cold, I may run out of oxygen. I must do something.

Just then the balloon rose into the damp woolliness of a cloud. I pulled on the valve rope and held it down until we dropped out of the bottom of the cloud again. There was no really great sensation involved but it immediately took my mind off the ordering of the world and I forgot my visions of Bulgarians drifting eastward and mingling with Uzbekistan belles: of Afghans sprinkled through Malay; Samoans bedding down in San Francisco; New York admen alighting in Ouargla or Biskra; Threadneedle Street clerks coming to rest in Chelyabinsk.

Of course, a certain fatalism would be necessary in balloon navigation, as I was finding out, and perhaps more comprehensive understanding and practical experience than I at that moment possessed. For, although it was becoming warmer and the ground was obviously closer, I had no way of judging my descent or predicting its cessation.

What alarmed me more than the apparently swift descent was that the winds aloft were somewhat different in direction to those on the ground and I was now being carried across the shore and out into the lake. I let go the grapnel but a mere dozen pounds seemed to effect little immediate change in the rate of descent. I dispensed with one of the wine coolers and opened the wine and poured myself a glass in the dark, before it should become too warm without its ice, but without sight of the amber liquid, the bubbles, the glitter of crystal, it was a depressing, pointless drink and I threw the rest of the bottle overboard.

Looking back on the shore I could discern the dark height of cliffs and knew that once the land lost its appearance of flatness I must be very low indeed. I threw over some ballast—a fifty pound bag worth about thirty thousand dollars. I began to hear the sound of waves quite clearly. I threw over another thirty thousand dollars worth of ballast and the descent was obviously checked.

I'll have to watch that, I thought. Be more judicious about expending gas through the valve. Costly. But lots more where that came from.

The balloon seemed to have levelled off at about three thousand feet to judge by its position relative to the glow of the city behind us. Ideal. And if the lake underneath was a bit awkward in an emergency, at least I was not being spied on from the ground and arousing Unidentifiable Flying Object scares. And the other side of the lake would be a matter of less than two hours away.

I settled down to my chicken sandwiches and champagne, seated on my hard bags of gold. The shapeless, misty cloud seemed to have lowered swiftly and by the time I had finished my snack I was completely surrounded by fog. It was clammy, chilly and soundless. There was no horizon. I could only hope that the wind had remained stable so that I would make a landfall no later than dawn. I nodded for a few minutes—perhaps five, perhaps ten; not long. I was jolted into alertness by a splash of water in the face. Rain?

Not under that enormous umbrella. Condensation from the cloud running down under the envelope? Very likely—except for a slap on the bottom of the basket and a fine spray atomised through the wicker side. Cautiously, I peered over the side. Waves almost within arms' reach.

Without a thought I threw over a bag of coins and then another. We jerked aloft but I could feel the impetus quickly diminishing. There was nothing to see in the mist but it was possible to note the descent through the vapour. I peered out with close attention. We hovered. We began to sink. We began to sink at a goodly speed, if not precipitously.

There is something wrong, I thought. Something wrong with the gas valve, perhaps. And there is a rip panel for spilling out all the gas, instantly, on landing. Could it be leaking? Nothing to do about it, anyway. Or did that fool Desmond actually put a bullet through the envelope? Or is the balloon of such ancient vintage that the gas is seeping out through every rotten pore?

In any event, I was sinking into the lake but where in the lake I did not know. There was no possibility of help unless the jets which had begun to thunder past me could find me in the limited visibility. Was I showing up on radar as some enormous bouncing bomb aimed at Watkins Glen from over the pole? I had no time for speculation. The water was in sight again, a hundred feet below.

Over went a bag which checked my descent to a slow sinking. I held another bag poised on the edge of the basket and let the coins trickle slowly through my fingers. The lifting capacity for hydrogen, I remembered from the manual, was 1.21 kg. per. cu. metre or one and two-third pounds per cubic yard. I was losing gold at the rate of twenty pounds per minute, I judged, which meant losing gas at the rate of either twelve or thirty cubic yards a minute. I'm terrible at fractions. How long could I last? Figures meant nothing at a time like this. There was nothing to do but keep feeding gold to the waves and try not to sink below a hundred feet. I kept up this outpouring for perhaps an hour until the moment came when I groped on the floor of the basket and found only a champagne cork.

I gazed at the water as it rose to meet me. With some asperity I plucked off my shoes and threw them overboard. I stripped off my coat, my shirt, my trousers, my socks. All went into the waves. No hope. No hope for the chance, the coincident, early fishing boat, the random derelict skiff; even a log, a branch. No.

The basket touched the water, began to drag. I sprang to its edge and clambered into the balloon's rigging, hooking a leg over the ring from which was suspended the basket. I snatched at the knife attached to a rope for emergencies. I cut away the basket's supporting ropes. We soared, briefly, a few hundred feet but in a few minutes were at the surface again. I hung on to the rigging as I settled into the water. As my weight relieved the balloon it still supported itself, its side bulging in like a sail, and I was dragged slowly through the water.

I seemed to have no thoughts. No regrets about the loss of the fortune. No serious, emotional dismay at my predicament. Just the unthinking feeling that one goes on this way as long as is physically possible. No active imagination about the moment when one's grasp is insufficient to guarantee survival.

It was hard work hanging on and absurd, but the alternative of letting go was, of course, unthinkable. In a way, it was a condition to which I had long been accustomed.